Acclaim for
Finding Hope

Romance Writers of America Golden Heart finalist

"This book is undoubtedly the best Emma Carlyle book I've read. I loved the characters, loved the story. I stayed up half the night to finish the book. Five stars." —Amazon reviewer

"This was a really cute story. The characters were interesting and the story was fresh. Good job!" — Amazon reviewer

"Who couldn't love Scotty, Woody, and Teddy? I confess I chose this book because I love Lois Winston (aka Emma Carlyle) and I have triplets. I enjoyed the book because it was well written and without any bias against Hope when she agrees to ba a temporary nanny for the triplets even though she was hired to be a member of the architectural firm. She saw the need and agreed to help. No negotiating special privileges as many heroines would do! I also liked the way she spoke her mind and was decisive...I love the way the author wrote the triplets. Her spelling to enhance the special speech of a three year old was a significant clue that she understood young children. Their growth under Hope's care was heartwarming and I am sure I wasn't the only one rooting for a happy ending!" — Amazon reviewer

"This is a heart felt love story. I loved the book. Ben and Hope had been through hell until they met. It was as if the universe was just waiting for them to meet because they were meant for each other." — Amazon reviewer

Everyone was looking at me. Ben stood at the opposite end of the room. With his arms folded across his chest and his unruly mop of hair falling over one eyebrow, he looked far too innocent. And incredibly sexy. When our eyes met, the corners of his mouth turned up in a rakish smile that reminded me of Harrison Ford back in his Han Solo and Indiana Jones days. I turned back to Edwina, trying desperately to ignore the shiver skittering up my spine. So much for visualizing Ben Schaffer as short and bald with a beer belly that made him look nine months pregnant.

Books by Lois Winston

Anastasia Pollack Crafting Mystery series

Assault with a Deadly Glue Gun
Death by Killer Mop Doll
Revenge of the Crafty Corpse
Decoupage Can Be Deadly
A Stitch to Die For
Scrapbook of Murder
Drop Dead Ornaments
Handmade Ho-Ho Homicide
A Sew Deadly Cruise
Stitch, Bake, Die!
Guilty as Framed
A Crafty Collage of Crime
Sorry, Knot Sorry

Anastasia Pollack Crafting Mini-Mysteries

Crewel Intentions
Mosaic Mayhem
Patchwork Peril
Crafty Crimes (all 3 novellas in one volume)

Empty Nest Mystery Series

Definitely Dead
Literally Dead

Romantic Suspense

Love, Lies and a Double Shot of Deception
Lost in Manhattan
Someone to Watch Over Me

Romance and Chick Lit

Talk Gertie to Me
Four Uncles and a Wedding
Hooking Mr. Right
Finding Hope

Novellas and Novelettes
Elementary, My Dear Gertie
Moms in Black, A Mom Squad Caper
Once Upon a Romance
Finding Mr. Right

Children's Chapter Book
The Magic Paintbrush

Nonfiction
Top Ten Reasons Your Novel is Rejected
House Unauthorized
Bake, Love, Write
We'd Rather Be Writing

Finding Hope

LOIS WINSTON
Writing as Emma Carlyle

Cover design by L. Winston

ISBN-13: 978-1-940795-17-1

"We need women who are so strong they can be gentle, so educated they can be humble, so fierce they can be compassionate, so passionate they can be rational, and so disciplined they can be free."
— Kavita Ramdas

DEDICATION

In loving memory of the real Ben Schaffer,
always and forever my hero.

ONE

The Christmas I turned six, I watched *The Nutcracker Suite* on television. During a commercial break, I bounced off the sofa, lifted my hands over my head, and twirled to a chorus of *plop-plop, fizz-fizz, oh what a relief it is.* "I want to be a ballerina," I announced loud enough to drown out the sonorous voiceover that followed the jingle.

My father snorted behind his newspaper.

"Short, chubby, pigeon-toed girls with swaybacks and no rhythm don't grow up to become ballerinas," said my mother, never one to mince words or mollycoddle her offspring. The clickety-clack of her knitting needles emphasized each blunt word.

I thrust my hands onto my hips. "Mrs. Cullpepper said if we work hard enough, we can grow up to be anything we want."

My father lowered his paper. "Someone needs to give Mrs. Cullpepper a remedial course in genetics."

"What's *netics*?" I asked.

"A subject your teacher didn't pay enough attention to when she was in school. She's got no right filling your head with such nonsense."

I stamped my foot. "It's not nonsense. I'm going to be a ballerina. You'll see."

"So will you," he said, turning his attention back to the sports section. "You'll be a secretary like your mother until you get married and have babies."

Refusing to give up on my new dream, I pestered my parents for weeks. I whined. I pleaded. I cried. To no avail.

"Enough!" said my mother one night. "We're not made of money, and I'm certainly not wasting any on something as foolish as dance lessons. I don't want to hear another word about it."

So I never took ballet lessons at Madame Verushka's School of Dance, I never wore a frilly pink tutu and matching satin toe shoes, and I never danced the role of The Sugar Plum Fairy.

When I was nine years old, I came home from school one day and announced, "We're having a talent show, and I'm going to sing the song from *Annie*."

My mother laughed. "You can't carry a tune. You'll make a fool of yourself."

The next day I climbed the steps to the auditorium stage and belted out what the music teacher announced was the most off-key rendition of *Tomorrow* she'd ever heard.

"I told you so," said my mother when I arrived home in tears. "You set unrealistic goals for yourself, Hope. Then you fall apart when you fail. When will you learn?"

Apparently not by the time I was eleven. That was the year I decided I'd become an astronaut. Until my father took me to Kennywood and plunked me on the roller coaster—the big one.

"NASA doesn't accept astronauts prone to motion sickness," he said as I set foot on terra firma and proceeded to hurl my cookies. "You'll be a secretary, Hope. Like your mother. Stop wasting time on daydreams." And just to make sure, for my birthday that year he bought me a secondhand PC computer and a touch-typing tutorial.

Forget women's lib. Forget college. We were a meat-and-potatoes working class family descended from a meat-and-potatoes working class family. While college kids were burning their bras and draft cards and discovering the joys of sex and raw veggies, my mother had been in the kitchen, learning to cook the life out of string beans.

Mom and Dad reasoned that what was good enough for them was good enough for us. They had lived through the Age of Aquarius unscathed by free love and flower power. Dylan could sing his gravelly lungs out, but the times weren't a'changin' any time soon in our little corner of America where the Rust Belt merged with the Bible Belt.

Charley, Jr. would follow Dad and countless generations of Morgan men into the steel mills of western Pennsylvania. Faith and I (and yes, had Charley arrived as a girl, we would have been Faith, Hope, and Charity) were expected to master nothing more complicated than the intricacies of shorthand and land ourselves husbands prior to our twenty-first birthdays. Once married, we would have babies and cook mushy string beans in a kitchen spotless enough to eat off the floor, continuing in the time-honored tradition of our female ancestors.

We were the product of low expectations, and none of us had enough backbone to buck the Morgan philosophy of How-It's-Supposed-To-Be-In-The-World-No-Matter-What-Those-Damn-Liberals-In-Washington-New-York-And-Hollywood-Say because Dad was a firm believer in Man-of-the-House Mentality. Or so he and Mom constantly told us.

Which is why for my first twenty-odd years I lived the life mapped out for me by others. And why now at the age of nearly thirty-four, I was in the middle of my first job interview that required a hell of a lot more than the ability to take dictation and type sixty words a minute.

"Professor Antonelli speaks very highly of you."

I held my breath. I could feel the *but* hovering in the air between me and the Prada-clad woman seated on the opposite side of the table in the glass-enclosed conference room. Would Marion Merrick dismiss me without so much as a quick glance at the contents of my portfolio?

"He's very kind." I wasn't sure what else to say. Should I flip open the leather presentation book to expose the first of my renderings? Was the president of Schaffer-Merrick waiting for me to do so, or would she consider the move presumptuous? Although proud of what I'd accomplished, I still battled the ghosts of various relatives who deemed me a lesser species and tried to browbeat me into a barefoot-pregnant-and-in-the-kitchen existence. You can take the girl out of the western Pennsylvania doublewide, but sometimes it's hard to take that doublewide out of the girl.

It had taken me twelve years of part-time study to achieve what others at Carnegie Mellon University normally earned in five. No class had covered the finer points of interviewing. I knew the protocols for seeking a secretarial position, but this was different. This was my dream job, and I couldn't shake the feeling that one false move might jeopardize my chances.

I'd cut off my right arm for a chance to work with Ben Schaffer, the architecture world's brightest young star. Well, maybe not my *right* arm. I needed that one for drawing. However, I'd gladly sacrifice my left arm. Then again, so would every other graduate of CMU's architecture program.

With Schaffer-Merrick's reputation, Marion could have her pick of architects, designers, draftsmen, and artists. I wouldn't let her intimidate me. I'd worked too hard to get to this point, and my talent spoke for itself—if only she'd give me a chance to prove it. I tore my gaze away from the unopened portfolio and stole a glance at the woman who held my fate in her French manicured hands.

Raising one perfectly waxed eyebrow, Marion trapped me in an icy blue stare. "Bullshit! Antonelli's a mean son-of-a-bitch who's as tight with praise as he is with a dollar." Her gaze raked over me. "You're a hell of a lot older than his usual conquests. Not to mention..." Her voice trailed off with a wave of her hand that didn't take a mind reader to interpret. *Not to mention heavier and less attractive.*

The insinuation pissed me off. And the unspoken but implied insults didn't sit too well with me, either, especially coming from a woman who looked like an Anna Rexia cult member. "Are you implying I slept with Professor Antonelli?"

One corner of Marion's lips cocked upward. "Did you, or are you really as good as he claims?"

Back in Pittsburgh, Professor Antonelli had warned me about Ben Schaffer's tough-as-nails wife and partner. "I have no doubt they'll grab you up the moment they see your work," he had assured me. "But you'll need to develop a thick hide to survive at Schaffer-Merrick, Hope. Ben is very likable and a real charmer, but I hear Marion can be an extremely difficult woman."

Difficult? The word didn't begin to describe the woman. If I were a man, her remark would constitute sexual harassment. But then again, maybe this was Marion's way of finding out just what I was made of. If I could handle her, I could handle the most temperamental of clients. Deciding I had nothing to lose at this point, I squared my shoulders, returned her steely glare, and stated, "I'm that good." Then I flipped open my portfolio to prove it.

When her mouth curved up in a slight smile, I knew I'd met the challenge. Marion dipped her head to study the watercolor renderings displayed within the acetate pages of the presentation book. Confident that my work would carry me the rest of the way, I allowed myself to breathe.

"Are you still living in Pittsburgh?" she asked as she continued flipping through the pages.

Yes! I fought to contain my excitement. Such a question could only mean one thing. Marion Merrick was going to offer me a position at the elite New York firm. "I live outside of Pittsburgh, actually. I commuted to CMU."

She stopped mid-flip and glanced up, spearing me with a look that stated in no uncertain terms that she didn't give a flying fig about the details of my life.

"But I can leave at any time," I quickly continued. "My lease is month-to-month."

"Good. You'll start Monday." She picked up the phone. "Edwina, come wrap this up," she said after a slight pause. Then without another word—not so much as a salary offer or a welcome-to-the-company handshake—she rose and exited the conference room.

I stared after her in disbelief. I'd never met a woman like Marion Merrick. Disdainful cold conceit best summed up her persona. And she looked the part as well—from her perfectly coifed, not-a-hair-out-of-place French twist down to her four-inch Bottega Veneta stilettos. Hey, I may hail from the sticks, and maybe the only designer labels I can afford are those featured at Walmart and Kmart, but I like to keep up in case I hit the lottery with that one Mega Millions ticket I allow myself each week.

Anyway, it seemed obvious that Marion never considered I might turn down the job offer—had there actually been an offer. Not that I would have, but all the same, Marion was damn sure of herself.

The sound of a chortle startled me. "Wish I had a camera to capture the expression on your face, honey."

A statuesque woman with an hourglass figure, flawless coffee-colored skin, and a shaved head stood in the doorway. She wore large gold hoops in her ears and an amused expression on her face.

"Excuse me?"

"Never mind. You'll get used to her." The woman dropped a thick file folder of papers on the table in front of me and grabbed the seat Marion had vacated. Reaching across the table, she clasped my right hand in hers and gave it a friendly pumping. "Edwina McCann. Office manager and staff shrink. Welcome to Schaffer-Merrick. Or Heaven-Hell, as we natives refer to it. How badly did she rattle you?"

Heaven-Hell? I grinned at Edwina. "On a scale of one to ten? I'd say a solid fifteen. I...I didn't realize I had been offered a job until she told me to start Monday. As a matter of fact, I got the distinct impression she didn't like me. And we never

6

discussed...well actually, we didn't discuss anything! Am I really hired?"

Edwina laughed. "Honey, you were hired the moment Ben saw the samples of your work Arturo Antonelli mailed him. Trust me. I was there. His exact words to the Queen Bee were, 'Grab her.'"

"Grab her?"

Edwina winked. "Ben knows talent. He wasn't about to lose you to one of our competitors."

I leaned back in my chair and shook my head. Interesting that the office manager had little regard for the president of Schaffer-Merrick but held the creative genius of the firm in high regard. Still, it seemed odd that Edwina would speak so frankly to a complete stranger. "Everything happened so quickly. I feel like I just stepped off a roller coaster. I think I need to catch my breath. What did you mean by Heaven-Hell?"

"Schaffer-Merrick. Heaven-Hell. You'll understand soon enough, but don't worry, honey. Her Royal Highness spends most of her time out of the office wining and dining prospective clients."

Edwina twisted in her chair, scowling at the closed conference room door. "Wish I knew how she manages to stay a size zero when she spends so much time at Nobu and The Four Seasons. Me? I have to do five hours of penance at the gym if I so much as glance at a soufflé. Which reminds me." She checked her watch. "It's past lunch, and I'm famished." She stood, scooping up the file folder and tucking it under her arm. "My treat. We'll tackle all this over some rabbit food and a couple of skinny lattes. Then I'll introduce you to the rest of the chain gang."

I followed as Edwina breezed through the large, open area of the fifth-floor loft that housed the architectural firm of Schaffer-Merrick. "This is Hope, everyone," she called out as she hurried past drawing boards and computer stations. Then she waved her arms to encompass the well-lit studio and the half-dozen people who had raised their heads at the sound of her voice. "Hope, this is Le, Tony, Paco, Zeke, Nigel, and Freddie—not necessarily in that order. I'll introduce you individually later. After I fill myself with weeds and seeds and my drug of choice."

"Better watch it, Winnie," said a tall string bean of a man with a long ponytail and wire-rimmed glasses. "You've already gone over your caffeine quota for the month, and it's not even half over. I heard The Queen Bee mention something to Ben about sending you to Coffee Drinkers Anonymous."

Edwina laughed. "Sure. When she enrolls in Bulimics Anonymous."

"Winnie!"

"Relax, sugar. She left ten minutes ago for a twelve-thirty with The Italian Stallion."

We exited the building, and Edwina led me down the street to The Java Joint, a small café on Third Avenue between Twenty-first and Twenty-second Streets. I raced to keep up with her fast-paced strides. Everyone seemed to operate in overdrive in Manhattan. I was used to the small mining and farm towns of Western Pennsylvania. The daily commute from Butler County into Pittsburgh for class had been a huge adjustment for me, but compared to New York, Pittsburgh was...well, a burg.

"Everything on the menu is scrumptious," said Edwina after we were seated at a table by the window, "but the Portobello quiche is to die for—*if* you're not counting fat, and calories."

Contrary to Marion's snide implications, I'd lost my baby fat years ago, and once I discovered there was more to cooking than the Morgan menu of gravy-smothered artery cloggers, I'd maintained what most people outside of New York, Paris, and Milan considered an average figure. Still, since Edwina apparently fought an ongoing battle with the bulge, I didn't want to rub her nose in it by ordering the quiche. So I settled on the Dieter's Delight.

After we placed our orders with the waitress, Edwina pulled a sheet of paper from her folder and passed it across the table. "This is what we're offering as base," she said. "There's also the standard benefits package—health insurance, dental, a small term life insurance policy, and flexible savings plan. We can go over all that back at the office."

I stared at the figure on the page and fought to keep from frowning. The salary sucked. Big time. I'd expected at least fifteen percent more than Schaffer-Merrick's offer. With tens of thousands of dollars in college loans still to pay off, how could I survive in Manhattan on such a low salary? Fighting to keep my voice level and professional, I said, "To be honest, I was hoping for more. I realize I'm right out of college, but I do have years of experience in the industry. That should count for something."

I had discovered my true calling while working as a receptionist/secretary for a Butler County architect. Who would have thought all those years of idle doodling had been a latent gift yearning to be set free? But Mr. Hagarty, my boss, had recognized my talent and encouraged me to develop it. "And this might be considered a generous offer in some parts of the country," I continued, "but—"

Edwina finished my sentence. "But how do you live in New York on that?"

"Exactly."

"You don't," she said. "You find a nice little apartment in the burbs and commute like millions of others. Hell, even Ben and The Queen take the train every day. From Jersey. Me? I'm a Brooklyn girl. Born and bred. Still live there."

The waitress arrived with our coffees. "About time," said Edwina, polishing off half the super-sized latte before coming up for air. "Besides," she continued, "this figure only represents base. It's not like that's all you'll have to live on for the year."

"I don't understand. I thought by base you meant starting salary for someone in my position."

Edwina raised an eyebrow. "Your resume said you put yourself through school while working for an architectural firm. How can you not know about base?"

"I received a straight salary."

"Sure, as a secretary, but what about the other members of the firm? The architects and designers."

"Mr. Hagarty is a one-man operation. I was the only employee."

"That explains it." She waved her hand in annoyance while taking another lengthy sip. "But you'd think with what CMU charges for tuition that they'd give you some practical info along with all those boring treatises on Bauhaus."

She drained her coffee before continuing. "Architecture firms work like law offices. Everyone gets a modest salary. Then, at the end of the fiscal year bonuses are handed out based on the year's profits. The more successful the firm is, the greater the financial rewards to the employees. With the business we've been pulling in, you can expect at least ten percent more come the end of December. And that's only because you won't have been with us for a full year."

I glanced at the figure on the paper in front of me and mulled over Edwina's words. I really did want to work with Ben Schaffer. Even though I'd never met the man, his innovative designs and creative genius had already turned him into a living legend before his fortieth birthday.

I did a bit of mental arithmetic. With what I'd had to pay for tuition each semester, I'd lived on far less. If I could find an apartment near public transportation and shopping, I wouldn't need the added expense of a car. New York and New Jersey auto insurance rates were legend enough that even those of us who had never set foot in either state knew of them. And I did have a six-month grace period before all but one of my student loans came due.

I took a deep breath. "You wouldn't by any chance know of someone with an inexpensive apartment to rent, would you?"

The office manager winked. "As a matter of fact, honey, you're in luck."

~*~

Forty-five minutes later we returned to the loft to find the entire staff huddled around my portfolio in the conference room. Heads nodded and tongues clucked in approval as a man, leaning over the center of the table, slowly flipped the pages that contained the culmination of the past twelve years of my life. As Edwina and I entered the room, six heads raised and turned in our direction. The chatter subsided, the silence broken only by the slow-moving ripple of the acetate sheets.

One by one the staff members turned toward the man whose attention hadn't veered from my work. Someone cleared his throat, and the man finally tore his gaze from the page he had been studying and glanced up at me. "Ah, here's my new da Vinci," he said, lifting his nutmeg-colored, tousled head. His mocha eyes twinkled as he extended his hand. "I'm Ben Schaffer, and you must be Hope Morgan."

Holy short circuit, Batman! Every neuron in my brain sputtered to a halt at the sound of that deep baritone. The man didn't speak his words; he caressed them. Think James Earl Jones blended with Patrick Stewart and just the slightest dash of Sean Connery. Ben's voice flowed with a richness of tone and timbre that sent my insides galloping. Reason deserted me as my mouth went dry and my ability to think came to a screeching halt. I stared at his extended hand, incapable of moving a muscle or kick-starting my own tongue.

What the hell was the matter with me? Okay, my dream had come true. I was really going to be working for this man whose designs I so admired, but why was I suddenly acting like a starstruck groupie meeting Bruce Springsteen or Bon Jovi? Hell, I was a nearly thirty-four-year-old widow. I'd left teeny-bopper crushes behind years ago.

An eerie silence filled the room. Ben was the first to break it with a joke. "Look, no buzzer," he said, holding up his hand, palm outward, and wiggling his fingers.

A rush of laughter erupted around me; Edwina jostled me from behind. "Earth to Hope," she whispered in my ear.

I shook myself free of the stupor. As a surge of heat rushed up my neck and settled in my cheeks, I segued from silent dummy to yammering idiot. "I...I'm sorry," I stammered, then giggled, before finally offering Ben my right hand. "I guess I'm just a bit overwhelmed. I can't believe I'm going to be working for you. I've admired your work for so long, Mr. Schaffer." *Jeez!* I cringed at the sound of my own words. I might have put teenie-bopper crushes behind me decades ago, but I had just resurrected my own inner groupie.

One of the men standing behind Ben groaned. "Shit. Another hero worshipper. Didn't we have enough of that with those damn interns last month? You'd better not let this start going to your head, Ben."

Ignoring him, Ben grasped my hand with both of his. "Ben," he said. "We're very informal around here, Hope."

The moment our hands met, every cell in my body picked up a band instrument and began playing *the 1812 Overture* at deafening volume. Drums rolled, cannons boomed, rockets flared. The hairs on the back of my neck stood at attention. Sensations unlike any I'd ever experienced shot from the tips of my fingers straight down to my toes. Having already branded myself a starstruck, blithering idiot, I clamped my mouth shut, but the damage was already done.

One of the other employees was quick to confirm my fear. "Definitely another member of the Ben Schaffer Fan Club. Maybe we'd better stand in line to get his autograph now before he stops having anything to do with the little people."

"Knock it off, guys," said Edwina. "Cut the newbie a break."

"Ignore them," said Ben, still grasping my hand. "They're short on social graces but long on talent. Welcome to the team, Hope."

"Yeah, don't mind us," said the bespectacled beanpole Edwina had bantered with earlier on our way to lunch. "We don't get out much."

Ben graced me with a mischievous mega-watt smile. "It's my sworn duty to keep the world safe from Tony and the rest of these reprobates. I lock them in their cages every night before I leave."

"If we're good, we get five extra crumbs each week," an Asian woman off to one side added. "And by the way, speaking of lacking in social graces, since no one else has bothered with introductions, I'm Le. Welcome aboard. It's nice to have another female around to help even out the gene pool. Winnie and I have gotten tired of being outnumbered."

Interesting how she omitted Marion, I thought, as I acknowledged the greeting with a smile and a weak, "Hi, Le."

What was wrong with me? If I wanted these people to accept me as an equal, I'd better start acting like one. Since good-natured bantering seemed an established form of behavior for the staff, I forced out some of my own. "Well, I suppose if you've also got a cage for me, I don't need to worry about finding an apartment."

Everyone in the room burst out laughing, Ben loudest of all. "Hope," he said, "I'm glad you're joining us. You're going to fit right in."

TWO

Ben left the office that evening feeling good about his decision to hire Arturo Antonelli's latest protégé. By bedtime his euphoria had faded. Throughout the next day, as the hours dragged on, his mood continued to darken until a black cloud of anger hung over him. All thanks to Marion. That night as he sat in the unlit den, stewing over the whereabouts of his AWOL wife, he tried to pinpoint the exact moment when their relationship had soured. In the beginning he and Marion had everything going for them. With talents, goals, and personalities complementing one another, he had believed theirs had been a match made in Heaven—both personally and professionally.

And the sex hadn't been bad, either.

So what had gone wrong?

Ben noticed the initial signs shortly after they established the firm. Whereas Marion once had many outside interests and friends, after becoming president of Schaffer-Merrick, she lost interest in anything that wasn't business related. Although they were both driven to succeed, Marion's drive bordered on obsession. No matter how many awards the firm won, no matter how many top clients Marion signed, no matter how large their fortune grew, it was never enough.

Ben grimaced. He didn't like the woman his wife had become.

Hearing the sound of her key in the front door, he rose to meet her. "Where the hell have you been?" he asked as she stepped over the threshold.

Marion dropped her purse and briefcase on the ornately carved Victorian hall bench and kicked off a pair of those damn eight hundred dollar, four-inch heels she insisted on wearing—even with jeans. Leaving the shoes where they landed, she headed up the sweeping oak staircase. "You knew I had a meeting with Giovanni. We discussed it before I left."

Ben stared at her back. "Your meeting was yesterday afternoon."

"Giovanni had some second thoughts about the New Orleans location, given the extent of damage from Hurricane Katrina and the BP spill. He's worried about the impact of future disasters. He requested I fly down with him to meet with the city engineers." She glanced over her shoulder at him. "I do have a responsibility to maintain the firm's integrity and high standards, Ben. Besides, we can't afford to antagonize our largest account."

"And what of your responsibilities here?"

Halting halfway up the stairs, she turned to confront him. "It's not like we don't have help! I'm your partner, not some goddamn *hausfrau*!"

Ben shook his head as he climbed the stairs behind her. "Why didn't you answer your cell? I called at least a dozen times."

Marion shrugged. "The cell died. I didn't have my charger with me."

"What? No one else had a phone you could use to let me know you were going out of town. I was worried."

Marion responded to his concern in a voice rising several octaves and an equal number of decibels. "I'm a grown woman. I don't have to account to you or anyone else for my every move. I swear, Ben, sometimes you act exactly like my father!"

The accusation stung. "Lower your voice, Marion. That's not true, and you know it." Nothing could be further from the truth.

"Do I? The tactics are different, but you're just as much a controlling son-of-a-bitch as he was."

Ben clenched both his jaw and his fists. Marion's father had completely ignored the late-in-life daughter he'd never wanted. All her life she felt compelled not only to prove she was as good as her brothers but that she was better. Smarter. More successful. And somewhere along the way Marion had transferred her hatred of Prescott Woodrow Edmondson Merrick the Third to him. "I have always encouraged and supported you."

"Encouraged? Supported? Ha! Coerced is more like it. Whatever Ben wants, Ben gets." She stabbed him in the chest with her index finger. "In triplicate!"

"Don't do this, Marion."

"Don't tell me what to do!"

He reached for her hand. "Marion, please. You can't mean what you're saying."

Avoiding his gaze, she yanked her fingers from his grasp and continued up the stairs. "Don't I?"

"I always thought we had the same dreams."

"No." She flung her arms in a sweeping gesture. "This was your dream, not mine."

"Damn it! You chose this house."

"I don't mean the house, and you know it. You owe me, Ben. Triple time. I sacrificed a hell of a lot for you, so don't start complaining when I run off to pacify some temperamental client."

Giovanni Scarpetta did have a reputation for being high-strung and demanding. When the elderly Italian playboy and department store baron had decided to expand his empire across the Atlantic, Marion aggressively courted and won the account. Schaffer-Merrick had designed both the U.S. headquarters and each of the seven mega-stores soon to be built across the country.

Although his wife refused to take crap from any man, Ben noticed that when Giovanni Scarpetta said jump, Marion asked how high.

Ben sighed. "We used to be such a great team, you and I. I'm sorry you regret what I consider our greatest collaboration. I've tried to be patient and understanding, Marion. I know the last few years haven't been easy for you. I had hoped..." Ben stopped. Any hope he'd held in that direction had long since died. Their marriage was a sham. The very thing that held them together was also the catalyst driving them apart.

He'd tried everything. On his own. Marion had refused to take part in any sort of counseling or therapy—with him or without him. Holding his breath, Ben forced himself to utter the one question he dreaded asking but knew was time to ask. "Do you want out?"

She paused at the entrance to the master suite. For several long excruciating seconds, she stood with her back to him but said nothing. When she spoke, she ignored his question. "Giovanni wants his American investors to meet us. He's having a dinner Friday night and wants a new set of renderings to show them."

Ben shook his head. In typical Marion fashion she changed the subject, preferring to focus on Giovanni, a minor count—or so he claimed—who was turning into a royal pain in the ass. One of the many shrinks Ben had consulted said it was because anything personal was too painful for Marion to confront. "What's wrong with the set of drawings he has?"

"He doesn't like them. The new girl starts Monday. You'd better have Zeke get her started on them right away." She entered the room, closing the door behind her.

After a few moments of staring at the polished wood, Ben continued down the hall to the guest room.

THREE

Was it possible to fall in lust in a split second? I couldn't shake the feelings that had invaded me Thursday afternoon and refused to let go. A smile, a handshake, and a sexy-as-sin voice had reduced my insides to warm honey. *Warm honey?* Jeez, I was beginning to sound like some character in a romance novel. Hell, molten lava was more like it! If I had to daydream in clichés, why not jump right into the get-down-and-dirty reality of what those daydreams really were—erotica with a capital E.

Maybe I'd just been without for too long. Here I was in my sexual prime, according to Masters and Johnson, and I was living the life of a nun. Not that I'd had time for any sort of social life, sexual or otherwise, the past twelve years. Juggling a full-time job, a demanding course load, and an hour-long commute to and from campus three times a week left little wiggle room for anything other than breathing. Early on, I'd given up sleep for studying. Eating was usually accomplished at my desk while proofreading blueprints or in the car on my way to class.

Let's face it: My resistance was at an all-time low. I was ripe for a kamikaze mugging from the first sexy guy who crossed my path.

"I'm a frigging idiot," I muttered, wrestling an overstuffed chair from the back of the U-Haul I'd driven from western Pennsylvania to Garwood, New Jersey. "The last thing I need is to be fantasizing about hot monkey sex with my *married* boss."

With neither the time nor the energy for a relationship the last dozen years, I'd relegated sex to the back burner of my life. Now those simmering hormones had decided to ignite into a full-blown and totally unacceptable conflagration between my legs. Damn. First paycheck, I'm buying myself a vibrator.

"Are you crazy?" a voice shrieked from behind me.

Great. I've moved into a town of Puritanical mind readers! But the clairvoyant sounded an awful lot like Edwina McCann. I glanced over my shoulder to find Winnie, one hand on her hip, the other holding a cup of Starbucks, frowning at me. She was flanked by three other members of the Schaffer-Merrick staff—Tony, the bespectacled beanpole and resident computer guru; Paco, the space planner; and Zeke, the firm's project coordinator.

"I had a feeling you planned to tackle something like this on your own," said Edwina.

Paco and Zeke relieved me of the chair while Tony grabbed a carton off the curb.

"Oh, so you didn't just happen to be strolling in the neighborhood?" I asked, swiping at a trickle of sweat with the sleeve of one of my many seen-better-days T-shirts. Then I offered Edwina and the rest of the cavalry a grateful smile. My brother-in-law Dwayne and a few of his buddies from the plant had loaded up the small rental truck for me the day before, but I'd anticipated struggling on my own at this end.

"Ulterior motives," said Zeke, a compact, muscular man who looked like he did his share of weight training and would have little trouble hoisting my sofa up two flights of stairs—by himself. "We have a huge presentation to give on Friday, and Ben wants you to redo all the concept renderings your predecessor prepared. We can't risk you injuring that precious drawing hand, can we?"

"Well, whatever the reason, I appreciate your thoughtfulness." I turned to Edwina. "I suppose Aunt Minnie is keeping you abreast of my progress?"

"One of my best spies," she said, referring to her middle-aged aunt who owned the small three-story corner building. Her pet store, *Minnie's Mouses and More*, occupied the ground floor, with Minnie McCann residing on the second floor. I had rented the recently vacated third floor walk-up. Although not much to look at, the rooms were spacious, the location convenient to shopping and transportation, and the price suited my tight budget.

"Nigel and Freddie got suckered into overtime at The Castle today," said Edwina. "Otherwise, they would've come, too. And Le's kids have a soccer match this afternoon, but she promised to drop off lunch before the game. Pizza with the works."

I raised both eyebrows. Weight-obsessed Winnie scarfing down pizza? This I had to see.

She smirked. "I wish. Packed my greens before I left." She tilted her head, draining the remainder of the coffee. Then, pitching the empty container into a curbside trashcan, she hoisted a carton of kitchen utensils onto her shoulder and followed Tony up the stairs.

I brought up the rear, a table lamp in each hand. How lucky could I get? A dream job and coworkers willing to give up a Saturday to lug furniture and hoist boxes.

Professor Antonelli had often bragged about Ben, his former undergraduate student, but I'd learned about the other members of the team from a year-old copy of *Architectural Digest*. The six-page spread had profiled the cutting-edge firm of Schaffer-Merrick, documenting its meteoric rise.

The diverse group of thirty-eight-year-olds had met in graduate school. After graduation they each worked at other firms for a few years, gaining experience and contacts. Five years ago Ben and Marion, already married, took a huge gamble. Quitting their lucrative positions, they merged Ben's creative genius and Marion's marketing skills to form Schaffer-Merrick. The others quickly signed onboard.

And now this tight-knit group of friends had put out the welcome mat for me. I grew giddy thinking about my good fortune. It had been a long time coming for me. Not that I hadn't worked my booty off, but sometimes hard work and sacrifice mean nothing if there isn't a bit of luck to go along with it. And luck hadn't exactly been my kissing cousin for over a decade.

"By the way, what's The Castle?" I asked, setting the blue cracked glaze ginger jar lamps on the floor in a corner of the living room.

"What Winnie dubbed Ben's and Marion's place," said Tony. He speared her with a watch-your-mouth glare before continuing. "They purchased a rundown Victorian in an historic section of Westfield right after they were married. It's taken them more than eight years to fully restore it. Nigel offered to put in a rose garden for them. He dragged Freddie along to help with the grunt work."

"Nigel? He's the landscape designer, right?" I conjured up an image of the slight man with a brilliant smile and a Jamaican accent.

"And Freddie's our interior designer," added Winnie. "Tall Fabio-looking hunk. He and Nigel are a couple."

"Oh."

"Yeah, I know." She sighed. "What a waste of testosterone."

"Hey, ladies, I've got plenty to go around, if you're looking," offered Paco, trudging up the stairs, an end table resting across his shoulders.

"Save it for your wife, Casanova." Zeke nudged him from behind. "Where do you want these, Hope?"

"One on either side of the sofa."

Zeke maneuvered around Paco, heading for the opposite end of the room. "You heard the lady, studmeister. Move it."

By the time Le, the firm's engineer, arrived with the pizzas, all my furniture was in place, and the various cartons of household items were stacked in their appropriate rooms. Tony had even unpacked my computer and stereo equipment and wired everything up.

"How can I thank you?" I asked, as they prepared to leave. "I thought this would take me all weekend. That's why I drove most of the way last night."

"Just arrive fresh and rested Monday morning," said Zeke. "You have a hectic first week ahead of you. Sort of a baptism by fire."

Paco snorted. "Sort of?"

"Don't spook the newbie," said Winnie. "She'll do fine."

"Right." I forced a casual optimism into my voice and resisted the urge to gnaw at the inside of my cheek. "No problem."

I had plenty of confidence in my ability to produce stellar renderings for the Scarpetta account. But why did I get the feeling the others knew something I didn't? Something they didn't want to tell me quite yet. Just how many renderings were we talking about and how detailed? Pencil sketches or full-fledged watercolors? And how large? I was afraid to ask. I didn't want to come across as a slacker, but Zeke's baptism by fire analogy and Paco's comment about it were turning my stomach to battery acid. Or maybe that was the three slices of pepperoni pizza.

For twelve years I'd kept a daunting schedule, but I'd only taken two or three classes a semester. Working full time, I couldn't handle more. Not to mention the mind-boggling tuition that stretched my budget to the brink of bankruptcy, even with the aid of Wally's modest life insurance policy and assorted student loans. At any rate, my course load was relatively light compared to that of full-time students whose level of assignments were more in keeping with an actual working environment.

Failure wasn't an option, though. I was determined to complete the concept art on time even if it meant working through the night. Lucky for me, I was used to going without sleep. And since I'd already been informed that the demanding Giovanni Scarpetta hadn't cared for my predecessor's work, I was bound and determined *my* renderings would blow his mind—as well as Ben's. And earning a few brownie points with Marion couldn't hurt, either.

~*~

Thanks to a combination of nervous anticipation and the inability to shut down my overactive imagination, I tossed and turned most of Sunday night. When I wasn't fantasizing inappropriate scenarios featuring my new boss (I *really* needed a social life or that vibrator—maybe both), I stared at the digital display on my alarm clock, counting down the hours and minutes and seconds until I stepped across the threshold of the fifth-floor Manhattan loft and settled in as the newest member of Ben Schaffer's team.

Yes, I was anxious to prove myself worthy of my new position, but I also couldn't wait to see Ben again. Not to work my seductive charms on him. Like that would happen, even if I had any! No, my more rational side hoped my regression into school-girl-crush-mode, and the subsequent erotic day and night dreams they'd induced, had been an overreaction to meeting a man I'd admired for several years and now had the good fortune to be working for. As I've said, I'm not used to luck landing in my lap.

Anyway, normal day-to-day contact would rid me of the hero worship/groupie thing and show me the real Ben, warts and all. Thursday's illogical hormonal reaction aside, he had to have them. The warts, that is. All men did. At least I hoped so because those damn hormones were planting some crazy ideas in my brain—ideas impossible to pursue. My mother didn't raise me to steal another woman's man.

For my own good, though, I had to exorcise myself of this unacceptable and decidedly unwelcome infatuation that had grabbed hold of me. And the sooner the better. So why then couldn't I access the rational side of my brain and erase the image of that incredible hunk with his devastating killer smile? Common sense eluded me. My higher reasoning skills abandoned me, packing up and fleeing the chaotic ruins of what was once a sensible brain.

Life would certainly be simpler if Ben Schaffer were short and bald with a beer belly that made him look nine months pregnant.

FOUR

Ben spotted Hope standing on the platform as the NJ Transit train pulled into the Garwood station. This was her first day on the job, and she looked nervous as hell.

He remembered his own feelings of inadequacy twelve years earlier. Filled with overconfidence after graduating at the top of his class and landing a job with a prestigious firm, every ounce of self-assurance fled him that first morning as he nervously waited for the bus into the city. Luckily, several senior staff members, apparently remembering their own first assignments, had come to his rescue, befriending him and quelling his fears.

How could he do any less for his own new employee? Rising from his seat, Ben made his way to the back of the car and called out to her as the train screeched to a halt. "Good morning, Hope."

Her face brightened at once. She stood in the morning light, a warm spring breeze blowing through her light brown hair, her expressive hazel eyes wide with surprise. Fresh and eager, ready to take on the world. He envied her. So much had changed in his own life over the past few years, so many bright hopes now threatening to suffocate under layers of neglect and disappointment.

Focusing on her smile, Ben found himself yearning to turn back the clock and start anew. *I wish you your dreams, Hope Morgan, and the wisdom to recognize false promises.*

"I didn't expect a welcoming committee," she said.

"A committee of one, I'm afraid. Marion has a client meeting this morning. She won't be in until later this afternoon." Ben stepped aside, allowing her to precede him into the car.

"When I saw you waiting on the platform, I started thinking about my own first day of work," he said, settling into a seat beside her. "I remembered how nervous I was—the new kid on the block, feeling very intimidated as I walked through the doors of Beckwith Hobart Associates. I had convinced myself they'd made a huge mistake and would realize it the moment I sat down at my drawing board. I expected to be fired by lunch."

"But they hadn't, and you weren't?"

"No, but I rationalized that as well. I decided the bigwigs were too embarrassed to admit their mistake. I envisioned them feverishly reworking all my designs every night rather than owning up to their hiring blunder. I'm certain they breathed a huge sigh of relief the day I handed in my resignation."

When Hope laughed, Ben reassured her. "No mistakes were made concerning you. You can relax. I wasn't about to let one of my competitors grab someone so talented."

Color flushed her cheeks; she lowered her gaze. "That's what Edwina said on Thursday."

Ben shook his head. "Winnie. I love the woman like a sister, but she's got a mouth as big as The Bronx. Did she at least wait until you had accepted our offer or has my secret cost me in a higher salary?"

"Am I under oath?"

Ben chuckled. He had hired Hope Morgan sight unseen. Her talent would mesh perfectly with the rest of his team. Now he saw that her personality would, too. And he admired her perseverance. A woman who wanted something so badly that she spent twelve years of her life pursuing it was a woman he wanted working for him. That kind of dedication came cheap at any price.

Ben believed that his firm achieved the success it did from more than the individual talents of its staff. His employees, together since the firm's inception, were all longtime friends. Jen's departure had created a dilemma. He had agonized over the ability of an outsider to fit into this close-knit group. He now cast that particular worry aside.

"How was your first weekend in New Jersey?" he asked. "If I remember correctly from reading your resume, you've lived your entire life in western Pennsylvania?"

She nodded.

"Quite a shock, I'll bet."

"In some ways I feel like the proverbial fish out of water. And in other ways it's like being a kid let loose in the toy store."

"What do you mean?"

"There are so many choices here. We had a Walmart on the outskirts of town, a Kmart a few miles farther down the highway, and not much else other than a small grocery store on Main Street. The nearest supermarket was ten miles away and the nearest mall a forty-minute drive. Now I'm living within a block of two supermarkets that would take up all of Main Street. I've never seen so many different brands of macaroni! I'm a stranger in a strange land."

"You'll get used to it. In a few months you'll get annoyed when the supermarket runs out of that particular brand of macaroni you've decided you like best."

She laughed. "I think it will take me at least that long to try out each brand."

He changed the subject. "What about family? Are you adjusting to being away from them? I imagine that can't be easy for you."

The laughter left her eyes. She turned to stare out the window as the train made its way through the suburbs toward the city. "I have no family."

FIVE

"None?"

I girded my proverbial loins and turned back to face him. I still had trouble speaking about the past, but maybe it was best to get it out of the way now rather than run the risk of an ambush in front of the entire staff. "No close relatives. Lots of distant cousins and such. Back in Rusty Mud Creek just about everyone is related to everyone else in some way if you bother to trace back far enough."

Maybe that would be enough to sate his curiosity. And maybe he hadn't noticed the quiver in my voice. I *really* didn't want Ben Schaffer—or anyone for that matter—poking further into my past. I'd worked too long and too hard to bury the pain. If I'd had the resources, I would have moved away a dozen years ago. Maybe that would have prevented further tragedy, but I couldn't afford both school and a new life where no one knew me.

Life choices always come down to money. So I concentrated on school and the future and sucked up the memories that assaulted me around every ramshackle corner of Rusty Mud Creek. I'd learned to choose my battles, and I tried my damnedest to make peace with my inner demons. Sometimes I succeeded.

Like now. Because Ben accepted my brief explanation and asked no further prying questions.

~*~

Within hours of my first day on the job, I fully understood Edwina's Heaven-Hell reference. When Marion was present, the tension level in the loft skyrocketed. Although the office manager was the only employee who felt no qualms about vocalizing her dislike for the company president, the others expressed their feelings in both body language and sideways glances to each other.

I could almost hear a collective sigh of relief whenever Marion left the loft. Subdued whispers immediately transformed into laughing banter. When Marion wasn't around, a near circus-like atmosphere prevailed with Ben often acting the part of ringmaster.

"Heads up!" he called, early in the afternoon of my second day on the job.

"Incoming!" yelled Paco.

Edwina quickly ducked out of the path of an intricately folded paper airplane. The projectile skimmed above my head, landing on the floor beside my stool.

"Looks like Ben's decided it's time for Hope's initiation," Winnie said, stooping to pick up the aircraft.

"My what?" I spun around in my chair. Puzzled by the strange comment, I watched as Winnie folded back one of the plane's wings, then groaned.

"What's it today?" asked Nigel. "Knock-knocks or elephants?"

"Light bulbs," said Winnie. Shaking her head, she offered me a pitiful smile. "Poor girl."

"Huh?" I glanced around. Everyone was looking at me. Ben stood at the opposite end of the room. With his arms folded across his chest and his unruly mop of hair falling over one eyebrow, he looked far too innocent. And incredibly sexy. When our eyes met, the corners of his mouth turned up in a rakish smile that reminded me of Harrison Ford back in his Han Solo and Indiana Jones days. I turned back to Edwina, trying desperately to ignore the shiver skittering up my spine. So much for visualizing Ben Schaffer as short and bald with a beer belly that made him look nine months pregnant.

"Our fearless leader can't let go of his adolescence," explained Winnie. "He has this awful habit of subjecting us to dreadful jokes, rotten riddles, and the most appalling puns you'll ever hear. However, if you know what's good for you, you'll laugh." She punctuated her statement with a wink. "Ready?"

"I suppose I have no choice?"

"None."

I held up my hands in surrender. "Bring on the firing squad."

Winnie cleared her throat. "Okay. Here goes. How many suburban weekend do-it-yourselfers does it take to change a light bulb?"

Somewhere in the dark recesses of my brain, I'd heard this joke. I closed my eyes and knitted my brows together in concentration. If only I could remember the punch line.

In the background I heard one of my coworkers whistling the *Final Jeopardy* theme.

"Give up?" asked Winnie.

Never. I shook my head. If this were some kind of acceptance test, I was bound and determined to pass with flying colors. "No,

I've got it." My eyelids sprang open. "The answer is one, but it takes three weekends and half a dozen trips to the hardware store."

"Way to go, Hope!" yelled Tony as the room filled with loud cheers and applause. Winnie slapped me a high-five.

"Now it's your turn," said Ben, approaching my drawing board. He glanced briefly at my work-in-progress watercolor, an interior view of Scarpetta's corporate offices. "Beautiful," he said.

Heat rose to my cheeks. *Jeez!* Every time the man complimented me or my work, that damn teeny-bopping inner groupie in me escaped. I stammered my thanks.

He retrieved the airplane from Winnie and handed it to me. "You have to come up with another light bulb joke. Write it somewhere on the airplane and send it off to someone else in the room."

I set aside my watercolor brush and picked up a pencil. Not someone who usually remembered jokes, I wracked my brain for one. If this was a routine occurrence at the firm, I'd have to start surfing the web for inventory. Finally, I remembered one I'd heard about engineers. After scribbling the question under the opposite wing, I sent it soaring in Le's direction.

Unfortunately, I wasn't as adept at flying paper airplanes as my boss. The plane climbed for several yards then banked steeply to the left. Catching on a swoosh of air as the front door opened, it took a sudden nosedive, crash landing against Marion's right shoulder as she entered the loft.

The room grew deadly silent. Without saying a word, Marion stooped to retrieve the airplane and crumpled the paper in her fist. Her gaze sweeping the room, she pierced first her husband, then each of her employees with a glare cold enough to freeze molten lava. Then she headed for her office, depositing the remains of the airplane on my drawing board as she passed.

An uneasy calm settled over the room. I dropped the balled paper into my wastebasket and returned to my watercolor. Out of the corner of my eye I caught a glimpse of Ben and Zeke exchanging glances, both their expressions grim. Around me the other members of the team quietly returned to their tasks.

The author who'd written the *Architectural Digest* article about Schaffer-Merrick had portrayed Ben, Marion, and the others as longtime, close friends. Boy, had she been off. At least where Marion was concerned. Talk about inventing the facts. Like a Park Avenue socialite forced to associate with street people, Marion kept her distance from the others and her nose raised firmly in the air.

Had Marion ever been part of the Schaffer-Merrick *gang*, and if so, why was there now such an impenetrable barrier between herself and her former friends? I doubted the Marion I knew had ever participated in one of Ben's spontaneous jokefests or any other tomfoolery. Ben seemed as much outside his wife's invisible stone wall as any of their employees.

Thankfully, Marion spent a good deal of each day away from the office. Unfortunately, though, when she was in the loft, she took to spending a good deal of time hovering over me. The woman scrutinized every one of my brush strokes. At first I thought she was waiting for a chance to find fault with my work. I fought to control the seething annoyance churning inside me. In contrast, each time Ben checked on my progress, he offered nothing but praise over the way I transformed his sterile architectural drawings and Tony's CAD layouts into paintings fit for a gallery showing.

Not to sound cliché but I put my heart and soul into my

watercolors. After a lifetime of yearning to be special at something, I'd discovered my real talent almost by accident. And I was good, damn it. I knew it, and no amount of intimidation on Marion's part was going to start me second-guessing that conviction. I'd worked too hard to overcome a lifetime of inadequacies, thanks to well-meaning but uneducated and stuck-in-a-time-warp parents.

No, there was *nothing* wrong with my work.

Finally, after being subjected to three days of silent inquisition, I worked up the courage to challenge Marion. "Is something wrong?" I asked, turning to confront her as she hovered over my shoulder yet again.

I thought I saw a fleeting glimpse of nervous anxiety pass across her pale blue eyes, but if so, the insecurity quickly disappeared, replaced by a mask of indifference. "Of course not. I was merely checking on your progress."

Not satisfied, I pressed her further. I couldn't shake the feeling that Marion really didn't like either me or my work and I wasn't sure which. Maybe both. "Then you're pleased with the results so far?"

"I'm satisfied that the client will be pleased. That's all that matters. That and finishing on time for the presentation Friday," she added.

I glanced at the wall clock. The first three watercolors had taken two full days, and that included considerable overtime each night back at my apartment. The fourth was proving equally time-consuming, and there was no reason to believe any of the others would work up any quicker. I gritted my teeth. "You'll have the art on time, Marion." Even if it meant pulling all-nighters for the rest of the week. I wasn't going to give this woman an excuse to fire me.

Her stiff posture relaxed slightly, and I thought I caught a near-imperceptible smile as she nodded before heading back to her office. "Oh, by the way," she said, pausing and turning at her door, "I'm leaving the office at twelve o'clock on Friday. Ben won't be in at all, so you'll have to be finished before I leave."

I nodded, waiting until she closed the door behind her before I groaned.

"Don't let her get used to coercing you like that," said Edwina, coming up behind me. "Given the chance, she'll walk all over you."

"What choice do I have? I'll never finish by noon Friday if I don't put in some heavy-duty overtime. You've all said how important this account is to the company."

Edwina glanced toward Marion's departing back and wrinkled her nose. "So *she* says." Leaning down, she whispered, "It's a load of crap, honey. I do the billing, and we were seeing strong profits way before that over-the-hill Neapolitan playboy waltzed into our lives. We don't need him *or* his fake nobility—not to mention those hissy fits of his.

"Hell, there was nothing wrong with the first set of renderings. He's only demanding new art because he likes yanking everyone's chain. Especially Marion's. For the life of me, I can't figure out why she puts up with it. She sure doesn't take that kind of crap from anyone else."

I had wondered about the first set of renderings—and my predecessor. "What happened to your previous staff artist?" I asked, no longer able to contain my curiosity. Winnie was so outspoken about everything else. Surely, she'd divulge the circumstances surrounding the sudden departure of the last occupant to sit in my chair.

"Jen? Nothing dramatic. Her husband was transferred to L.A."

"And she left so suddenly?"

"She gave two-weeks' notice, but Ben told her it was all right to leave immediately. She wanted to find a house and get her kids settled before the school year started. Since we weren't scheduled to make any new presentations for several weeks, there was no reason for her to hang around."

"And then Scarpetta demanded a new set of renderings."

"Consider it your baptism by fire," said Zeke as he and Ben approached on their way out the door.

"Winnie, how about if you let Hope get back to work so she can catch a few Z's this week?" said Ben, stopping to study the current watercolor.

"Aye, aye, captain!" Edwina saluted the two men with her ever-present cup of coffee, casting a wink in my direction before leaving.

"Looking good," said Ben, nodding at the watercolor taped to the drawing board. He patted my shoulder. "If that Italian pain in my butt isn't satisfied with these, he doesn't know the first thing about good art."

Zeke concurred. "Yeah, Jen's stuff was good, but Hope's work is spectacular. You found us a winner, Ben."

"That's called buttering up the boss," Ben stage whispered to me. "Now he's going to expect me to pick up the check at lunch."

"Damn right," said Zeke as the two men strode toward the exit.

From my first day on the job, various staff members had stopped at my drawing board. I suspected they were checking out the new kid on the block, but as the week progressed, all of them continued to offer words of praise and encouragement. I took both their curiosity and their compliments in stride. After twelve years of studio courses, I was used to working in a fishbowl. What I wasn't used to was the fluttery feeling that continued to settle in the pit of my stomach whenever Ben appeared.

Think bald.

Think fat.

Think beer belly.

I always sensed his presence long before he approached. Some latent hormonal radar triggered inside me whenever he came within twenty feet. Or whenever I heard his deep sexy baritone float across the vast expanse of the loft. Or whenever the corners of his mouth turned up in that incredibly devastating smile that ought to be outlawed.

I prayed Ben had no idea of the turmoil he was creating inside me. And that I succeeded in carrying off the role of calm, cool, collected junior employee who went about her business totally oblivious to his killer charms. Especially when he spoke directly to me.

I couldn't remember ever feeling this way about my husband. But then again, I couldn't remember much at all about Wally Greeble in a make-my-toes-curl, release-the-butterflies-in-my-stomach sort of way. Wally was just Wally. Steady. Dependable. We were friends. We dated. My parents thought he'd be a good husband, a good provider. They campaigned for steady, dependable Wally, and being the obedient daughter, I didn't protest. We married three days after my eighteenth birthday and set up housekeeping in a doublewide on the outskirts of Rusty Mud Creek.

When the steel mill closed a year later, Wally enlisted in the Marines. After basic training, he was sent to Kuwait. He returned in a flag-draped coffin a week before my twenty-first birthday. His helicopter had crashed during maneuvers. That was the day I decided to stop listening to my parents and lead my own life.

The first thing I did was drop the Greeble from my name. As much as I cared for Wally, I never could see myself going through life as a Greeble. Before our wedding, I'd even suggested Wally change his Greeble to my Morgan, but Wally, like my parents, was too much of a traditionalist.

The second thing I did after becoming a widow was take Mr. Hagarty's advice and enroll in college. Not just the local county college, though. I applied to and was accepted at one of the most prestigious art and architecture schools in the country. And that's my story in a nutshell. At least all of it up to that one fateful night that I don't want to think about.

Getting back to Ben, though, in all fairness, he didn't treat me any differently than he did the rest of his staff. He wasn't coming on to me. This was all me. My problem. But even had Ben been available, falling for the boss was a cardinal no-no under any circumstances.

"I need a social life," I told myself. "One made up strictly of single, eligible guys." I'd fallen into the habit of talking out loud to myself. Since I didn't have money in the bank, this could only mean I was going crazy. But since I hadn't yet begun carrying on two-way conversations with myself and myself, I figured I still had some time before I transformed into a bag lady.

~*~

Friday morning. I swished my brush in the jar of cloudy water to remove the last remnants of paint, then patted the bristles with a paper towel. Leaning back, I smiled through bleary eyes at the final watercolor, now complete.

"And with over two hours to spare," said Zeke, glancing at his watch. "It's not even ten o'clock. I'd say you deserve the rest of the day off." He carefully lifted the tape from the drawing. "I'll mat this for you and get everything ready for Marion to take with her. Go home, Hope. You look exhausted."

Exhausted didn't begin to describe it. Did I even have the strength to walk the several blocks to the PATH train, let alone make it all the way back to my apartment? But the thought of my bed calling to me, acted like a shot of adrenaline. Once I sank into my mattress, I had no intention of rising until Monday morning.

I capped my tubes of paint and headed for the sink to wash out the palette and water jar. On my way, I passed Tony, a stack of assorted computer hardware and software balancing precariously in his arms. "Hey, wait a minute." I grabbed for a box that was about to slip from his hold and shoved the package back under his arm. "Okay. You're good to go."

"Thanks." He continued across the room.

I deposited my dirty tools in the slop sink and turned on the water.

A moment later Zeke yelled, "Look out!"

A loud crash echoed off the walls.

Edwina gasped.

Tony groaned.

Paco, Le, Freddie, and Nigel rushed over to see what had happened. The group stood in a circle staring at the floor. One by one they lifted their heads and turned their collective gaze in my direction.

A prickle of dread spread from my toes to my scalp. Only the sound of running water filled the otherwise silent room. I turned off the spigot and walked toward the group, forcing one foot in front of the other. Whatever had happened, I knew it was bad. Very bad. When I reached the spot where they stood, I froze. There at my feet lay the ruins of the painting I'd completed minutes earlier.

SIX

I stared in horror at the rapidly spreading dark puddle of coffee. Like the mighty Mississippi during a spring thaw, it engulfed everything in its path, morphing the American corporate headquarters of Scarpetta International into a muddy blur.

"I'm so sorry, Hope," said Winnie, her voice choking with tears, the empty coffee cup still in her hand.

"No, it's my fault," said Tony. "I shouldn't have been carrying so much at once. I couldn't see where I was going."

I bent and examined the painting.

"Is it salvageable?" asked Le.

No way. Had I worked the piece in acrylics or pastels, given time, I might have been able to doctor the stain that continued branching out from all directions. But a watercolor? Forget it. Even I wasn't *that* good.

Behind me I heard the staccato click-click of Marion's four-inch black and gold Bottega Veneta stilettos on the polished wood floor. The crowd parted, allowing her an unobstructed view of the damage.

"You'd better get started on another," she said, her eyes focused on the soggy mess. Her posture and tightly pursed scarlet lips conveyed her displeasure. She glanced at her diamond Rolex. "You only have two hours before I leave."

"You can't be serious!" I motioned to the ruined artwork. "This painting took nearly nine hours to complete."

Her look accused me of being a slacker. She huffed out a snort of irritation. "You have until five-thirty. Edwina will give you directions to the house. Be there before six-thirty." She turned to the others. "Don't any of you have work to do?"

Tony and Winnie stooped to pick up the strewn computer paraphernalia. The others scattered in various directions.

I wanted to scream. Instead, I stifled a yawn, muttered a few choice expletives under my breath, and headed back to the sink to fetch my equipment. Not only was I pissed, I was also thoroughly convinced there was a conspiracy afoot to keep my head from ever again coming in contact with my pillow.

On the way back to my drawing board, I passed Zeke. The project manager scowled at me. "You're in the big leagues now," he said. "This isn't school. The client doesn't care that the dog ate your homework. Shit happens. We can't afford anyone who won't give a thousand percent to get the job done right and in on time. No matter what."

"Hey, this wasn't my fault!"

"No one's blaming you."

"Does it matter? I'm still the one suffering the consequences."

"Only because you're the only one who can fix it."

"Yeah, right." I matched his scowl as I collapsed into my chair. I didn't care how bitchy I sounded. I deserved a large dose of compassion right about now, not a lecture on the inequities of life. I already knew how unfair life could be, thank you very much. And after nearly thirty-four years of suffering through life's inequities, I figured I was due a break. Only it didn't look like I was going to get one any time soon.

~*~

"Wow!" Eight hours later I stood on the sidewalk, staring at the majestic Victorian masterpiece that was Ben and Marion's home. The house, set back from the wide, tree-lined street and surrounded by a wrought-iron fence, reminded me of a dollhouse come to life. The three stories of rose-colored brick, trimmed in white, gold, and black, sat in the center of an acre of perfectly manicured lawn. On the left, a sweeping driveway led to a similarly painted carriage house, tucked away at the back of the property. Off to the right, the wraparound porch offered an ideal view of a newly planted rose garden.

Without looking at the slip of paper Winnie had given me, I knew I'd found *The Castle*. Pushing open the gate, I made my way down the path toward the front steps.

And cringed.

Then groaned.

Brick steps led from the sidewalk to a herringbone walkway that ended at a staircase leading up to the front porch. In my exhausted state of mind, the one, two, three—fifteen(!) steps might as well have been Mt. Everest, considering the effort I'd need to scale them. I'd already nearly missed my stop, having dozed off on the train, and only the blaring siren of a passing ambulance and the cool evening breeze had revived me enough to drag my body from the station to my final destination.

Even though my personal Energizer Bunny had run out of get-up-and-go hours ago—or was it eons at this point? I still had to force one foot in front of the other and hoist myself onto the porch. Thank heaven for a sturdy banister. Maybe if the gods took pity on me, I could play on Ben's and Marion's compassion and get them to drop me at my apartment on their way to their dinner meeting. Well, maybe Ben's compassion. I seriously doubted Marion had any.

The thought of hiking back to the station and waiting for the train—not to mention the walk at the other end and two steep flights of stairs to my apartment—was enough to make me consider curling up on one of the Schaffer-Merrick porch chairs for the night. Hell, the verandah was so large, they'd never even notice me. And at the moment, the white wicker settee with its overstuffed cabbage rose cushion looked more inviting than my bed—if for no other reason than the settee was a few short steps away while several miles stood between me and my mattress.

As I contemplated the possibility, the front door swung open. "Good. You're here." Marion sounded as though she'd just run a marathon—in her Bottega Venetas. Although she didn't look it. Not a hair on her head would ever dare consider coming loose. Her makeup looked like she kept Bobbie Brown on retainer, and her black cocktail dress—skimpy enough to double as a slip during the day—looked like Dolce & Gabbana had stitched it directly to her size zero figure. I figured I could buy out Macy's entire lingerie department for what that wisp of silk cost.

Marion might look drop-dead gorgeous, but her outfit certainly didn't qualify as appropriate business attire, and that wasn't my Rusty Bible Belt upbringing talking. I'd seen more fabric covering the bodies of nude Greek sculptures. But that was Marion's business. And Ben's. Certainly not mine. All I wanted was to collapse onto the nearest bed.

Marion pulled the brown paper-wrapped watercolor from under my arm. "Don't just stand there. Come in, Hope. I need another favor."

Another favor? As if I'd had a choice about working nonstop the past week! Not to mention accomplishing a miracle by creating a replacement watercolor in a timeframe that would qualify me for Olympic gold if the IOC ever added a watercolor event. "A favor?"

"Our housekeeper developed an allergic reaction to something she ate and was rushed to the hospital. There isn't time to get someone else from the agency. Unfortunately, Ben is very fussy about that sort of thing and won't allow just anyone."

"Of course I'm fussy about that sort of thing!"

I glanced up at the sound of Ben's voice. He stood on the top step of the curved oak staircase that led from the foyer to the second floor. No man had the right to look that good in a tuxedo. Even if he currently looked thoroughly disgusted. With hands planted firmly on his hips and deep creases etched into the corners of his mouth and across his brow, he addressed his wife. "I told you I'd stay home, Marion. You're far better at these functions than I am. It's Friday night. I'm sure Hope has plans."

Marion glared at him. "Your presence is needed this evening." Then she turned to me. "If you have a date, he can come here."

"No, but—" The only date I had was with my bed, but why would anyone need a house sitter for a few hours? Surely, they had an alarm system. And besides, this was Westfield, New Jersey, not Newark.

"Good, then it's settled," said Marion. "We won't be gone more than four or five hours. They're upstairs."

"They?" Now I was really getting confused. *They who?*

"Prescott, Woodrow, and Edmondson," said Marion, heading for the door. She glanced back over her shoulder at Ben. "You *know* Giovanni doesn't like to be kept waiting. We have to leave. Now."

"Wait!" My head was spinning. None of this made any sense to me.

Marion turned back, her face pursed in annoyance. "What is it now?"

"Who are..." I thought for a minute. Who did Marion say was upstairs? "Prescott, Woodrow, and uh..."

"Edmondson."

"Right. Edmondson."

"Our sons," said Ben. He cast a quick glance over his shoulder before heading down the staircase.

Sons? "Oh, I didn't realize—"

"Of course not," said Marion. "Why would you?"

"Well, I..." I shrugged. "No reason, I guess."

"You've had a rough first week, Hope. If you don't feel up to this, just say so," said Ben. "We'll understand."

I glanced from Ben to Marion. *He* might understand, but I had the feeling that if I turned Marion down, my life at Schaffer-Merrick would become far more Hell than Heaven. "It's okay," I said, swallowing the yawn that fought to explode from inside me. "No problem. I'll just go up and introduce myself." I headed for the stairs.

"I'll take you up," said Ben.

Marion stamped her foot. "We're already late!"

"Wait in the car, Marion. I'll only be a minute."

Perfectly matching crimson blotches of rage broke out on

Marion's perfectly made-up face. She opened her mouth but after eyeing me, clamped her lips into a tight line. She spun on her heels and slammed the front door in her wake.

His shoulders sagging, Ben turned back toward the stairs. If this was how these two behaved in front of me, a nearly total stranger, how did they act when alone? Throw the Wedgwood and Lalique at each other? So much for that *Architectural Digest* article.

Without a word, I followed Ben up the steps and down a long hall to the doorway of a nursery. Three toddlers were sprawled on the thick navy carpeting, a huge pile of LEGO scattered among them.

"I wants to build a space fowt!" said the first child, his lower lip pouting.

"Na-huh. We builded a fowt last time," said the second, shaking a head of hair the same nutmeg color as his father's. "I wants to build a skyscwaper."

"Did not!" said the third. He placed his hands on his hips, daring his brothers to defy him. "We builded a space *station* last time. A fowt's diffwent."

I turned to Ben. "Triplets?"

Smiling at the fracas, Ben nodded. Then he cleared his throat. Dropping the blocks, the three children stopped arguing, scampered to their feet, and raced toward him.

"Daddy, tell them we'se building a skyscwaper!" pleaded the second child.

"No! A fowt, Daddy!" argued the first, his large hazel eyes filling with tears.

The third child, slightly taller than his brothers, was the first to notice me. He, too, had enormous hazel eyes, and at the moment they were studying me with suspicion. "Who's she?" he finally asked.

The other two boys stopped arguing and also turned to stare at me.

"This is Hope," said Ben, kneeling to his sons' level. "Hope, meet Woody, Teddy, and Scotty." Ben placed a hand on each child's head as he spoke their names.

"Hi, guys!" I glanced over at the pile of LEGO. "You like LEGO, huh?"

They each nodded.

"Me, too."

"You do?" Teddy eyed me skeptically.

"Mommy don't," said Woody.

Behind me, I heard Ben sigh. I guess that sort of summed up everything about him and Marion and their relationship right there. From what had transpired downstairs, Marion didn't seem to possess a maternal bone in her Size Zip anorexic body. Had she and Ben been too busy planning an architectural dynasty to discuss children prior to marriage? I suspected the triplets were an unwanted and unwelcome result of failed birth control—at least for Marion.

Just another of life's cruelties. So often people who want children can't have them, and people who don't want them wind up with half a hockey team. Somewhere along the way the cosmic egg man definitely screwed up on the delivery. Marion should have gotten my sister Faith's dud-filled ovaries and Faith should have been blessed with Marion's fruitful ones.

"Well, different people like different things," I said to the boys. "From what I hear, you like skyscrapers, right, Woody?" The child nodded. I turned to Teddy. "And you like space forts?"

"Uh-huh."

I pivoted to address Scotty, who still eyed me warily. "What about you, Scotty? What do you like to build?"

"Dinosauws."

"Well, then, that's perfect." I clapped my hands together. "You can all build the interplanetary headquarters of Dino-Trek. They have a huge skyscraper complete with a dinosaur observation tower inside a space fort that protects them from MegaRex, the giant android tyrannosaurus."

"Huh?" All three boys wrinkled their brows and stared in bewilderment at me.

I turned to Ben. "Don't tell me your sons don't know about the planet Dinosaurian and the brave space-traveling Dino-Trekkers?"

"I guess I didn't think they'd be interested."

The three toddlers climbed over their father. "Tell us! Tell us!"

Laughing, Ben rolled backwards and allowed the boys to scramble onto his tuxedoed chest. "I think Hope knows much more about the planet Dinosaurian than I do," he said. "Maybe if you ask real nice, she'll babysit for you this evening and tell you all about it."

Three pairs of pleading hazel eyes gazed up at me. "Will you?" asked Teddy.

"Hmm." I cocked my head. Knitting my brows together, I tapped my chin with an index finger and studied the ceiling. "I was going to wash my hair..."

"We gots shampoo," offered Scotty, his original suspicions lost in the excitement. "The kind that doesn't make you cwy if you gets it in your eyes."

"Well, then..." I glanced toward Ben. "Are they good boys?"

"We'se weal good!" said Woody, answering for his father. "Wight, Daddy?"

"The best," said Ben, standing up. "But you have to promise to listen to Hope and go to bed when she tells you. Okay?"

Holding their collective breaths, the boys nodded in agreement. They were so adorable, waiting solemnly for me to make up my mind. I wrapped my arms across my chest and leaned against the wall to support a body that was ready to collapse at any moment. I willed a shot of energy into my system. Where it came from, I have no idea, but how could anyone say no to these kids? Okay, I could think of one ice queen quite capable of ignoring them. All the more reason to offer the little guys some much-deserved attention. "Okay. I'll stay."

My decision was met with a chorus of cheers. Ben bent and planted a kiss on the top of each child's head. I suspected he'd much rather spend his evening playing LEGO with his sons than wining and dining with Giovanni Scarpetta. At least the heirs to the Schaffer-Merrick Empire had one loving parent.

I was equally certain Marion would not be pleased when she saw her husband's disheveled tuxedo.

SEVEN

It's over.

Five hours later Ben sat alone behind the wheel of his Lexus SUV and stared across the darkened lawn at his house. The house Marion had insisted on buying yet no longer wanted. He thought of the three little boys asleep in the upstairs nursery and cringed at the memory of her brutal words. "They're your sons, not mine. I never wanted them."

Marion's admission shouldn't have rocked him. She had carried too much baggage into their marriage to ever love any child, much less three. Especially three boys. The moment she had insisted on naming their sons after Prescott Woodrow Edmondson Merrick the Third, the father who had never wanted her—the father she still tried to please, no matter how many times he rebuffed her efforts—Ben should have known the relationship was doomed. He wasn't a shrink. Why had he deluded himself into thinking he could solve his wife's problems by pressing her into having children?

He leaned his head against the steering wheel and took a deep breath. She hadn't blindsided him this evening. He'd seen it coming for years. If it hadn't been Giovanni Scarpetta, it would have been someone else. If not now, a month from now. Or six months. Or a year. The writing had been scribbled all over those damn Victorian walls. He'd just refused to read it.

Marion had never wanted a husband. What she wanted—needed—was a father to love and accept her. To praise and compliment her. To wrap his arms around her and extol her virtues and talents to anyone who'd listen.

Giovanni Scarpetta was the perfect father figure. Thirty years Marion's senior, he provided her with all her father had denied her. And in return the phony duke—or count or whatever the hell the little shit claimed to be—got to enjoy the pleasures of a beautiful, younger woman.

Marion would make the perfect trophy wife for Scarpetta. Not only would she look good dangling from his arm, but she'd also be a professional asset as well, fully capable of stepping in as the president of Scarpetta's new American division. A real win-win situation for both of them. With Ben and the boys the big losers.

Or were they? Marion had never shown the least bit of maternal instinct toward her children. She barely tolerated them, treating them with the same contempt her father had shown her. In return for the quickie divorce she wanted, she was willing to give up all claims to everything she and Ben shared—the house, the business, the children. Especially the children. Marion wanted no part of them.

Well, she could have her uncontested divorce. Let her fly down to some Caribbean Island in Scarpetta's private Lear jet and file whatever papers she needed to. The sooner the better. He'd tried to save her from herself and failed. Now she was Scarpetta's problem.

Ben switched off the engine and headed up the walk. It was time he got on with his life. Three little boys were depending on him.

EIGHT

"Hope?"

"Hmm?" Even in my dreams Ben's voice caressed me like warm molasses sliding down a stack of pancakes. I giggled at the trite metaphor and reached for his hand, the one massaging my shoulder, and snuggled my check against his palm. This was a nice dream. So real.

"Hope, wake up."

I didn't want to wake up. I liked this dream, liked the warm whisper of Ben's breath kissing my skin, the tips of his fingers skimming my lips.

He yanked his hand away.

My eyes flew open. "Ben!" I scampered to a sitting position on the floor, my back pressing up against the footboard of one of the beds. Clutching a makeshift pillow to my chest, I felt what had to be the equivalent of the Santa Anna winds swooshing up my neck to my cheeks, cheeks that were now probably as red as the giant, furry Elmo in my arms. Ben knelt beside me, his jacket hooked over his shoulder, his tie unknotted and draped around his neck. In the dim light I saw the puzzlement on his face and could only hope the shadows kept him from seeing the embarrassment on mine.

"What are you doing sleeping on the floor?"

I rubbed the Sandman's grit from my eyes and swallowed back a mega-yawn. "I didn't mean to fall asleep. The house is so large. I was afraid I wouldn't hear the children from downstairs if one of them woke up."

He smacked the side of his head. "I forgot to point out the monitoring system to you. I'm sorry. You can hear the nursery from any room with the flick of a switch." He pulled Elmo from my grasp. "You could have at least helped yourself to a pillow from one of the guest beds."

I reached up and massaged the stiffness that had settled in my neck and frowned at the big red Muppet. "Guess that explains the crick."

"I'm sorry I kept you so long," he said. He stood and offered me his hand.

I nearly moaned out loud from the tingle that shot up my arm and quickly spread to an area of my body that had no business having any awareness of my boss. *That does it. First thing tomorrow I check out the local singles scene. This nun is vacating the convent.*

"Why didn't you tell me you were too tired to babysit?" He turned to his sleeping sons. One by one he adjusted their quilts, stooping to place a kiss on each child's cheek.

"You were in a bind. Besides, Marion really wanted you at that dinner meeting."

Ben made a snorting noise of sorts that took me by surprise. "She did at that."

As we descended the steps, I noticed the tense set of his jaw, the frown lines that had settled into his face. Edwina's opinion to the contrary, I knew how important the Scarpetta account was to Marion and therefore must be to Ben. I had a sneaking suspicion the evening hadn't gone well, but I felt it would be presumptuous to ask about it. After all, I'd only been with the company a week. If Ben wanted to divulge the details of the evening, he would.

Instead, he caught me off guard with a question of his own. "Where's your car? I didn't see one parked out front."

"I sold my car before moving here."

"Then how—"

"I took the train."

He reached into his pants pocket and withdrew a set of keys. "Here. I can't leave the boys alone to drive you home. Take my car."

I stared at the keys. *Leave the boys alone? Where was Marion?* Something was definitely wrong in the kingdom of Schaffer-Merrick. I raised my chin and saw confirmation etched in Ben's face. "I don't mind taking the train. It's only one stop."

"The inbound trains don't stop in Garwood this time of night, and you're not walking three miles." He reached for my hand, placed the keys in my palm, and folded my fingers over them. "Go home. Get a good night's sleep. You can bring the car back tomorrow morning."

"All right." It was evident Ben was in no mood for conversation. The man appeared ready to snap from...something. I had no way of knowing what had transformed the normally easygoing Ben Schaffer into a study of carefully restrained anger, but it didn't take a doctorate in Freudian psychology to figure out his wife was at the heart of it. I mumbled, "Good night," and headed for the front door.

"Hope?"

I paused, my hand on the doorknob, and turned to face him. "Yes?"

"Thank you."

"No big deal." The lighthearted cheeriness in my voice sounded hollow and fake, even to my own ears. The foyer filled with a tense silence. Not knowing what else to say and afraid of uttering something inappropriate, I was about to make my escape when I remembered the earlier phone call. "Oh, I almost forgot. The hospital called. Your housekeeper didn't have an allergic reaction."

"Then what was it?"

"Her appendix. It ruptured."

Worry swept across Ben's face, momentarily wiping away the anger, but then it became the catalyst that ignited his fuse. Slamming his fist into the wall, he shouted a long stream of profanity—all directed at Marion.

Not knowing what else to do, I ducked out the door.

NINE

From the window, Ben watched Hope drive away in his car. He'd probably scared the shit out of her with that outburst. He supposed he owed her an explanation, but any words that came to mind only opened the door to questions he wasn't willing to answer. Not tonight. And certainly not to someone he barely knew. She'd find out soon enough. Everyone would.

He'd screwed up big time, and three innocent little boys would suffer the consequences.

His thoughts drifted to the way he had found Hope asleep on the floor of the nursery. Her sensitive concern for his sons overwhelmed him. And glaringly pointed out their own mother's shortcomings.

With a sigh of defeat, he headed upstairs.

TEN

After a night spent tossing and turning, I arrived back at Ben's house the next morning shortly after nine o'clock. At five I'd finally given up hoping all those damn sheep would cooperate and send me off to Slumberland.

After a quick shower, I spent the early hours before dawn emptying some of the cartons still stacked in various rooms of my apartment. For someone who had averaged a mere four hours sleep each night of the previous week, I had expected to remain comatose well into Saturday afternoon. But that was before the unsettling events of the previous evening, events that kept screaming for my mind's attention no matter how many thousands of sheep I counted.

Each time I closed my eyes, I saw the pain etched into Ben's face. What the hell happened between him and Marion last night? And how could any woman have such disdain for those three adorable little boys? My sister Faith would have killed for triplets. Too bad fate had other plans for her. And for me.

As I stood on the porch, poised to ring the doorbell, I momentarily thought about slipping the keys through the mail slot and making a dash for the train station. I dreaded having to face Ben this morning—ignorance being bliss and all that rot. I should have insisted on calling a cab last night—and waiting on the porch for its arrival.

I had no idea if Marion had already returned, but if she hadn't, I certainly didn't want to be anywhere near this house when she finally arrived home. After Ben's brief tirade against his wife last night, I anticipated a display of fireworks to rival the most spectacular of Fourth of July celebrations.

Okay, so now I could add coward to the rest of my numerous character flaws. Although I doubted anyone would blame me if I ran, in the end I ratcheted up my courage and rang the bell.

ELEVEN

Saturday morning proved Ben had shortcomings of his own when it came to his kids. Who would have thought making pancakes could be *this* difficult—and messy? Ben stared at the fallout. The boys, spattered from head to toe with raw batter, held their collective breaths, no doubt waiting for him to explode. And although the thought had crossed his mind—and he might benefit from the release—he wasn't about to blow up in front of his children. Instead, he shook his own batter-dappled head and tossed what remained of the blender-chewed rubber spatula into the sink. Throwing his arms up in defeat, he turned to the boys and asked, "Who wants breakfast at McDonald's?"

A chorus of *me*'s answered him.

"Well, we can't go looking like this," he said. "To the showers, men." He lifted the boys one-by-one off the kitchen counter and was about to lead them up the back stairs when the front doorbell rang. "Don't move, and don't touch anything," he warned them, heading for the door. As it was, he faced a massive cleanup, but at least the mess was presently contained to one room. Ben wanted it to stay that way.

"Coming," he yelled as the bell chimed a second time. When he swung open the heavy oak door, he was surprised at first to see Hope standing on his front porch. "Oh, the car," he said, half mumbling to himself. "I forgot."

"Am I too early?"

Ben followed her gaze, from his T-shirt to his hands, and then his jeans. After the spatula had caught in the blender and spewed pancake batter in all directions, he had attended to the boys. Only after he viewed himself through Hope's eyes did he realize how extensively he, too, was covered in flour and raw pancake mix.

He picked at a clump of batter drying on his chin. Damn stuff felt like caked mud. "No, come in. I need to get us all cleaned up, though."

"Have a visit from the Ghostbusters?" she asked, following him back to the kitchen.

"Certain people should never be allowed in kitchens," he told her. "I'm one of them."

"I'll say!" He watched her large hazel eyes grow even larger, ogling first the boys, then the kitchen. "What happened?"

"Daddy goofed," said Woody.

"Daddy's funny," added Scotty.

"I'm hungwy," said Teddy.

"We'll go out for breakfast after I get us all cleaned up and we take Hope home," said Ben. He herded the boys toward the stairs. "This will take a while," he told her. "Make yourself at home."

TWELVE

Make yourself at home? Not likely. I surveyed what was probably once a pristine kitchen. Tornado Ben had left an upended box of pancake mix, broken eggs, and spilled milk—not to mention clumps of lumpy batter sticking to every vertical and horizontal surface—in his wake. "Yuck! Next time stick with Cap'n Crunch," I offered. "Dry."

"Now you tell me! Where were you an hour ago, Suzie Homemaker?"

A better question, I thought, watching Ben's tight jeans-clad butt disappear around the bend of the staircase, was—*where is your wife, Ben Schaffer?*

"Damn," I muttered. "Control your roving eyes, Hope! *And* your unacceptable fantasies." After giving myself a swift hypothetical kick in my own posterior, I fished a waterlogged sponge out of a pot soaking in the sink. Maybe if I kept busy....

Morgan women are raised for a life of cooking, cleaning, and raising babies. I may have bucked the system, but domestic training started early in Rusty Mud Creek. Faith and I were dusting furniture before we were out of diapers. So while Ben and his boys showered, I repaired the damage done by their less-than-successful culinary escapade, cooked a stack of blueberry pancakes, and set the table with glasses of juice all around as well as milk for the boys. After a puzzling few minutes, I'd figured out how to operate Ben's state-of-the-art coffeemaker and set the dials to *brew*.

At the sound of four sets of feet tramping down the back steps, I removed the platter of pancakes from the oven.

"What the—!" Ben stood at the base of the stairs, eyeing the extreme kitchen makeover. Droplets of water glistened in his nutmeg hair.

Behind him, three wide-eyed boys, scrubbed clean and now outfitted in jeans and T-shirts, stared in awe. "Hope cookeded pancakes, Daddy!"

"So she did," said Ben. He shook his head. "And then some." After settling the boys into their seats, he asked, "Bucking for a raise already, Ms. Morgan?"

I spun toward the griddle and busied myself by removing the last of the pancakes to the serving platter. "Whatever works. You would have been chiseling dried batter for weeks if you left the cleanup until later."

"That explains the maid service," he said, removing the platter from my hands. He grabbed the serving fork I'd placed on the table and began spearing several pancakes onto each boy's plate. "What about the catered feast?"

How do you explain Morgan genes to an outsider? Especially an outsider married to someone like Marion. He'd never understand. So I shrugged as he divided the remaining pancakes between his plate and mine. "The boys wanted pancakes, didn't they?"

"Which they would have gotten at McDonald's." Ben added a river of syrup to each of the boys' stacks.

I wrinkled my nose. "Cardboard on a griddle?"

"Hmm! Yummy," said Teddy, shoving an overloaded, maple syrup-drenched forkful into his mouth.

"Don't talk with your mouth full," admonished his father without looking at him. Ben's gaze remained firmly riveted on me as he took his seat and motioned for me to do likewise. "Thank you," he said.

Somehow those two simple words flustered me as much as the few times he had innocently touched me. Damn it!

Think bald.

Think fat.

Think beer belly.

"I'll get the coffee," I said, rushing to the counter. This was getting out of hand. If I couldn't tamp down my gaga genes, I'd be forced to quit my job. Ben was a smart guy. Sooner or later, no matter how hard I tried to hide my drooling, he'd notice the telltale signs of rampant crushitis. Better to concentrate on his flaws. Flaw. Since I'd yet to find more than one. The guy might be sex on a stick, but he wasn't a perfect ten. The klutz factor, as evidenced by his kitchen exploits, had knocked him down to a solid nine-point-nine.

"By the way, for future reference," I said, placing a steaming cup of java in front of him, "it's generally not a good idea to insert utensils into a whirring blender."

"Thank you, Hope. I'll make a point of remembering that."

I felt his gaze on me as I took the seat opposite him and began to attack my pancakes. Between mouthfuls I joked with the boys, encouraging them to develop a better working knowledge of the kitchen than their father possessed. "The way to a woman's heart is through her kitchen," I said. "Remember that."

Ben chuckled. "Do you have younger siblings?"

I stopped chewing mid-mouthful. Hadn't I told him I had no family? "Why do you ask?"

"You're so relaxed and at ease with the boys. I thought maybe you were used to being around younger children."

"Mommy don't cook, neiver," said Scotty. "Only Fwitzi. She cooks good stuff. Like cookies."

The other two boys nodded in agreement.

I could have kissed Scotty for his timely change of subject. I had no desire to pick at family scabs with Ben or anyone. Even after all this time, the wounds were still too fresh, and I'd already bled enough to satisfy the thirstiest of vampires. "Who's Fwitzi?" I asked.

"Our housekeeper and nanny," explained Ben. "Frederica Fitzgerald. Fritzi. Or Fwitzi if you're three years old and still mastering the mother tongue."

"Fwitzi makes pancakes, too, Hope," said Woody, "but she gots a sick pendix."

"Your pancakes are gooder," said Teddy.

"Better than McDonald's?" I asked, raising an eyebrow in Ben's direction when all three boys agreed.

~*~

After Ben dropped me back in Garwood, I spent the remainder of Saturday and the better part of Sunday organizing my apartment, something I hadn't had time to do after moving in, thanks to the Scarpetta renderings. Like a good Morgan woman, I scrubbed the kitchen and bathroom until they sparkled. I lugged four bags of groceries from the supermarket and continued unpacking the remainder of my boxes.

By Sunday afternoon I was down to one small carton that hadn't been opened since I'd sealed and labeled it over three years earlier. I knew the contents—all that was left of a family and past I couldn't bring myself to confront.

I remembered packing up the few framed pictures that had somehow survived that awful day. I hadn't been able to deal with the guilt then and still couldn't. Maybe someday I'd have the courage to open the box and release all those ghosts. For now, even after nearly four years, the wounds were still too raw. I dragged the carton across the polished hardwood floor and shoved it under my bed.

With the heavy work behind me, I turned my attention to the beautification program I'd mapped out for the apartment. Hoisting my portable sewing machine onto the kitchen table, I set about constructing matching bathroom window and shower curtains from the pastel chintz I'd purchased on sale before leaving Butler County. Stitching ruffles hardly qualified as rocket science, though, and once again, I found myself drifting to an image of Ben's triple X-rated sexy smile.

I couldn't remember a crush ever consuming me to such an extent. It *was* just a crush, wasn't it?

Of course, it is, you idiot!

My feelings for Ben were no different than the time I fell madly in love with Tom Cruise. Although, I'd never actually met Tom Cruise, and the crush had occurred back when he starred in *Top Gun* and had lasted all of three weeks, and I'd been all of eight years old. But still, a crush was a crush. I'd gotten over Tom, and I'd get over Ben. I'd better, if I wanted to maintain my sanity. And my job.

I removed the valance from under the presser foot and groaned. Yup, I had it bad. The casing I'd just sewn into the hem of the valance was all the proof I needed. I reached for the seam ripper.

Maybe the gym down the street offered aerobics classes for singles.

THIRTEEN

Ben was struck by Hope's easygoing nature and the way she interacted with his sons—as if she had known Scotty, Woody, and Teddy from the day they were born. Better than their own mother. The boys cowered in the presence of Marion. With Hope they bloomed. And giggled. In three years, Marion and her sons had never shared a spontaneous outburst of laughter. Around Hope, the boys didn't stop laughing. The realization made Ben giddy. His sons were giggling! And it was all because of the bubbly brunette who had taken it upon herself to clean his kitchen and cook their breakfast.

Maybe with Marion gone, the boys would laugh more, cower less. He hadn't yet told his sons their mother wasn't coming back. They hadn't questioned her absence this morning, but that didn't surprise him. Even when she was home, Marion had little interaction with her children. He doubted they'd miss her.

"Daddy?" Woody had asked as they ate Hope's spontaneous breakfast feast.

"Hmm?" Ben broke from his reverie and turned his attention to his son.

"If Fwitzi gots to stay in the hospital, who's gonna cook for us?"

"Hope, silly," replied Scotty. He offered his brother a don't-you-know-anything smirk before shoving another forkful of pancake into his mouth.

Ben had glanced over the rim of his coffee cup at Scotty's matter-of-fact solution. Too bad life wasn't that simple. "Hope has work to do at the office," he said. "We'll eat out or bring in." He envisioned a few days of pizza and Chinese, not the best diet for three growing boys, but they'd view it as a rare treat. Besides, it was only a temporary glitch. In an age of laser surgery and managed health care, Fritzi would be back at her duties in a few days, a week tops. They'd manage.

Or so he thought until he stopped at the hospital after dropping Hope back at her apartment.

"Six weeks!" Flabbergasted, Ben stared at the doctor. Surely, he had misunderstood. He'd heard of heart patients going back to work two weeks after a quadruple bypass. This was only an appendectomy, for cripe's sake. "You can't be serious."

"Six weeks, Mr. Schaffer. Mrs. Fitzgerald needs that time to regain her strength. She's pushing sixty, and she's just been through a serious operation. Her appendix ruptured. She was damn lucky she got to the hospital in time."

Ben turned to the woman propped up in the hospital bed. She barely had any gray streaking her light brown, tightly permed hair. "Sixty?"

She nodded.

"I had no idea. You don't look a day over fifty."

"Ah, Ben, I can always depend on you to say the right thing. It's those boys of yours who keep me young."

"And they'll age you very quickly if you go back to work too soon," warned the doctor.

"Will you be able to manage without me, Ben?"

He patted her hand. "Don't worry. We'll be fine. I'm sure the agency can send a short-term substitute. You just concentrate on getting well."

"My sister wants me to come stay with her in Tampa."

"I'll make the arrangements," he said. Forcing himself to smile, he bent down and kissed her on the forehead. "Get some rest. I have to collect the boys before they destroy the visitors' lounge and send that nice Candy Striper running to a nunnery."

"My little angels? They wouldn't dare!"

Six weeks! Ben's life had just gotten a whole lot more complicated. Not wanting to worry Fritzi, he hadn't mention Marion's desertion. Knowing his overprotective nanny, she would have bolted out of bed and headed straight back to Westfield, her open-backed hospital gown flapping in the breeze as she jogged through the Watchung Reservation and across Route 22. Ben figured there was time enough for him to drop the missing Marion bombshell after Fritzi returned from Florida.

However, his assurance to Fritzi aside, he wondered how the hell he and the boys would manage for the next six weeks. Frederica Fitzgerald ran his home like a Fort Dix drill sergeant. Hell, Ben wasn't even certain he knew where to find the washing machine in the sprawling Victorian, and the boys' hamper was already overflowing with batter-soaked PJ's and wet towels.

Even if the agency had a list of temps, he'd have to muddle through on his own until at least the middle of next week. It was

Saturday afternoon, and he couldn't even get in touch with the placement service until Monday. By the time he interviewed and hired someone, it might be Wednesday or Thursday. *If* he was that lucky. *And* assuming he found an acceptable candidate. He wasn't about to leave his children in the hands of just any babysitter.

~*~

Unfortunately, first thing Monday morning Ben's luck turned from horrible to downright rotten. "No one at all?" he asked Edwina.

"'fraid not, Ben. The last agency I called said they have a waiting list of families. Every qualified nanny on their books is already placed. Want me to try another service?"

Ben shook his head. "Don't bother. You've already called half a dozen. If there *is* an unemployed nanny out there, she's probably no Mary Poppins." He glanced across the room to where the boys were busy building a LEGO fort with Freddie and Nigel. "I'm not about to hand my kids over to a babysitter no one else will hire."

Ben rubbed his temples in a vain attempt to ward off a growing migraine. "Damn!" he said, keeping his voice low enough so the triplets didn't hear him. "I can't even drop them at pre-school and come in for a few hours. By the time I got here, I'd have to hop back on the train to pick them up."

"It's only six weeks," said Winnie. "We can take turns keeping an eye on them here."

"Yeah, they're good kids," said Tony. "Really, Ben, we can manage."

Ben was overwhelmed by the generosity of his friends. They had taken the news of Marion's defection as if they had expected it all along. Maybe they had. Maybe he was the only one who had hidden from the truth for so many years. "Thanks, guys. I appreciate the offer, but this is no place for three-year-olds. The novelty will wear off, and they'll get bored. We're not set up for daycare. Besides, with Marion gone, I'm going to have to wine and dine prospective clients. I can't very well order Happy Meals all around."

"True," said Zeke, "and we should have the signed contract on the Woodmere Resort by the end of the week. Things are going to get hectic around here."

"Not for Hope," said Le, tapping a mechanical pencil against her lower lip. "She won't have much to do for a few weeks."

His engineer had a point. Hope's work began after all of theirs wrapped up. As always, Le's practical mind cut to the heart of the issue. Ben glanced at his watch. "Where is Hope, anyway? It's nearly ten o'clock."

"According to the radio, a transformer blew outside the tunnel," said Paco. "Everything's backed up. She's probably stuck on the tracks."

"Why not ask Hope?" suggested Tony. "You said the boys really like her, and she lives close enough. If anything came up here before she has to start on the Woodmere art, she could work from your house."

Yes, the boys liked Hope. Ben had noticed the instant rapport from the moment his new employee had entered the nursery Friday evening. And he couldn't forget how touched he'd been by her concern for their wellbeing—so much so that she had camped out on their bedroom floor. "Because Hope was hired as an artist, not a babysitter," said Ben. "It wouldn't be fair. From what I've seen of her, even if she didn't want to do it, she'd still agree. My God, the woman nearly killed herself for us last week, remember?"

"It's not a perfect solution," said Winnie, "but I don't see where there's much choice at this point. And it *is* only temporary. We'll all pitch in to help her."

He was certain they would. His staff's loyalty went far beyond friendship—for him and for each other. Ben had noticed how they'd welcomed Hope like a long-lost sister. After only a week she was as much a part of the team as anyone else in the room. These were good people. The best. He had no fears that they were trying to dump his problem on the newcomer. Still, he wasn't naïve. Their plan could backfire in his face. Lawsuits were filed and won over far less every day.

Zeke had apparently been thinking along the same lines. "Look, I don't want to sound like the voice of doom and gloom here, but as much as everyone likes Hope, we really don't know her."

Winnie began to protest, but Zeke held his hand up to silence her. "Yes, she pitched in the past week, far more than she should have had to, but how do we know she didn't feel coerced into agreeing? This is her first job outside of secretarial work. Maybe she feared losing it if she balked. You drop this bombshell on her, and she might run straight for the nearest law office. Do we really want to risk finding ourselves in the middle of a harassment lawsuit?"

"I think you're wrong about Hope," said Winnie.

Zeke offered her a wry smile. "The way I was wrong about Marion?"

Le gasped. She and the rest of the staff stared in disbelief at Zeke, then turned to Ben.

He shook his head. He couldn't get angry with Zeke for speaking the truth. Ben was the one who had chosen not to listen all those years ago. "All right," he said. "Let's get the I-told-you-so out of the way and move on. Zeke's right, and we all know it. About Marion, at least. I was blind, and I made a mistake. It's in the past, and we have to move on from here. The trouble is, I don't see where I have any other options at this point. We're just going to have to hope he's wrong about Hope."

Tony nodded in agreement. "I'm with Winnie, Ben. Hope's the logical choice."

"For what?"

FOURTEEN

Seven pairs of eyes simultaneously studied their laps. Throats cleared. Feet shuffled. Fingers fidgeted. All indicators reinforcing the suspicion that I'd been the topic of a serious conversation. And the fact that no one looked all that happy couldn't bode well for me. I knew I was late, but surely, they'd understand about the train. Didn't most of them commute to work? Or was it something much worse?

My morning orange juice and coffee turned to battery acid in my stomach. Had Giovanni Scarpetta hated my watercolors? Enough to cancel his contract with Schaffer-Merrick? Did Ben have to cut back on expenses? Tony said I was the logical choice. The logical choice for what? To be let go after only a week?

Not knowing what else to do, I stammered an apology for being late. "Something was wrong with the train. We sat on the tracks for over an hour. A downed power line, I think."

"Transformer blew," Paco mumbled.

No one else spoke. Tony became lost in the intricate grain

patterns of the maple conference table. Winnie shuffled and reshuffled a sheaf of loose papers. Paco began a systematic removal of invisible lint from his khakis. With rapt fascination Le picked at her cuticles. Zeke pushed away from the table and sauntered over to where Freddie and Nigel played with Ben's sons.

Only Ben looked at me, his brow creased, his mouth set in a tight line. His silent stare said it all. For whatever reason, I was about to be fired. In front of the entire staff. Not wanting any of them to see the tears beginning to dampen my eyes, I shifted my attention to the LEGOs scattered around the triplets.

"Hi, Hope!" called Scotty, the first of the boys to notice me. "Look what we're making."

"It's a dinosauw skyscwaper," said Woody. "Nigel and Fweddie are helping."

"We made a giant space fowt, too," said Teddy, holding up a large multi-colored construction.

Nigel nodded toward me, then motioned to Freddie. Both men rose from the floor. Along with Zeke they crossed the room to join the others at the conference table. Like a firing squad lining up. Public execution. Maybe Ben had brought his kids in to keep me from making a scene.

I waved to the triplets. It was then that I realized the Schaffer-Merrick team was shy one Merrick. Had Marion ever come home?

"I'll come see in a minute," I told the boys. "Keep building." Then, sucking up any vestiges of courage lurking beneath my epidermis, I turned to Ben. "I'm the logical choice for what?" I repeated. "The ax? Have I done something wrong? Is my work not good enough?"

A look of genuine bewilderment crossed his face. "No, of course not. Why would you think that?"

The others cast surreptitious glances in my direction. Why wouldn't I with the way everyone was acting? I gnawed on the inside of my cheek. "You're all looking at me like I'm about to be fired."

Ben rose and pulled out a chair for me. "Have a seat, Hope."

Now he really had me worried. I perched on the edge of the chair, too nervous to sit back, too tense to breathe. I clasped my hands in a death grip and stared at my white knuckles.

Tony pulled his attention from the table grain and reached over to pat my shoulder. "Relax, Hope. This isn't the Spanish Inquisition."

"Glad to hear that," I said, my voice high-pitched enough to shatter any crystal within a five-mile radius. Because from where I sat they all looked like graduates of the Torquemada School of Business.

"Oh, for God's sake," cried Winnie, slamming her coffee cup onto the table. "You're giving the poor woman a heart attack!" She turned to Ben. "Spit it out already!"

Ben cleared his throat. For the first time I noticed that he appeared as nervous as I felt. "Actually, Hope, we...that is, I...I need your help."

"You're part of the team now," said Le, her words charged with an unspoken challenge, "and we've always been there for one another. Ben has a problem, and you're the logical solution. You can't say no."

"Le!"

"She can't, Ben!" Le jumped to her feet and leaned across the table, her nose coming within inches of Ben's. "You have no other choice right now."

The corners of Ben's mouth dipped into a scowl. Le retreated but continued to stand, hands on her hips. "Le didn't mean to sound so harsh, Hope." He glared at his engineer, his expression demanding an apology.

"No, of course not," she said, settling back in her seat. "I'm sorry, Hope. It's just that we're all worried about Ben and how he's going to manage. I think...that is, we all think you're the best short-term solution."

Ben lowered his forehead onto his hands. "Believe me, Hope, if there were any other way..." Then he raised his head, and I lost it. One look into his eyes and I knew I'd agree to anything he asked. Go over Niagara Falls in a barrel? No problem. Scale Mt. Everest in a bikini? Piece of cake. Bungee jump off the Brooklyn Bridge during a Nor'easter? In a New York minute. I was a lump of Play-Doh in the man's hands. *Damn! Damn! Damn!* Someone pass me whatever pill will cure me of this infatuation.

Ben broke into my self-flagellation and brought me back to the present, and as yet, unnamed dilemma. "I'm afraid Le's right," he said. "You're my only hope."

His words sent me reeling into the past, and I remembered the last time someone had spoken those same words to me.

"Please, Hope, you're my only hope."

My sister Faith had wanted a baby. Not just any baby, though. The kid had to be a miniature combination of Morgan and McKinnon genes. Don't ask me why. Neither family could boast an outstanding leaf hanging from its family tree. No founding fathers or Nobel Laureates doggy paddled in the chromosomal soup of either clan. Not even a B-list celebrity. Just your run-of-the-mill blue-collar beer bellies.

However, along the road to conception, Faith and Dwayne had hit a major snag: Faith's eggs were duds. So she had turned to me to supply the Morgan component for the Petri dish.

The memory filled me with pain and triggered the isolation and loneliness that always lurked beneath the thin Happy Hope veneer I presented to the world.

I stared at Ben. Whatever was going on, he was hurting. His friends were trying to help him. I didn't understand how or why, but for some reason they had all decided I was the solution to his predicament. And since whatever it was, it apparently didn't entail my imminent dismissal—or another round of egg harvesting—how could I refuse? "What do you need?" I asked.

"A nanny."

A nanny? Maybe I should have tried to get more sleep over the weekend. Obviously, I was having trouble with my cognitive skills, a sure sign of exhaustion. I blinked, hoping to unclog whatever detritus was clouding my brain and blocking my ears.

"It's only temporary," said Winnie.

I stared at Ben. "I don't understand."

"Just until Ben's housekeeper comes back," Winnie continued, crossing the room to stand beside me. She placed her hand on my forearm. "Of course, we don't want you to feel you're being pressured into something you don't want to do, but you'd sure win our eternal and undying gratitude. Especially Ben's," she added with a wink. "Sure couldn't hurt come bonus time."

"Winnie!" Zeke speared her with a reproving glare.

Flabbergasted by the odd request, I repeated the words. "A nanny?"

"We'd all help as much as possible," said Le. "Especially me. I'm only a mile away."

Ben cleared his throat. Everyone turned in his direction. "Why don't you all clear out of here and let me talk to Hope alone."

Winnie and Tony ushered the triplets from the room. Le, Paco, Nigel, and Freddie followed close behind. Only Zeke held back.

"You, too, Zeke."

"You sure, Ben? Maybe it would be a good idea if I stayed."

"I don't think that's necessary. I can handle things from here." Zeke hesitated, finally leaving only when Ben scowled at him. But he left the conference door open.

Ben rose, walked over to the door, and closed it before beginning a stream of invectives that began with a muttered *goddamnfuckingshit*, then got swallowed up in a low growl when he slammed his fist into the wall. Finally, with a long, drawn-out sigh, he took his seat, lowered his head, and began to speak. "Marion walked out Friday night. On me. On the boys. On the firm."

I gaped at him, unable to even mumble an *I'm sorry*. I hadn't realized the extent of his and Marion's problems. How could I, being so new to the firm? But from my first day in the office, I picked up on the friction between them. And between Marion and the rest of the staff. Jeez, you could cut all that tension with the proverbial knife. And it didn't even have to be a sharp knife. A blunt cheese spreader would slice just fine.

Yet even after Friday night, I chalked up Marion's behavior to a minor speed bump in the rocky road of long-term relationships. Hell, all married couples go through bad patches from time to time. Wally and I had come to verbal blows on several occasions during our short time together. The stress of infertility had nearly destroyed my sister's marriage. And as much as my parents liked to think they displayed a united front, when the lights were out, I had often heard more than I wanted to know. Houses in Rusty

Mud Creek aren't built with the thickest of walls.

Unlike Ben and Marion, though, my family and I had time apart from our spouses during the day to cool down and calm down. It couldn't be easy living and working with the same person twenty-four/seven. Add triplets to the mix, and the pressure had to multiply ten-fold, if not more.

But even so, how could any mother walk out on her children? Ben wasn't a monster. Infatuation or no infatuation, I knew that when a marriage dissolved, both parties were partially to blame. But whatever Ben's shortcomings—aside from being a kitchen klutz—I couldn't believe they were great enough for Marion to sacrifice her children.

He had stopped speaking and seemed to be waiting for me to say something. So I voiced my thoughts. "Maybe Marion just needs a little time away. No matter what she might have said, all parents love their children."

He gritted his teeth and spoke through a clenched jaw. "Don't toss me crumbs of hope. You don't know the half of it. Don't know Marion."

"But—"

"Trust me. She's not coming back."

"You can't know that. People make mistakes. But we learn from them. Sometimes, lots of times, things work out." My voice trailed off. Was I talking about Marion or myself? And do they work out for the best or just work out? I couldn't come to terms with my own past. What right did I have offering advice to Ben?

Rising from his chair, he strode over to the floor-to-ceiling windows that looked out over Twenty-second Street. "At this moment Marion is in the Caribbean obtaining a quickie divorce that I will not contest. Within the next few weeks, if all goes according to her well-orchestrated plans, she will become the president of Scarpetta America and the new Mrs. Giovanni Scarpetta."

I gasped.

Ben returned to the table and sank back into his chair. "Marion's not coming back. Ever. She doesn't love me or our children and wants nothing more to do with us or the company we built."

When I was four years old, my father accidentally slammed the car door on my arm. The pain was a mere twinge of discomfort compared to the vice grip that presently constricted every one of my internal organs. I bit down on my lower lip and turned my head away, glancing at the abandoned LEGO buildings. I knew all too well the pain of losing a parent, but death had torn my life apart, not selfishness. My family hadn't abandoned me.

Marion's behavior was despicable, and I hated her for what she had done—would do—to her kids. No doubt Ben would survive Marion's betrayal. But would Scotty, Woody, and Teddy? What right did any woman have to bring children into this world, then toss them aside like a worn-out pair of her precious Bottega Venetas?

Unable to fathom such a self-centered attitude, I turned back to Ben. Maybe I hadn't understood him correctly. "You mean she's giving you custody but she'll still have visitation rights, won't she?"

He shook his head. "She doesn't want any."

Unbelievable! "Ever?"

"Ever."

"How could any mother deliberately walk away from her own children? Does she hate you that much?"

For several seconds Ben sat silently contemplating his clasped hands before finally emitted another heavy sigh. I noticed he was doing that a lot. Sighing. And when he wasn't sighing, he was muttering a lot of *hells*, *shits*, *damns*, and worse under his breath. But they seemed directed more inward than outward, as if he were verbally flogging himself, not his soon-to-be ex-wife. "Marion doesn't hate me. She left for other reasons, reasons I don't want to go into. I'm certain she would have waited had she realized the extent of Fritzi's condition."

From what I'd seen, I doubted Marion would keep something as trivial as a sick housekeeper from interfering with her agenda. Ben was trying to convince himself, not me.

He paused again briefly, and at first, I thought he'd finished with his explanation, but then he continued. "I know it appears that way to you, but Marion isn't a malevolent person. Her actions stem from unresolved, complex issues and a pain she's suffered her entire life. In the end, I realized that nothing I could have done or said would have changed the outcome. I'm sure this is hard for you to understand, not knowing the full story, but Marion deserves our pity, not our hate. I'm as much or more to blame for what's happened as she is."

I couldn't believe he was defending the bitch. "How can you say that? I know couples break up all the time, and it's rarely just one person's fault, but mothers *don't* abandon their children like this, Ben!"

He sighed yet again, this time combing his fingers through his hair before balling his fists and rhythmically pounding his thighs in a steady staccato as he stared off into space. "They do if they never wanted those children in the first place. I never should have forced a family on Marion. I can't be bitter. I've been blessed with three wonderful sons. I need to think of them and not dwell on the mistakes of the past."

"And that's where I come in?"

He raised his head, his eyes begging like an abandoned and abused cocker spaniel. "It was Le's idea. You have to understand, the rest of the team is very protective of the boys and me. We've been together a long time, and we think of each other as family. I would never have considered Le's suggestion if I hadn't already exhausted every other available option and come up cold."

"You're saying you can't find another nanny?"

He shook his head. "We tried all morning. None of the agencies has anyone available." He clenched his jaw and exhaled his frustration. "Look, I realize babysitting doesn't exactly fall under your job description—"

"Exactly? Playing Mary Poppins didn't come within a light year of the job I was hired to do."

"And you could sue the pants off me if you felt you were being coerced into this—"

I held up both hands. "Wait. As much as I'd like to be a team player here and help you out, you've got the wrong person. Believe me. I have no formal training. I've never taken so much as a single course in Early Childhood Development."

"You wouldn't have to—"

"My brother was only two years younger than me, and the few cousins I have are all much older."

"You mean to tell me you never babysat as a teenager?"

"Sure, I babysat, but that was eighteen, twenty years ago, and most of the time the kids were already asleep when their parents left the house. Or they were a lot older than your boys."

Ben attacked my excuses. "Most parents have little experience when they start out, Hope, and I've seen you with the boys. You have a natural affinity with children. I don't want you to think I'm talking you or myself into this, but I have confidence my sons would be in loving hands with you."

"I'm really not qualified to do this, Ben. I've never even changed a diaper."

"You wouldn't have to—"

"We're not talking diapers here, are we? Because I don't do diapers."

"No diapers." But he looked a bit too guilty as he said it.

"Why do I get the impression you're leaving out a very large *but*? No pun intended."

"Sometimes they don't quite make it to the bathroom in time," he mumbled.

"Great. Please tell me we're talking pee here and not poop."

He hesitated a bit too long. "*Mostly* pee."

I wriggled my nose. Potty habits aside, though, I had rattled off my string of negative nanny attributes more for self-preservation. Without his knowledge or any attempt on his part, Ben had mounted a full-frontal assault on my too long-suppressed libido from the moment we met. An assault I'd vowed to fend off.

My current strategy was to hit the singles scene ASAP and exorcise this man from my libido. Having him tell me he's available and wants me to move in with him for a week or two definitely threw a monkey wrench into my game plan. After all, I'm a flawed human, not Superwoman. The man had no idea what he was asking of me. If the pope were a woman, even he would have a tough time controlling himself around Ben Schaffer under these circumstances.

But those three little guys had gotten to me. And really, what other argument did I have other than, "I'm sorry, Ben, I can't be a nanny to your children because I've wanted to jump your bones from Day One, and how could I watch your kids if we're fucking each other's brains out?" I was pretty certain divulging *that* volatile bit of information would definitely not be the wisest of career moves. Instead, I inhaled a deep breath and asked, "How long are we talking here?"

"The doctors won't let Fritzi come back to work for six weeks."

"*Six weeks?*" He expected me to live with him for six weeks? Impossible! A week maybe. Two weeks would be a stretch. Six weeks? I'd never survive. Although Ben had invaded my dreams—both waking and sleeping—for the past week, I knew the feelings weren't reciprocated. Shouldn't be. Wouldn't be.

In the Schaffer-Merrick family everyone was a brother or sister. And I, as the junior member of the firm, was looked upon as the little sister, even if there were only a few years separating me from the rest of the staff. Ben thought of me as a new kid sister. If he thought of me at all. It wasn't his problem that my long dormant libido had suddenly decided to come out of hibernation at such an inopportune moment and with a totally inappropriate man.

I had to stop thinking like a teeny-bopper. Ben was in the middle of the most serious crisis of his life, and all I could do was focus on the itch between my thighs? What did that say about my maturity? Over the years I'd survived a hell of a lot worse than hormones with a one-track mind.

Because my father had instilled the wrath of God in me and my mother had filled me with enough fear from stories of failed birth control and unwanted pregnancies—always about friends of friends of friends she knew or stories she'd heard fourth-hand, I'd remained a virgin until my wedding night. And I'd slept alone since Wally's death. Not that I'd had time for so much as a one-nightstand the past twelve years. But even though both Masters and Johnson and my own body said I had entered my sexual peak, surely, I could survive another six weeks without scratching that particular itch. Nuns did it all the time, didn't they?

Taking another deep breath, I asked, "Do the boys know Marion isn't coming back?"

Ben shook his head. "Not yet. I'm wrestling with what to tell them. And how."

I shifted my gaze to the window. Ben was asking for six weeks. Six weeks that could mean a world of difference to three little boys. Not to mention their devastated father. I closed my eyes and prayed I wasn't making the biggest mistake of my life. "Okay." I'm either a total glutton for punishment, I thought, or definitely certifiable. "Under one condition."

His face lit up. "You'll do it?"

"If you meet my condition."

"Anything."

"You have to promise to stay away from all kitchen appliances."

FIFTEEN

If the exterior of Ben's sprawling three-story Victorian reminded me of a dollhouse, the interior only reinforced that opinion. "These rooms aren't exactly decorated with young children in mind," I said, following him as he familiarized me with the layout of the house.

I'd seen little of the other rooms on my two prior visits. Friday night I'd gone from the front hallway directly to the children's bedroom. Once they were tucked in, I curled up on the floor at the foot of their beds where Ben later discovered me—sound asleep. When I returned his Lexus the following morning, I'd remained in the kitchen.

"Marion didn't allow the children in most of these rooms," he said.

And just how had Marion reinforced that edict? I'm not sure I wanted to know. I glanced over my shoulder. The triplets had followed close at our heels during the tour but always hovered in the hallway outside each room.

Marion had created a museum, not a home. Furnished in period pieces, each room evoked the Victorian philosophy of "more is better" with a preponderance of bric-a-brac and collectibles. Antique porcelain figurines, crystal, china, and assorted other clutter filled every shelf, corner, nook, and cranny. Lace shawls, doilies, and antimacassars were draped across tables and upholstery. Marion had even placed glass display cases, filled with collections of everything from butterflies to antique buttons, throughout the house. The only things missing were the "Do Not Touch" signs and the velvet ropes across the doorways.

I waved my hand to encompass the front parlor. "Is all this authentic?" Heavy burgundy velvet drapes, edged with gold silk fringe, hung from either side of the lace-covered windows. A fleur-de-lies patterned gold silk wallpaper lined the four walls. Ornately carved chairs and loveseats, upholstered in a gold, burgundy, and cream stripe, formed a formal-looking, uninviting sitting area in front of a large marble-mantled fireplace. I counted four Tiffany lamps along with massive silver candlesticks and innumerable, breakable knickknacks.

"Down to the last gewgaw," said Ben. "Our home was Marion's passion."

Marion's passion but certainly not Ben's from the lack of enthusiasm in his voice. Did he not share his wife's love of antiques, or was his emotionless monotone a result of her desertion? Once again, I glanced at the triplets. Shouldn't they have been their mother's passion? I'd bet my first month's paycheck that they'd spent most of their short lives confined to the nursery and kitchen, even though the house was large enough for a family of twelve. The thought angered me. "This may be a spectacular house," I muttered, "but it isn't a home."

Ben uttered a sound close to a growl. I hadn't meant to voice my thoughts out loud. He glared at me.

"I'm sorry. I had no right to say that."

He shook his head. "Don't apologize. You're right." He leaned one hand against the door jamb and lowered his lips close to my ear. "I have to admit, after you left Friday night, I had an incredible urge to smash every piece of glass and china throughout the house."

I knew the feeling. Only there was little left for me to smash when the urge had taken hold of me. "What stopped you?"

"I was afraid I'd wake the boys."

His eyes mirrored the anger that consumed him. And the guilt. My fingers itched to reach out and comfort him, but it wasn't my place. Besides, it would only make my own situation that much worse. Here I was only an hour or so into my temporary nanny gig, and I knew, beyond a doubt, that getting through the next six weeks was going to prove even more difficult than I'd originally suspected. The man pushed too many of the right buttons in me. Or in his case, the wrong buttons.

"Is Marion coming back for any of this?" I whispered.

Ben kept his voice low enough to prevent the boys from hearing him. "She came Saturday afternoon to pick up what she wanted."

My jaw dropped. Nothing in my life's experiences had prepared me for a woman who cared more about things than her own sweet little sons. Although I felt like screaming, I mouthed my next question. "What did she tell the boys?"

"Nothing. She requested they not be here when she arrived. I took them to the hospital to visit Fritzi."

"*What?!*"

Ben shot a quick glance over his shoulder at his sons before responding. "I don't think this is the time or place for this discussion."

I bit down on my bottom lip. "You're right. I'm sorry."

"Let's finish up here," he said, leading me from the parlor to the library. "I still have to make arrangements for a rental car."

"A rental car?"

"You don't have wheels. Marion took her Jag. I'm giving you the LX to use for the next few weeks. After the boys are in bed tonight, we'll go over everything else."

~*~

I had assumed *everything else* would include how to handle the boys' questions concerning their mother, but this was one area Ben had trouble confronting. "I don't know what to tell them!" he said later that evening when I again asked him about it. Raking his hands through his hair, he sprang from his seat and began pacing across the kitchen floor.

I watched him for several minutes as he wore a path from one end of the room to the other. Like the rest of the house, the kitchen mirrored Marion's Victorian compulsion. The floor was covered with small black and white hexagonal tiles, the kind found in retro bistros. The appliances, although state-of-the-art, were designed as Victorian reproductions. A claw-foot oak pedestal table with six matching high-back chairs, occupied the center of the large room.

Spread across the surface of the table were various papers listing everything I'd need for the next several weeks—names, phone numbers, addresses, schedules. Ben had drawn detailed maps showing me how to get from the house to the boys' pre-school, the supermarket, the pediatrician's office, the pharmacy, the library, the mall. Extremely organized, he had thought of everything. Everything except an answer to my most important question.

I pushed the sheets of paper aside and rose, stepping in front of him to block his path. Unless Ben physically moved me aside, he had to face both me and my question. Standing toe to toe, I placed my hands on my hips and craned my neck to look him in the eyes. "Damn it, Ben! Sooner or later those boys are going to start asking questions, and I need to know how you want me to handle it. This is not exactly my field of expertise, you know. I agreed to stay with your kids, but I'm no shrink. And I'm definitely no mind reader."

His shoulders slumped. Sorrow clouded his eyes. "How can I tell my children their mother never wants to see them again? Can you imagine the traumatic impact that will have on them?"

"Is it necessary to be so blunt?"

"How else do I explain what's happened? I can't just say we're getting a divorce. What do three-year-olds know of divorce? And when they do get old enough to understand, what happens when they ask why she never comes to visit? Or why they don't live with her some of the time?" He looked at me, as if I had the answers to his questions. Like I knew more than he did. But I had no answers for him.

"They're bright little guys," he continued. "They have friends at school whose parents are divorced. How long before they figure out their situation is different? Wrong?"

I thought back to the way Marion had spoken of her sons Friday night—how she hadn't even said goodnight to them, knowing she planned never to see them again. "Look, Ben, maybe I have no right to say this, but I have to wonder whether Marion's departure will leave much of an impact at all on your sons."

"What do you mean?"

"If the boys lost you, that would be one thing, but from what I've witnessed, she wasn't much of a presence in their lives, was she?"

He didn't answer, just stared at me, so I pressed on, hoping I wasn't shooting myself in the foot as I shot off my mouth. "Other than a few references about their mother not liking LEGO and not cooking, your sons didn't mention Marion all Friday evening or Saturday morning. And not at all today. Correct me if I'm out in left field here, but I have a sneaking suspicion your housekeeper has been more of a mother to them than Marion ever was. Hell, she never even said goodnight to them Friday, knowing she planned never to see them again. So I have to ask, how likely is it that they'll need more than a brief explanation to questions they may not even ask?"

"Marion certainly wasn't the maternal type," he admitted. "She never had much to do with them when she *was* here."

"Did she tuck them in at night?"

He shook his head.

"Read to them?"

"Never."

I knew the answer to my final question before I even asked it. "Hug them?"

"You've made your point, Hope." And with that Ben stormed out of the kitchen.

~*~

The next day, after dropping the boys off at pre-school, with the window rolled down and a gentle spring breeze whipping through my hair, I began driving with no particular destination in mind. Trading my position at the firm for a babysitting stint came with one definite plus—Ben's Lexus SUV. Considering my cargo, he had decided it made more sense to give me what he said was one of the safest cars on the road while he drove the rental to and from the train station.

Without a car of my own, exploration of my new environs had been limited to whatever venues were serviced by New Jersey's public transportation system—such as it was. Being without a car hardly posed a problem in Manhattan. The suburbs, however, were a different story. They were designed for owners of gas-powered transportation.

The sensible hemisphere of my brain told me I should spend the few hours the boys were in pre-school doing the grocery shopping. I assumed Ben's housekeeper kept the pantry and fridge well stocked, but after nearly four full days without her services, three growing boys and their father had pretty much depleted the larder of the basic food groups—not to mention whatever junk food Fritzi normally kept on hand. This morning I'd been reduced to scraping the dregs from a jar of peanut butter in order to make sandwiches for lunch. And they were quite vocal when they realized dessert would consist of an Oreo per child—all that remained in the cookie jar.

"You're lucky there's one for each of you," I told the whining threesome. "It's better than nothing. There's ice cream in the freezer. You can have that as a snack when you come home, okay?"

The promise of double-chocolate-fudge-ripple had stopped the complaints.

Yes, I should go to the supermarket, but it was such a beautiful day, and I yearned for a bit of freedom.

I'd expected a short vacation between graduation and the start of my career. Mr. Hagarty, my old boss, had insisted on it. "I'm laying you off, Hope. Collect unemployment while you job hunt." That along with an additional two-weeks vacation pay was his graduation gift to me. He'd balked when I offered to stick around to train my replacement. "What? You think I can't handle it? I trained you, didn't I?"

That was the Friday before my Sunday graduation. In the middle of sending out resumes the following Tuesday afternoon, I received the call from Professor Antonelli that would change my life. Less than a week later I was working at Schaffer-Merrick. I spent my first week slaving round the clock as a pawn in Marion's scheme to leave Ben. And now two days into my second week, I found myself playing the role of nanny/housekeeper/cook to my suddenly single boss and his three sons.

Some rest.

In two-and-a-half weeks I'd segued from Magna Cum Laude to Mary Poppins. Marion's decision to walk out on Ben and the triplets had turned my life upside down. In more ways than one.

The hell with the supermarket. I'd buy food after I picked up the boys. I needed some *me* time. Time to be alone. Time to think. So I hopped onto the Garden State Parkway and headed south.

Forty minutes later I pulled the Lexus into a vacant parking space on the tree-lined main street of a small shore town. Leaving my sneakers and socks in the car, I rolled up my jeans, locked the door, and headed toward the nearly deserted beach for a much-needed solitary walk.

But I found no answers, no peace. Only more uncertainty and a shoreline strewn with broken shells and seaweed. So I climbed back into the car and drove back to Westfield.

~*~

I was surprised to find Ben standing on the porch when I arrived home with the boys.

SIXTEEN

Ben slept little the previous night. In reality, he hadn't slept since Marion walked out on him Friday evening. Last night was worse, though. Besides the stress and shock of Marion's desertion, his conversation with Hope kept replaying in his mind. For someone who didn't have children of her own and claimed to have little experience with them, she was perceptive as hell about them.

Not to mention kind beyond words. She could have turned him down. Should have turned him down. He'd given her every opportunity to do so. Instead, she'd agreed to his highly unusual and—as Zeke repeatedly reminded him—professionally questionable request. At this point all Ben could do was pray Zeke's fears were unwarranted.

His gut told him Hope was as genuine as she appeared, and he should discount Zeke's paranoia about lawsuits. From what he saw, Hope wasn't the lawsuit type. Then again, his gut had originally told him all sorts of things about Marion, and look where that had gotten him. Zeke, damn him, had been right about

Marion from the moment she'd enter their lives all those years ago. Too many years later Ben saw what his friend had seen from the start. But then, Marion wasn't Zeke's type, and he'd never let his prick get in the way of his brain.

Ben stood in the shadows of the porch watching and listening as Hope turned into the driveway. Over the rumble of the engine and the crunch of tires on gravel, he heard...*singing?* Four voices, all high-pitched and slightly off-key, were belting out a lively rendition of *Rubber Ducky*. Well, one voice was singing *Rubber Ducky*. The other three were singing a slightly different version—*Wubba Ducky*.

Did she tuck them in at night? Read to them? Hug them?

Hope's questions reverberated in his head. A basketball size lump formed in his throat. No matter how much he had tried to make up for Marion's disinterest in her children, he was only one loving parent. His boys deserved two. And his selfishness had stolen that from them.

Hope tooted the horn and waved. As Ben walked down the steps to meet them, he watched as she carefully lifted each child from his car seat and hugged him before setting him down on the driveway.

Hug them?

No, Ben had never once seen Marion hug her sons.

"Daddy!" The boys all shouted at once as they tackled his legs.

Following behind the children, Hope eyed him cautiously. "Is something wrong?"

"No, why?"

"It's only a little after three. We didn't expect you until dinnertime."

Ben led the way up the front steps. Opening the door, he

stepped aside. The children scampered down the hall to the kitchen, but he stopped Hope at the entrance. "Have they mentioned Marion at all today?"

She shook her head.

"I thought about what you said last night. I can't put off telling them any longer."

"We were going to the supermarket after they had a snack. I promised them a special treat for dinner."

Ben cocked an eyebrow. "You should have gone while they were in school. How did you plan to handle three little boys and a cartload of groceries by yourself?"

Hope stepped across the threshold and headed down the hall toward the kitchen. "The same way I've seen countless mothers handle a trip to the supermarket," she said over her shoulder. "Through coercion and bribery. If that doesn't work, I'll resort to violence."

There was far too much mirth in her voice to take her seriously. Somehow Ben didn't think Hope had it in her to swat a fly, much less a child. "We're going to have to do something about that biting sense of humor of yours," he said.

"We?" She removed a carton of ice cream from the freezer and placed it on the counter. Ignoring Ben, she turned her attention to the triplets. "Anyone know where the ice cream scoop is kept?"

"I do," said Teddy.

"Good. Will you get it for me, please?" Teddy headed for one of the drawers. She turned to the other boys. "Woody, would you get spoons, please? And Scotty, please get the napkins." Then she spun around and confronted Ben. "You can get the bowls, Professor Higgins."

"Huh?" Scotty stopped pulling napkins from the holder and

turned toward Hope. "That's not Daddy's name. It's Ben. Ben Schaffer."

Ben laughed. "Hope was making a grownup joke." He nodded in her direction. "Touché, Miss Doolittle."

Once again Ben found himself studying Hope as she interacted at the table with his sons. Sweet and easygoing, she had seduced his normally reticent children from the moment they met her. The boys had fallen under her spell and were coming alive in ways Ben hadn't believed possible. Hope wasn't just a ray of sunshine in their lives, she was the whole damn blinding ball of fire. If he didn't watch out, he'd find himself drawn in by her incandescence as well.

And he knew there was no way in hell he could allow that to happen.

"We dwawd cards for Fwitzi," said Teddy, breaking into his thoughts.

Ben smiled at him. "I'm sure she'll love them." Yesterday he had called the pre-school and informed the boys' teacher of the upheaval in their lives and that Hope would be taking them to and from school for the next few weeks. Not knowing what kinds of changes in behavior they might manifest, he had wanted Mrs. Bretton prepared. "We can bring them to her when we go visit."

"Tonight?" asked Woody.

Ben glanced over at Hope. He wasn't at all certain how the boys were going to react after he told them about their mother. And he still hadn't informed Fritzi. He wanted to wait until after she was fully recovered to break the news to her. However, if he told the boys, he'd have to tell their nanny—which was another reason he wished he could put off the unsavory task.

"Why don't we see what time it is after we finish dinner?"

Hope suggested, as if reading his thoughts. "It might be too late to go tonight. People in the hospital need lots of sleep. They go to bed earlier than little boys."

"No way!" said Scotty.

"Way," said Hope.

With skepticism written all over his face, Scotty eyed Hope, then looked to his father, hoping no doubt, that he'd counter Hope's statement. "Would Hope lie to you?" he asked his son.

"Hope don't lie. Lying's naughty."

"Well, then?"

Scotty cocked his head toward Hope. "That's weal early."

"Hmm," she answered him. "Sure is."

~*~

"You don't know Fritzi," Ben said a short time later as he cleared the table. The boys had gone to wash their hands. With any luck he would have about thirty seconds of privacy before they scurried back. "She'd refuse to go to Florida when she's released on Saturday. The doctor was adamant about a six-week recovery period."

Hope grew thoughtful. "I suppose there's no way of keeping her from seeing the boys before she leaves?"

"What am I supposed to do? Pick her up at the hospital and drive her directly to the airport?" Ben shook his head. "Besides, it wouldn't be fair to her or the children. They're very close."

"Close enough that the boys wouldn't want to do anything that might keep her from getting well?"

"Of course."

Hope smiled. "There's your solution, Ben. You simply tell the boys not to mention anything about Marion leaving because the doctor said people who have been in the hospital aren't supposed to hear bad news for a while. It might make them sick again."

"You're asking me to lie to my children."

Hope's hands flew to her hips. Her chin jutted out. Her eyes blazed with fire. "How is it a lie? Haven't you ever heard that stress can impede recovery?"

Stupefied, all Ben could do was stand gape-mouthed in front of her. The children returned, jostling each other as they raced into the room. He turned to watch them, realizing with a start that they would never risk acting so boisterous when Marion was home. She hadn't tolerated such raucous behavior, and at an early age the boys learned they dared not upset their mother.

His sons were running in the house! And laughing! Without fear. He turned his gaze to the woman who had precipitated this wonderful metamorphosis in such a brief amount of time. "How did you get so wise?" he asked.

She didn't answer him. Instead, she grabbed a sponge and began wiping the table. "I'm taking the boys to the supermarket," she said. "We'll be gone about an hour."

"I'll come with you."

"If you want," she said, her tone clipped as she pitched the sponge into the sink.

Ben was taken aback by her sudden change in attitude. Talk about getting the frost treatment. He'd given her a compliment, hadn't he? Maybe Zeke was right. He'd better watch what he said and where he stepped around Hope Morgan. And he'd better keep a close eye on things to make sure she kept those mood swings in check around his kids. The last thing he needed was a bipolar babysitter. His boys had suffered enough trauma from a loveless mother.

Ben made a mental note to ask Winnie to continue the temp

nanny search. Maybe someone would turn up. Someone professional. Someone with experience dealing with children. The sooner Hope was back at her drawing board, the better.

Damn, he hated when Zeke was right. And he sure as hell wasn't looking forward to any further I-told-you-so's.

SEVENTEEN

I was amazed by Teddy's, Scotty's, and Woody's reaction to a trip to the supermarket. They acted like we'd entered Toys R Us—the big one I'd seen at Times Square. Complete with an indoor Ferris wheel. The boys *oohed* and *aahed* up one aisle and down the next, finding all kinds of goodies their father couldn't refuse them.

I eyed the contents of the quickly filling cart and shook my head. Sugary cereal, cookies, candy, potato chips, soda. Ben had allowed his children enough junk food to turn a hundred zombies hyperactive. "I think we need to concentrate on a few nutritious items now," I said.

"What's that mean?" asked Woody.

"It means fruits, veggies, milk, chicken, and fish."

"Fish!" Scotty screwed his face into a grotesque mask.

Teddy matched his brother's grimace and added a loud, "Yuck!"

Woody stuck out his lower lip and remained silent.

I turned to Ben. "I could use some help here. Unless of course, you want to turn your children into Twinkie-brained dolts."

He frowned at me, then the items in the cart. "I guess I did let them get a bit carried away."

"A bit?"

His eyes narrowed; his voice tightened. "Okay, a lot." He steered the cart into a U-turn and headed back the way we'd come. His voice sounded a false joviality as he said, "To the produce aisle, men." Teddy, Woody, and Scotty followed, dragging their feet and voicing their displeasure at the prospect of yucky vegetables.

I stared after them, too confused to move. What had gotten into Ben? He'd done an about-face back in the kitchen and now seemed to have a giant chip on his shoulder over something. Chip? Hell. The guy was acting like a sequoia was perched on his shoulder.

"Hey, lady, are you going to stand there blocking the aisle all day?"

I jumped. "Sorry." I stepped out of the way of a harried-looking woman struggling with an overloaded cart and a toddler in full tantrum mode. The woman muttered a mild obscenity as she pushed past me. Shrugging off both the comment and my own confusion, I scurried off to catch up with Ben and the boys.

I found the four of them gathered in front of a display of string beans. Ben held open a plastic bag while each boy deposited a small handful of beans. "Not enough," I said eyeing the paltry number of string beans in the bag. "Two more big handfuls each."

"You're quickly losing points with the pee-wee set," Ben muttered.

"I guess Teddy, Scotty, and Woody just aren't Dino-Trekker material."

"Huh?" All three pouting boys stared at me.

"All the Dino-Trek space guys love veggies. That's what gives them the power to fight mean old MegaRex."

"No way!" Doubting Thomas Scotty voiced his opinion of my theory. Then, apparently remembering the earlier conversation where his father had convinced him I wouldn't lie, he asked, "Weally, Hope?"

I nodded. "Really."

Scotty grabbed a large handful of beans and added them to the bag. Then another. His brothers followed suit as Ben watched the bag fill. The tightness in his face seemed to relax a bit. "What's next?" he asked, his voice less harsh as he wrapped a twist-tie around the bag.

I grabbed a bag of baby carrots and a head of Romaine, then pointed toward the acorn squash.

"What's *that?*" asked Woody, turning his nose up.

"Acorn squash." My answer was met with another chorus of complaints. "You eat it with brown sugar," I said. "It tastes like warm pumpkin pie."

"How can a veg'ble taste like pie?" asked Teddy.

"Pumpkin's a vegetable," I told him.

Scotty opened his mouth, about to issue forth his third *no way* of the afternoon but stopped short. "But I likes pum'kin pie," he said.

"And I bet you'll like acorn squash."

His eyes looked doubtful, but he didn't argue. Teddy and Woody watched and waited for their brother's reaction to my pronouncement. When Scotty, the obvious leader, raised no further objections, they remained silent.

"Actually, I believe pumpkin is a fruit," Ben whispered as we headed for the poultry aisle.

I looked at him. "No way. It's a squash. Squash is a vegetable."

He shook his head. "Way. It's a fruit."

"Oops." Not that I'd ever taken a botany class but who would've guessed? Hopefully, the boys would like the squash and forget my less-than-accurate vegetable lesson. After all, Hope never lied. Or so we'd told them.

Twenty minutes later we stood in line at the checkout counter. I frowned at the contents of the cart.

"What's wrong?" asked Ben.

"I'm wondering if we bought enough milk."

He hoisted the gallon container and studied it as if the milk might divulge some deep, dark secret. "I don't know. Maybe I should run back and get another." He returned the milk to the basket and headed for the dairy section.

"Are you triplets?"

I spun around. An elderly woman with rheumy, pale gray eyes and tight blue curls addressed the boys. Talk about bad dye jobs! Someone should point that woman in the direction of a good salon.

The boys shifted closer to me, warnings about talking to strangers apparently having been drummed into them by their father and teacher. I doubted Marion had ever bothered to warn her children about anything other than keeping their hands off her precious collections. "Yes, they are," I answered for them.

"They're precious," said the woman, "and such a perfect blending of you and your husband. I can see both of you in each of them. They have their father's features except for the eyes. So round and expressive and such an interesting blend of colors. Just like yours."

I stared at the boys. They were looking up at me, puzzlement clouding each face.

"That lady silly," said Scotty.

For a moment I continued to stare at the boys, focusing on three identical sets of gray-green eyes with gold flecks and a narrow band of brown around the perimeter of each iris. I'd noticed before that the boys had hazel eyes, but so did many other people. Their thick straight hair, in varying shades of nutmeg, along with the slant of their mouths and the shape of their faces, made them look like miniature versions of their father and no one else. Interesting how they didn't seem to favor their mother in the least. Not a single physical trait of Marion's showed in any of her sons.

I chalked up the woman's comments to advanced glaucoma or cataracts. "The nice lady just made a mistake," I said to Scotty.

I turned to the woman. "I'm not their mother."

She offered an embarrassed apology. "I...oh, my. I'm so sorry, my dear. I just assumed. Well, you must be their aunt, then?"

"No relation. I work for their father."

The conveyer belt began moving, and I started unloading the cart.

All three boys were giggling when Ben returned with another gallon of skim milk. "Someone tell a good joke?" he asked, scooting around the children and me to start bagging the groceries.

"That lady funny," said Teddy. He pointed to the end of the counter where the woman was beginning to unload her purchases onto the belt.

"You boys know it's not nice to make fun of the way someone looks," Ben whispered in a stern voice, but he looked like he was having a hard time keeping a straight face. Those blue curls really did look like the woman had mistaken a box of Jell-O for Miss Clairol.

"Huh?" Woody, Scotty, and Teddy scrunched up their faces.

"It's not the hair," I whispered. "The poor thing probably doesn't see very well." I stole a nervous glance in the woman's direction then frowned at the children. "And now I'm hoping her hearing is just as bad as her eyesight."

Ben kept his vision narrowed on the triplets, but he directed his question to me. "So if it isn't the blue hair, what do these three ill-mannered hellions find so hysterical about her?"

I shrugged. "She thought I was their mother just because we have the same color eyes. Apparently, your children find that amusing."

Ben's gaze slid back to her. "Marion's father and three brothers have hazel eyes," he said, between gritted teeth.

EIGHTEEN

Hazel eyes, thought Ben as he steered the car out of the parking lot. Yet another reason why Marion could never bring herself to love her children.

During the short ride back to the house, he contributed little to the lively conversation flying between his sons and Hope. He preferred to listen, drinking up his children's exuberance. Maybe he had jumped to the wrong conclusion back at the house. Damn Zeke for planting suspicions and doubts in his head. Didn't he have enough problems right now?

His thoughts turned back to Marion and the infrequent times the five of them had traveled as a family. Even as babies, the triplets had sat quietly in their car seats, somehow sensing not to anger their mother. They rarely cried and never laughed. Baby-talk babble was so infrequent that at first Ben worried the boys might be developmentally backwards. As they grew older, their silence around their mother continued. Marion had impressed on them her intolerance for jabbering. It gave her a headache.

Ben castigating himself once again for his own culpability. For most of his childhood he had felt like an outsider. Bounced between distant relatives and foster homes, he grew up longing for a family of his own. Marion had suffered deep psychological scars from her abusive father. Ben pressed her for children, convinced a family they created together would give them the unconditional love neither had experienced during their childhoods. Babies would fill the aching void in both their hearts.

At first Marion agreed, but when her fertility problems came to light, she seemed more than happy to drop the idea of having children. Ben, on the other hand, wouldn't give up and pleaded with her to explore various options. Finally, Marion had acquiesced.

When Ben learned they were expecting triplets, rather than one child, he was overjoyed at the prospect of an instant large family. Marion, on the other hand, was horrified. She bluntly told him she didn't want one child, let alone three, and accused him of using her. Their marriage plummeted downhill from there.

A series of belly laughs erupted from the backseat. The happy sound sliced through him like a jagged knife. He had prayed that Marion's attitude would improve as the children grew older. Instead, her cold intolerance of the boys grew worse. Periodically, he had tried to convince his wife to seek counseling, but she adamantly refused. This was his problem, she said, not hers. He was trying to mold her into something she wasn't. And each time Ben broached the subject, she silenced him with one final blow: *You're just like my father.*

As angry as Marion made him, in retrospect Ben was glad his wife walked out. Things would be different now. Better. Life would be filled with belly laughs, not nervous silence. No matter what, he'd make the past up to his sons. They deserved so much more than they had received in their short lives.

After pulling into the driveway and parking the car, he handed a lightweight grocery bag to each boy. Hope grabbed two bags, and Ben juggled the remaining four. When all the food was stored away, he turned to the boys. "Hope and I have an agreement." From the corner of his eye, he saw Hope toss him a quizzical look.

"What's a 'gweement?" asked Woody.

Scotty answered for his father. "It's something you gots to do cause you said so."

"Like a deal?" asked Teddy.

"Right. Like a deal," said Ben, ruffling Teddy's hair. "Hope and I made a deal."

Scotty glanced from Hope to Ben, then back to Hope. "What kinda deal?"

Ben grinned. To think that he once worried his children might be developmentally challenged! There was nothing slow about Scotty. The little guy's wheels were always whirring in that analytical brain of his. After their trip to the supermarket, Ben supposed his son was worried that the deal had something to do with vegetables. "Hope said she'd help us until Fritzi got better if I stayed out of the kitchen."

Scotty and Teddy giggled, but Woody offered Ben a serious face and asked, "Where's Mommy? Isn't she going to help?"

Inwardly, Ben cringed. From across the room, he saw Hope raise her eyebrows. He could almost hear the unspoken words: "Told you so. Now deal with it." Only this wasn't how he had planned to start *that* particular conversation. Actually, he still hadn't figured out a way of broaching Marion's departure to his sons. Maybe Woody's innocent question was the catalyst he needed.

"How about if the four of us clear out of the kitchen and let Hope start dinner? We'll go have some guy talk." He reached for their hands and led them out to the porch.

The boys climbed onto the wicker loveseat. Their tiny legs, not long enough to dangle over the edge, kicked up and down on the stuffed cushion. Ben looked down at his sons. Chins tilted upward, they were smiling at him. Their faces filled with trusting acceptance, they innocently waited for the bombshell he was about to drop.

Scooping Woody from the middle of the group, Ben squeezed between Scotty and Teddy, placing Woody on his lap. Teddy snuggled his way under Ben's left arm. Scotty leaned against his right thigh, his legs continuing their muffled staccato beat.

Ben cleared his throat. The boys turned expectant faces toward him. "You know how you have some friends at school who don't live with both their mommy and daddy?"

The boys nodded, but Ben could see creases of worry forming across their brows.

"Like Gweg's mommy and daddy?" asked Teddy.

"They gots divowceded," said Scotty. "Gweg lives with his mommy for school and his daddy for weekends."

Ben noticed Woody's lip begin to tremble ever so slightly. "Yes, like Greg's parents. But sometimes mommies and daddies get divorced, and one of them goes far away for a long time."

Woody's eyes widened in horror. His lip tremble increased, spreading to his entire body. Tears filled his eyes and spilled onto his cheeks. He wrapped his arms around Ben's neck and began howling. "Don't go, Daddy! Please! I don't want you to leave!"

Damn! He was handling this all wrong. He didn't want his

children to think *he* was deserting them. Weren't their lives screwed up enough?

Taking his cue from Woody, Teddy began wailing. His small arms squeezed Ben's arm in a death-grip. Between sobs, he echoed Woody's pleas, repeating over and over, "Don't go, Daddy. Please don't go."

Only Scotty remained dry-eyed. "No!" he cried, his face contorted in anger. He balled up his fists and pounded Ben's thigh. "You stay! You stay! Make mommy leave!"

"Mommy go," echoed Teddy through his tears. He sniffed back a fresh deluge and stared up at his father.

Woody buried his wet face in Ben's neck and nodded his head in agreement. "Daddy stay," he whispered. "Please stay. We'll be weal good."

Ben stared at his sons, too shocked to speak. A chill swept up his body. He had never realized the extent of their anger toward Marion. Suddenly, he found himself wishing she had walked out the moment they were born. He drew all three children into his arms, hugging them close to his chest. "I'll never leave you, guys. Ever."

Somehow Ben succeeded in calming down his sons and explaining that their mother, not he, was the one who had decided to move away. When the news penetrated, he saw the relief in their faces. But was it relief that he was the parent who was staying or relief over Marion's departure? Probably a little of both. The realization added to his mounting sense of guilt.

"Mommy don't wuv us." Scotty's words were spoken as a statement of fact, something the child had apparently accepted long ago. Teddy nodded in agreement.

"Will Mommy come visit us?" asked Woody. Ben wasn't

certain whether the question was spoken from a sense of longing or of dread. With Woody it was always hard to tell. He had craved his mother's attention more than his brothers, withdrawing further when she had ignored his attempts to please her.

Not knowing what else to say, Ben answered with the truth. "I don't know."

Woody sighed the sigh of an adult shouldering a heavy burden. Wistfulness clouded his face. For several seconds he stared out across the yard, saying nothing. Then he wiggled out of Ben's arms and ran into the house.

Ben found him in the kitchen nestled in Hope's lap. She sat on the floor, her back propped against the kitchen cabinets. Her long brown hair fell in waves over her shoulders, draping Woody in a silken blanket. In a soft, calming voice she comforted his son, rocking the boy gently in her arms, giving Woody the unconditional love his mother had denied him.

This is what his children had missed. This is what he had missed.

Hope raised her head toward him. From across the room Ben saw the tears glistening in her eyes. Here was a woman choked with emotion for a child she barely knew, a child whose own mother had never shown any feeling other than annoyance toward him. Ben felt tears gathering in his own eyes.

Behind him he heard Scotty and Teddy creeping down the hall. "Is Woody huwt?" asked Teddy, poking his head around Ben's legs.

"Not anymore," he answered, wrapping his arms around both boys.

NINETEEN

"So what happened next?" asked Zeke.

After a roller-coaster evening, the next day Ben was in desperate need of some adult male bonding and guy advice. So he grabbed his closest friend and second-in-command and headed for the local microbrewery. He might hate Zeke for his paranoid doomsday warnings of mayhem and lawsuits, but Ben couldn't deny that his longtime buddy had been dead-on when it came to Marion.

He told the rest of the group they were off to a client meeting. He wasn't ready to bare his soul to his entire staff—no matter how close they all were. Even if their sideways glances told him they suspected this *meeting* was far from business related.

Last night his already chaotic life had taken another hairpin curve, and Ben was still reeling. He was certain his friends, having known him so long and so well, had picked up on his tension.

Brewski's, a popular hangout packed with lunchtime regulars, had an open booth near the back of the restaurant. He and Zeke claimed it. Zeke, who never let anything dampen his gargantuan appetite, polished off half his foot-long sub and was on his second pint before Ben got down to what was really bothering him. He sat nursing the suds from his first beer and hadn't touched the club sandwich he ordered. "We ate dinner," he said, "the way a family is supposed to."

"Family?" Zeke raised an eyebrow.

Ben set his mug down in front of him and grimaced, remembering the conflicting feelings that had torn him apart throughout the meal—a meal filled not only with delicious food that his sons polished off without complaint, but laughter. So much laughter.

Hope was the complete antithesis of Marion. And it struck Ben that if he had to choose between the two women... well, there was little point going there. Circumstances prevented such useless meanderings of the mind. "It's as if Hope's always been a part of our lives. I don't understand it. The boys have only known her since Friday, and yet, they've accepted her unconditionally. They respond to her better than they do Fritzi, and you know how much they love her."

Zeke nodded. "Fritzi has always been more of a grandmother to the boys. Hope is closer in age to their friends' mothers."

"It's more than that. She's so open. So loving toward them. I guess I didn't expect her to respond with such heartfelt concern. After all, it's a temporary job, and one you all practically coerced her into accepting."

"Not me. I thought it was a bad idea, remember? But that's not why you decided to treat me to lunch, is it?"

Ben placed his elbows on the rough, slatted-wood tabletop and lowered his head into his hands. "We've known each other a long time, Zeke. You were there when I met Marion. You witnessed how she changed."

"Changed?"

Ben raised his head and stared at his friend. "Look, I know you never liked her much, but even you have to admit she's not the person she was back then."

Zeke smiled wryly. "You're memory's a bit fuzzy around the edges, Ben."

"What are you saying?"

"Nothing. Except that from the day you met Marion, you looked at her and saw only what you wanted to see. I told you I thought Marion was nothing but trouble the moment I met her, but you didn't want to hear it. So I shut up. I didn't want my dislike for her ruining our friendship.

"As far as I'm concerned, Marion was always a very confused, deeply disturbed woman. Maybe I shouldn't have kept quiet. I stood by and watched her grind your dreams to sawdust before you finally saw her for the person she's always been. I'm sorry, Ben."

Zeke's observation was one Ben had reluctantly come to on his own, only far too late. "Yeah, I suppose you're right." He shook his head in disgust. "No, you're definitely right. I've been so goddamn blind. And so cocksure. I thought I had all the answers. To Marion's problems. To my own loneliness. I should have had the sense to listen to you back then, before three innocent lives were damaged."

"Damn it, stop flaying yourself. Kids are resilient, and from what you're telling me, yours are already bouncing back in just a few short days. Besides, Marion was never enough a part of their lives to have inflicted any lasting damage. She hardly spent any time with them."

Ben smacked his hand on the table. "But that's the whole damn problem, isn't it? I thought having children of her own would erase all the psychological abuse she suffered at the hands of that bastard father of hers. Instead, she became just like him."

"Hell, that's classic Psych 101, man—the abused growing up to become an abuser."

"I must have cut that lecture."

Zeke chugged down the rest of his brew. "Look, Ben, from what you've told me, you should thank your lucky stars Marion kept her distance from the triplets. It could've been much worse. Besides, it's not like the boys have never known love. Remember, Marion had no one else to turn to as a child. No one loved her. That's not the case with Woody, Teddy, and Scotty."

Zeke was right. Marion's mother died in childbirth, a death her father blamed on the innocent infant he never wanted. Her older brothers were chips off their son-of-a-bitch father's block, taking pleasure in inflicting their own forms of torture on their unwanted sister.

As for himself, Ben may not have had loving parents to raise him, but the various relatives and foster families he had lived with were never unkind or abusive.

"The boys have you," continued Zeke, "and no one could love his kids more than you do. Except me, of course. But then again, I've got the two cutest little girls who ever graced the earth."

As miserable as he felt, Ben couldn't help but chuckle. Talk about viewing life through rose-colored glasses! Amanda and Crystal Ripley were sweet children, but unfortunately, Zeke's gene pool had prevailed over his wife's, and their daughters were miniature female versions of their pug-faced father.

"Plus, the boys have had Fritzi and the rest of us showering them with affection since the day they were born," added Zeke. He reached across the table and grabbed Ben's forearm. "So what aren't you telling me?"

Ben stared over Zeke's left shoulder, seeing the rest of last night replay in his mind. "I figured after all that happened yesterday, I owed Hope some explanation. At first, I didn't want to tell her. After all, it's not like she's been part of the group from the beginning."

"No, and as I pointed out on Monday, we really don't know much about her."

Ben ignored the verbal jab. "Yet, after a week in the office, it felt like she'd been with us since the beginning. There's something about the way she slipped right into the routine and pitched in without complaint when the need arose. Like any of the rest of us have always done for each other countless times."

Zeke snorted. "Yeah, well, I'm still not sure it wasn't because she felt she had no choice. So?"

"So, after the boys were in bed we sat on the porch, and I told her."

Zeke leaned forward. "Everything?"

"No, not everything." Ben rubbed his temples. His head was beginning to pound. He grimaced at his plate. Even though he had no appetite, he picked up one of the sandwich quarters and took a bite, washing it down with a swallow of beer. "There was no need to go into minute detail, but I told her about Marion's family situation. And mine. Our dreams for the company. For ourselves. And how everything fell apart after the boys were born."

"And how you blame yourself?"

Ben shrugged. "She sort of figured that one out for herself."

"Bright woman."

Ben met Zeke's gaze. "She cried, Zeke. She cried for me. For Marion. For the boys."

"And then?"

"I cried."

Zeke offered him a lecherous grin. "And then she comforted you?"

"No! It was nothing like that." Ben shook off the lewd innuendo. "She barely touched me. Just placed her hand on my shoulder until I regained control, but afterwards, when I looked at her, it was like seeing her for the first time."

"She turned you on."

Turned on was an understatement. Ben grunted, annoyed with himself and his mutinous body part. "All of a sudden, I realized I was rock hard. Luckily, by then it was dark outside, and she couldn't see what was going on south of the border. Not that she so much as glanced in that direction, of course."

"Of course." Zeke smirked. "Hey, I can't blame you, man. She's a looker." He paused for a moment, as if carefully considering his next words. "How long has it been, pal? Weeks? Months?"

"Since what?"

"Do I have to spell it out for you? Since you and Marion fucked."

Ben gritted his teeth. Bile churned in his stomach. "Not since before the boys were born."

"Jeez, man! I'm sorry. I had no idea." He studied Ben for a moment, his face solemn and thoughtful. Then his mouth turned up into a crooked smile. His eyes twinkled. "Well, there's nothing stopping you now. I'd say it's high time you remedied the situation."

Ben shook his head. "Not with Hope."

"Hell, I wasn't suggesting Hope. Don't even think of it! I'm still not convinced you did the right thing in asking her to take over for Fritzi. This whole situation could still wind up boomeranging back in your face. Hope could be a walking time bomb for all we know. Let's not add a Dorfman-Hewitt scenario into an already potentially volatile situation."

Ben winced at the reference. Chuck Dorfman might be his biggest competitor, but he didn't deserve the raw deal the courts recently handed him. What began as an innocent love affair with a secretary had ended as the sexual harassment suit of the decade. The poor guy would be paying for letting his dick rule his head for years to come. The way the courts were ruling, nowadays, a guy would have to be certifiable to have an affair with an employee. "Don't worry. I have no intentions of getting involved with Hope Morgan."

"Glad to hear it, especially since she's living under your roof, but do us all a favor, will you?"

"What's that?"

"Find someone else. And do it quickly. It's not healthy, man."

Ben never heard Zeke's reply. His attention was riveted on one of the many televisions scattered around the bar. "My God!"

"What?" Zeke whipped his head around. "What's going on? Another terrorist attack?"

"Shh!" Ben waved a hand to silence him. On the screen the reporter was detailing the events of the top story of the noon newscast.

"Informed sources tell *Eyewitness News* that well-known fertility specialist, Dr. Leo Bussey, has been charged with several counts of trafficking in stolen human eggs. For more information we turn to correspondent Andrea Currothers outside Dr. Bussey's clinic on Central Park West. Andrea?"

"Thank you, Pete. First, let me begin by stating that it is common practice and perfectly legal for an egg donor to be paid a sum of money for her time and inconvenience. It is also not uncommon for a fertility doctor to act as a go-between for couples seeking donor eggs and the donors themselves.

"However, according to reliable sources, Dr. Bussey found a lucrative way to circumvent the need for donors and pocket the huge sums of money paid to him by his patients for the donors' services."

"Do we know how this scam operated, Andrea?"

"Yes, Pete, a couple needing an egg donor would enlist Dr. Bussey's services. Instead of securing a donor, Bussey used a network of lab technicians at several fertility clinics across the country. These women stole eggs from their facilities and shipped them to Dr. Bussey."

The reporter referred to her notes before continuing. "From what I've been able to determine, at this point in the investigation there's no evidence of complicity between the doctor and any of his patients. All the recipients thought they were going through proper, legal channels to obtain their donor eggs, but the investigation is ongoing."

"Andrea, do we know how the police found out about the trafficking?"

"Sources tell us one of the lab technicians at an out-of-state clinic came forward."

"Are we talking fertilized or unfertilized eggs, Andrea?"

"We don't know, Pete."

"Do the police have any idea how long the operation had been going on?"

"No. However, Dr. Bussey apparently had some forewarning of the arrest. My source tells me the police believe he may have had time to destroy crucial records."

"So we have no idea how many families are involved?"

"That's correct. And because of Dr. Bussey's reputation and success rate, his practice wasn't limited to local couples. Patients throughout the tri-state area may be impacted by this scandal."

"But these were all couples planning to use donor eggs? So besides the financial scam, there are no other ramifications for them, correct?"

"The police can't be sure of anything at this point. The eggs were supposed to be fertilized with the husband's sperm, but many of the women may have been impregnated with eggs fertilized at the other clinics. We have no way of knowing whether Dr. Bussey limited his activities to couples seeking donor eggs. He may have also used the stolen eggs in his regular in vitro patients to increase their odds of having a baby. If the doctor was successful in destroying his records, these couples may never learn the truth."

"Where does the investigation go from here?"

"The D.A.'s office will try to recreate Dr. Bussey's patient list from interviews with his staff and by checking insurance company records, but many insurance companies don't cover in vitro fertilization, let alone the cost of egg donors. Couples who paid out of pocket won't show up on outside records."

"Are they talking DNA testing? That would be a massive undertaking."

"True. It would entail testing all the doctor's patients, the patients at the other clinics, and any babies born from the implantations. Many couples may refuse to take part for fear of losing their children. In the meantime, Dr. Bussey's lawyer has scheduled a press conference for one-thirty this afternoon to refute all the charges. Back to you, Pete."

The camera shifted to the anchor. "Thank you, Andrea. *Eyewitness News* will be standing by with further updates on this developing story as they break. Now on to our other top story..."

Ben leaned against the high-backed wooden planking of the booth and covered his face with his hands. "Jeez!"

"That's the doctor you and Marion used, isn't it?" asked Zeke.

Ben nodded. Lowering his hands, he stared at his friend. "What if the boys—?"

Zeke cut him off. "Not a chance, pal. Don't even think about it. Those kids look too much like you."

"Which means Marion and I could have other kids out there somewhere."

"How do you figure that?"

"Don't you think the bastard would use as many of his own patients' eggs first? Why pay for something he had available in his own office? He told us we had three viable embryos. What if we really had five? Or fifteen? Those kids are my responsibility, Zeke. I'm the one who talked Marion into going through with the procedure."

Zeke reached across the table, grabbed Ben's forearm and shook it. "Damn it, man. You've got enough on your plate already. Stop trying to turn yourself into a martyr. You have no responsibility in this. Besides, you don't even know if the guy stole any of your embryos, let alone whether they produced a child. Look at the odds. You dealt with him four years ago. Don't you think if he'd been involved in something as shady as this back then, he would've been caught before now?"

"I suppose you're right."

"Damn straight, I'm right. Just forget it."

TWENTY

After last night I knew I'd gotten myself in too deep with Ben and his kids. I never should have spied on them from the library window. The tears that streamed down my face as I listened told me I was getting too involved. I hauled around enough emotional baggage. No way did I need to stack someone else's trunks onto my already overloaded luggage cart.

At least the boys had their father's unconditional love to counter their mother's indifference. They were very young. They'd forget Marion. With time, the wounds she'd inflicted would heal.

Still, Marion really pissed me off. I had tiptoed back to the kitchen and taken out my anger on a cup of shelled walnuts, chopping the nutmeats into a fine powder. With each dull thud of the curved metal blade against the wood bowl, I visualized pounding some sense into the bitch. Or pulverizing her.

Ben said Marion wasn't to blame for what happened. He alluded to problems in her past. But what kind of trauma could create a monster who hated her own children? And it was hate. Pure and simple. Dressing Marion's treatment of her sons up in less offensive terms didn't negate what she'd done to them.

I grabbed a large knife and hacked the three miniature acorn squash in half. *Take that, Marion!* But it didn't help. Both my rage and my tears only increased as I scooped out the seeds and set the halves in a shallow pan with a small amount of water. After filling each center with a combination of chopped nuts, brown sugar, a pat of butter, and probably some tears, I covered the dish, placed it in the microwave, and headed for the powder room to splash cold water on my face.

When I returned to the kitchen, I found Woody hovering in the doorway. "Hi," I said.

He hesitated.

I bent to his level. He ran into my outstretched arms. "Stay," he said with a shudder and a sniff.

That's when I'd known I was really screwed. Full frontal assault type screwed. So much for thinking I'd come to terms with the life fate had dealt me. One needy kid in my arms, and I was feeling as sorry for myself as I was for him and his brothers.

I knew what he was going through. In a way I'd been there myself. He might be too young to articulate his feelings, but I knew he blamed himself for the mother who didn't love him. As did his brothers. Woody was the most sensitive of the three boys. And the one who tried the hardest to please. "It's not your fault," I whispered in his ear as I stroked the back of his head.

I knew then and there that I needed to create a life outside of playing Mary Poppins. Which is why the next morning I stood at the counter of the YMCA, filling out an application form.

"Are you interested in any of our singles events?" asked the woman behind the counter.

"Absolutely." I handed her the form and my credit card. She handed me a flyer listing the month's social events for singles. I planned to attend every one of them.

~*~

The following Tuesday night after cleaning up the dinner dishes, I said to Ben, "Bath and bed are on you tonight."

"They wear you out today?"

I tossed him the universal look for *duh*.

"Dumb question, huh?"

"Bingo."

"I'll handle them. Go veg."

I waved as I headed up the back stairs. "Actually, I'm going bowling."

Forty-five minutes later I scored my first strike. With my first ball. A guy with a Drew Carey body and a Jim Carey face, saluted me with a thumb's up. "Not bad. For a girl."

I responded with a tight smile, then took a seat as far away from him as possible. Definitely not the kind of guy I wanted hitting on me.

While I waited for my next turn, I observed the rest of the group. There were twelve of us, enough to make up four teams. We'd spent the first twenty minutes or so doing a round robin of introductions. Besides me, the only other newcomer was a forty-two-year-old recently divorced mother of four. The rest of the group ranged from late twenties to a widower who claimed he was forty-eight but looked like he was pushing sixty. Five men, seven women. Not great odds for those of us lacking a Y chromosome.

Worse after eliminating the Carey-Carey chauvinist, especially since I caught him picking his nose. And slimmer still, once I scratched off the geezer. Not that the age difference bothered me all that much. I'd spent my entire life deep in Blue Collarville. Now that I had a college degree and an actual profession (Okay, I'm putting the nanny stint aside for a moment. It's *temporary*. *Very* temporary.), I wasn't about to start dating a car salesman. I didn't care if he did sell Beemers. A car salesman is still a car salesman.

That left Chet, the thirty-seven-year-old high school biology teacher; Elvis, the forty-five-year-old accountant; and Jason, the twenty-nine-year-old stockbroker. All three of them zeroed in on me. I couldn't blame them for steering clear of the divorcee with the four kids. And I suppose they'd already struck out with the other women in the group.

"Hey, you've done this before," said Elvis, plopping into the molded plastic seat beside me.

I accepted the can of Coke he offered me and flipped the pull tab. "Thanks. Bowling is pretty much a Friday night staple where I come from."

"And where would that be?" asked Chet, taking the seat on the other side of me.

"Western Pennsylvania. North of Pittsburgh."

The three of us engaged in small talk for a few minutes until it was my turn to bowl again. I left a seven-ten split with my first ball.

"Tough break," said The Nose Picker.

I glanced up at the scoreboard. He'd bowled a nine his first frame, an eight his second frame. I hefted my ball, centered myself and waltzed one, two, three steps toward the foul line. Arm lowered. Arm back. Arm forward. Release. The ball straddled the very edge of the lane, half balancing over the gutter.

Behind me The Nose Picker snickered. "Gutter ball."

I continued to watch my ball skim along the edge of the polished wood. As it neared the seven pin, it arced slightly, clipping the pin at just the right moment and in just the right place to spin it into the ten pin. Exactly the way my father had taught me.

I turned around in time to see The Nose Picker's eyes bug out.

"Whoa, Mama!" cried Elvis as he marked the spare.

"Have any other talents?" asked Jason.

"A few."

"Maybe you'd like to discuss them over dinner tomorrow night?"

Elvis and Chet blasted Jason with a rapid-fire volley of daggers behind his back.

"Tomorrow night?" Where I come from guys who ask girls out for a weeknight first date do so because they're not sure they want to waste a weekend on them. Sort of a pre-date. And usually at some remote diner where there's no chance of bumping into anyone they know. Just in case.

"I...uhm...I'm tied up this weekend. Family wedding in Connecticut."

Which I'm sure he already had a date for *if* he indeed had a wedding to go to in Connecticut. Tripping over his tongue to come up with an excuse raised doubts with my inner jury. Jason, with his buff body and Brad Pitt blond good looks, didn't seem like the type of guy who went begging for companionship any weekend. Which made me wonder why he needed a singles group. But what did I have to lose? "Tomorrow night, then."

Tonight, I'd opened the cloister door. Tomorrow I'd officially vacate the premises. I gave both Chet and Elvis encouraging smiles, letting them know my social calendar contained plenty of blank pages. By the end of the evening, I had a dinner date scheduled with Elvis for Friday night and one with Chet for Saturday night.

Ben was going to get a lot of bathtub and bedtime practice.

~*~

And I was going to need a nap each day while the boys were in pre-school. But then I wouldn't get the laundry or marketing done. Not to mention meal preparations. And when was the last time I shaved my legs? Taking care of three active three-year-olds was no picnic. This was real work. I didn't remember being this tired when I juggled a full-time job and school. Fritzi must have a stash of secret elixir hidden somewhere in the house. Or be related to the Energizer Bunny. The woman was nearly twice my age. How did she manage?

As well behaved as the boys were—most of the time—they were still...well, three-year-olds. And each day as they became more accustomed to me, their new routine, and their mother's absence, they began to display typical three-year-old behavior (I looked it up online) —complete with sibling rivalry and temper tantrums. When they weren't arguing amongst themselves or staging group histrionics, they were thinking up new ways to get into mischief—an easy task for three creative children who lived in what amounted to a museum.

I had little time to myself. My reading consisted of Dr. Seuss, my television viewing, *Sesame Street*. By the time the boys were tucked in bed each night, I had no energy for even the most mindless of entertainment. What was I thinking accepting a mid-week dinner date?

And NJ Transit didn't help. At five-thirty Ben called to say he was stuck on the tracks outside of Newark. In a car with no lights.

And no air conditioning. He growled when I reminded him I had a date picking me up at seven o'clock.

And my date was far from happy when he arrived to find me wrestling with three overly stubborn bare-bottomed boys who refused to put on their PJ's. "We have a seven-thirty reservation," said Jason, checking his Tag Hauer for the fifth time.

I fastened the last snap on Scotty's Nemo PJ's and reached for Teddy. "I wants Shrek!" he said, grabbing a second pair of Nemo PJ's from my hand and flinging them across the room.

"Shrek is in the wash. You have your choice of Nemo or Buzz Lightyear." I turned to Jason. "I can't leave until their father gets home."

"Want Shrek!" Teddy stamped his foot.

"I thought you were some sort of architect," he said. "Not a nanny." He made the kind of face one makes after stepping in dog poop.

"I am. But I'm also helping out my boss for a few weeks."

"Why?"

"It's complicated."

"Where's Daddy, Hope?" asked Woody. He stared up at Jason, a combination of fear and suspicion knitting together the fine hairs of his eyebrows.

"Stuck on the train, Sweetie. He'll be home soon."

Jason scowled down at me. I was sprawled on the floor, shoving Teddy's legs into his Nemo pajamas. Scotty was jumping on his bed.

Jason wore an olive drab suit over a taupe linen shirt. A silk walnut brown tie and matching handkerchief that peaking from his breast pocket, completed the outfit. He scowled at my faded jeans and bleach-stained T-shirt. "You weren't planning on wearing that out to dinner, were you?"

"I can be ready in ten minutes."

He checked his watch again. "We won't make our reservation."

"So call the restaurant. Teddy, hold still." I grabbed for him as he darted away, still only half-dressed. As I chased him down the hall, I called over my shoulder, "Change the reservation. Teddy, get back here!"

I caught Teddy and hoisted him under my arm. When I returned to the nursery, I found Jason with his ear to his cell phone, his brow furrowed into a piercing glare aimed at Scotty and Woody. "Thank you." He flipped the cell phone closed. "They agreed to hold the table for us another half hour but no later."

I found it hard to believe that any restaurant in New Jersey would be that booked on a Wednesday night, but I kept my opinion to myself. No point antagonizing the first date I'd had in more than a decade and a half before we were even out the door. Besides, he was already pissed off if his sullen expression was any indication.

And as if our budding relationship wasn't strained enough, Scotty picked that moment to hurl a LEGO man at Jason, hitting him square in the jaw.

"You little bastard!" Jason lunged for the child, clamping a hand over Scotty's forearm and roughly shaking him.

Scotty let loose an ear-piercing shriek. "Ooow! Wet go! Hope!"

Teddy and Woody ran to their brother's defense, pummeling Jason's legs with their tiny fists.

"You a mean man!" yelled Teddy.

"Go away!" said Woody.

"Let go of him!" I screamed.

Jason glared at me, his hand still encircling Scotty's arm. "You saw what he did. He could've blinded me."

I pried Scotty from his grasp and pulled the other two away. They took refuge behind my legs. I stepped aside and confronted them. "Scotty, you know better. We don't throw toys. You could have hurt Jason. I want you to apologize to him. All three of you."

Scotty shook with rage, tears streaming down his face. "No!" He drew his leg back and kicked Jason in the shin.

Jason drew his arm back. "Son of a—"

"Jason!"

"What? This is my fault? These kids are monsters."

"We not monsters," cried Teddy. "You a monster!" He bent down, scooped up a handful of LEGO and chucked them, but this time Jason sidestepped the tiny missiles. "See? Someone needs to teach these brats a lesson. They need a good hard walloping."

I bent down and drew the boys into my arms. "Don't you dare lay another hand on them." I felt like kicking him in the shins myself. No, make that his groin. *And* hurling LEGOs at his thick skull. "I think you should leave."

He glared at the four of us as if we were beneath scum. "You're right. No piece of ass is worth this shit." And with that he stormed out of the nursery. A moment later I heard the front door slam.

"That man say bad words," said Woody.

"He not nice," said Scotty.

"No, he wasn't," I agreed. At least I now knew why Jason needed a singles group.

So much for leaving the cloister.

TWENTY-ONE

Ben arrived home hot and rumpled and cranky, an hour past his sons' bedtime. "Damn trains," he muttered, wandering into the kitchen. He pulled a beer from the fridge and took a long swig. "Are the boys asleep?"

"They fought against it for the longest time, trying to stay awake until you got home," Hope said. "But they finally conked out about ten minutes ago."

She sat at the kitchen table, eating a salad as she flipped through the latest issue of *Architectural Digest*. Ben took in her worn jeans and bleach-stained T-shirt, her messy ponytail, her face devoid of makeup. "I thought you had a date."

"I did," she said, not bothering to make eye contact with him. "But?"

She flipped another page. "Now I don't."

Ben pulled out a chair and sat down opposite her. "I'm sorry."

"You're not responsible for train problems."

"You knew I was on my way. It's still early."

"This has nothing to do with you, Ben." She speared a cherry tomato, pausing to speak before plopping it in her mouth. "I changed my mind."

"About going out tonight?"

Hope talked around the mouthful of tomato. "About the guy. He failed the Scotty-Woody-Teddy Challenge."

Ben raised both eyebrows.

"You can tell a lot about a man by how he treats cranky three-year-olds."

"You're angry."

She placed her fork on her plate and took a sip of iced tea. "No, I'm not."

He wasn't sure he believed her, even though her voice remained soft and calm and free of accusation. "But you're saying my sons are responsible for you canceling your date."

She stopped flipping pages and looked at him for the first time. "That's right."

Ben placed the sweating beer bottle against his throbbing temple. "Hope, it's been a long day. Let's cut to the chase, here, huh? What did my kids do?"

"They threw a three-prong temper tantrum." She pointed to the oven. "Your dinner's warming."

He removed a plate of lasagna and string beans from the oven. "Kids throw tantrums." But on the inside, he was all smiles. His boys wouldn't dare pitch fits around their mother. They were finally starting to act like normal three-year-olds.

"True." Hope finished her salad and pushed the plate aside as he grabbed silverware for himself. "Except I've noticed some violent tendencies creeping in over the last few days."

Ben froze. "Violent?"

"And unprovoked. Look, I admit I'm no shrink, but I'm worried they may be starting to act out three years' worth of pent-up anger."

The lasagna suddenly looked as tempting as twelve-day-old roadkill. Ben ignored the food and drained his beer. "Exactly what happened tonight?"

As Hope filled him in on the evening's events, every muscle in his body clenched. "And you were going to go out with this asshole? He'd better not step foot in this house again."

"What? You think I'd deliberately date an anal-retentive child-hater with passive-aggressive tendencies? I may have been out of the dating pool for a while, Ben Schaffer, but I'm not that desperate."

He stared at his plate and shook his head, not sure how to respond.

"Look," she continued. "I'm not condoning Scotty hurling a LEGO at Jason's head, but I've heard kids have a higher radar when it comes to adults. Maybe the boys picked up some bad vibes from Jason, and it was their way of protecting me. I don't know. I'm not sorry it happened, especially when I saw how he reacted, but there have been other incidents lately. Ones that do concern me. And should concern you."

"What kind of incidents? Why haven't you mentioned them before tonight?"

Hope rose and placed her plate and utensils in the dishwasher. She turned to face him, leaning against the kitchen counter, her arms crossed over her chest. "Because at first, I attributed them to four days of nonstop downpours and cabin fever. Did you ever consider that even though your house is the size of a minor Caribbean Island, only two of the rooms are furnished with the boys in mind? And one of them is this kitchen."

"They have a nursery that's better equipped than most schoolrooms."

"What they have is a Toys R Us furnished prison. Sure, they have a computer, a television, a stereo, and more toys than the North Pole, but children need to run around. Burn off steam. This house is anti-child. I don't need a degree in early childhood education to know that, and neither do you." She opened the cabinet below the sink and withdrew a large plastic bag. "Today's damage," she said, depositing the bag in front of him.

Ben opened the bag and withdrew four decapitated Capodimonte figurines, a cracked vase, a mutilated antique doll, five torn lace doilies, and a silk pillow that had somehow acquired a large black stain. Wasn't he paying her to watch his kids? "And where were you while this was going on?"

"Taking care of a necessary bodily function. That is allowed, isn't it?"

Why was she getting annoyed with him? "Of course it's allowed." He rose, leaving his dinner untouched. "Come inside."

Hope scooped up the broken bric-a-brac and followed him into the library, one of the few rooms on the first floor that afforded an environment conducive to a small amount of adult relaxation. Ben suspected Marion had decorated the floor-to-ceiling, bookcase-lined room with her impossible-to-please father in mind. With its dark mahogany paneling, massive desk, and hunter green leather wingbacks, the room screamed Prescott Woodrow Edmondson Merrick the Third. All it lacked was a group of stodgy old oil barons puffing away on Havanas.

"Have a seat," he said. She dumped the junk onto the coffee table and shivered slightly, hugging her chest as she folded herself into one of the massive chairs. Ben crossed the room to the gas-powered fireplace and flipped a switch. Within seconds a roaring blaze danced to life in the hearth, warming the cool dampness of the spring night.

"Marion's gone. The boys are no longer confined to their nursery. I don't care if they occasionally accidentally break a china doodad. They're just things." He paused, scowling at the Victorian clutter that surrounded them. "Frankly, I don't know why she didn't take all this crap with her."

"You're missing the point, Ben. I don't think we're dealing with accidents."

"What do you mean?"

"Look, maybe I'm crossing a line here. This is all foreign territory to me. You're my employer, and maybe I have no right to say this. After all, I'm not even the nanny, not really. Just a temporary replacement. So if you want me to keep my mouth shut, I will, but—"

"For God's sake, Hope, stop beating around the bush. Spit it out."

She nodded, hesitated a moment, then spoke. "I think the rooms and everything in them are a reminder of Marion. From what I've seen and from what you've told me, she cared more for her collections than she did her sons. Don't you think the boys realize that? They look around this house and, in every room, see proof of her neglect and lack of love. I think they're taking out their anger for their mother by deliberately destroying her precious trinkets and baubles."

Ben said nothing. For several seconds he stood unmoving, staring down at her. Then he strode over to the coffee table where she had placed the evidence. He lifted one of the headless figurines and stared at it. "So, Miss Morgan, you're now a psychologist?"

The moment the words left his mouth, Ben regretted them. Hope stared at him, wide-eyed and cowering in the weighty leather chair. What the hell was wrong with him? "Shit. I'm sorry. I have no right to take this out on you."

"Damn right," she muttered, her initial shocked expression turning to anger.

"Well, you know what?" He bounced the figurine in his palm like a pitcher getting a feel for the ball. "You're pretty observant." With that he flung the porcelain at the fireplace. With a loud crash it smashed against the tile surround.

One-by-one Ben assigned the other items to a similar fate, smashing the breakables, tearing apart the doilies and pillow. Then he snatched a Dresden vase off the mantle and hurled it across the room.

When he reached for a Tiffany table lamp, Hope leaped from her chair and seized his arm. "Stop it!"

Ben allowed her to remove the lamp from his grip. He sank into one of the chairs and lowered his head into his hands.

"Should I worry you're going to trash the entire house?" she asked.

Ben lifted his head and grinned at her. "You have no idea how good that felt. Maybe it's time to get rid of all this shit."

"Uhm, Ben?" Hope placed a hand on his shoulder.

"Hmm?"

"Don't you think it might be better to box everything up and donate it to a museum or something?"

He reached across his chest and patted her hand. "I suppose. It might be shit, but it's damn valuable shit." He nodded across the room at what remained of the butt ugly vase. "I probably just destroyed a few thousand dollars."

"If you've got that kind of money to burn, maybe I should ask for a raise."

Ben chuckled, but the laugh had nothing to do with Hope's words and everything to do with masking certain feelings beginning to stir in him. Shit. He didn't need this on top of everything else.

The moment he touched her he realized his mistake. The feel of her soft flesh under his palm was all it took to kick-start his too-long-neglected libido and smack him with the realization that he'd very much like to spend the night fucking her senseless. The same thought he'd had the other night on the porch, and it produced the same reaction. Once again, he was rock-hard thanks to Hope Morgan, and he was goddamn tired of seeking relief with a dog-eared copy of *Playboy* or *Penthouse* instead of the real thing.

If he knew what was good for him, though, he'd keep a judicious distance between himself and Hope. Zeke's warnings echoed in his head. His friend had been right about Marion, and Ben hadn't listened. Look where it got him. Maybe Zeke had a better-honed intuition when it came to women. If so, Ben wasn't foolish enough to disregard his warnings. He'd already struck out once. Big time.

But it sure as hell wasn't easy. Not when he and Hope were living in the same house five days a week, and every day she insinuated herself a bit more into his life.

"It's getting late," he said, "and I have some papers to go over before a meeting tomorrow." Shoving himself out of the chair, he flipped off the gas jet and headed toward the hall without a backward glance in her direction. He needed to get away from her before he did something stupid.

Once in the small second-floor bedroom he used as a home office, he found himself unable to concentrate on the proposal he was due to present the following morning. The computer layouts and text danced around the pages in blurry amorphous shapes. A throbbing bulge strained between his legs, mocking any attempt he made to focus either his eyes or his mind on his work.

Shit! Maybe Zeke was right. After three years of playing Willy Wanker Solitaire, he was so fuckstrated, it was a miracle he hadn't lost his sanity. Enough was enough. He needed an outlet, and he needed one fast. But not Hope. He pulled open his desk drawer and hunted around for the scrap of paper Paco had shoved into his hand several days earlier. Thanks to Zeke every male member of the office staff was now on a campaign to get him laid.

Ben stared at the name. Vanessa Glassman. Paco's wife's former college roommate. Thirty-two, recently divorced, and, according to Paco, hot with a capital sizzle. Ben reached for the phone. He could use a good dose of sizzle.

TWENTY-TWO

I guess Ben was feeling a bit guilty about getting home so late Wednesday night because he walked in the door Friday afternoon at four and told me to forget about dinner. He'd take the kids out for pizza. So I was on my own until Monday morning and had the luxury of three solid hours to get ready for my date with Elvis the Accountant. I just hoped I wasn't pampering myself with a facial, manicure and pedicure for a repeat of Wednesday's Jason fiasco.

After all, what did I know about this guy other than he was forty-five years old, good at math and bowled a one sixty-two? Hell, come to think of it, I didn't even know his last name. I'm sure he must have mentioned it, but I couldn't remember. Stojko? I slapped my forehead and uttered a silent *duh*. Elvis Stojko was a Canadian figure skater. Costello? No. He was a singer. The only other Elvis who came to mind was Presley, and I knew that was definitely wrong. I wondered if Elvis the Accountant put up with a lot of grief over his name. What kind of mother names her kid Elvis?

It didn't take long for me to find out.

"Mother is a big fan of The King." He said this within thirty seconds of arriving to pick me up for our dinner date and without me asking.

The theme from *Twilight Zone* started running through my brain. Were my thoughts of two hours earlier floating in a balloon above my head? "I didn't—"

"I know, but everyone gets around to asking eventually. So I figure it's easier to get it out of the way as soon as possible."

"Then why didn't you mention it Tuesday night when we first met?"

He shuffled his feet. "There are a few people in that group who like to give me a hard time."

I nodded in understanding. At the next singles function I now knew to steer clear of the Nose Picker *and* Jason.

"And no, I don't own any blue suede shoes," he said as we headed down the steps to his car.

Not that I was going to ask about the shoes, but as it turned out, he did own a vintage red and white Cadillac convertible, circa nineteen-fifty something or other, complete with huge tail fins and lots of polished chrome.

"Mother's," he said by way of apology. "She doesn't drive it anymore because of her arthritis, but she'd disown me if I ever sold it, and I don't see the point in owning two cars. Insurance rates in New Jersey are steep enough on one car."

"Kind of hard to shake the Elvis image when you drive around in something like this," I said. Especially with HOUNDOG vanity plates, I added to myself. I guess I should be glad Elvis didn't show up in a white sequined jumpsuit and cape.

Not that what he wore was more than a few ticks higher on the

Fashion-o-meter. Elvis the Accountant was in dire need of a visit from those Queer Eye guys. His pea green serge pants were shiny and threadbare at both knees and where his wallet bulged from his back pocket. His pale blue shirt was one of those pintuck pleated and embroidered numbers that tourists bring back from Mexico. White socks and black loafers completed the fashion *faux pas*.

I decided to give him the benefit of the doubt. Maybe he was colorblind. And maybe he had a sentimental attachment to the shirt. Although that didn't excuse the Salvation Army reject pants. After all, Elvis wasn't a starving grad student; he was a forty-five-year-old accountant. And a successful one at that, according to the little bit of personal info he'd divulged on Tuesday night.

I thought back to Tuesday evening. He definitely hadn't shown signs of being sartorially challenged at the bowling alley. Like most of the other men, he'd worn a pair of jeans and a T-shirt. And bowling shoes. But we were all wearing bowling shoes.

His jeans showed signs of wear, but most people pay extra for that look. His maroon T-shirt sported a logo and advertising for a local gardening center. A freebie from one of his accounts, no doubt. I hadn't thought anything of it at the time. In hindsight, maybe I should have.

I could see why Elvis worried about New Jersey insurance rates. He drove like a little old lady, doing twenty in a thirty-five mile an hour zone, oblivious to the road rage building up in the drivers trying to pass his enormous boat of a car. Luckily, we were on the road for less than ten minutes.

"Mother and I eat here often," he said, opening the car door for me after finding a parking space. Okay, he gained back a couple of points. You don't often see guys opening doors for women anymore. At least Mother—or someone—had taught Elvis manners.

"They have great chicken chow mein," he continued.

I turned to read the sign on the storefront window he pointed to:

Chow Chow Now
All-You-Can-Eat Chinese Buffet
$8.99/person
Lunch or Dinner

All-You-Can-Eat-Buffet? Hell, I wasn't expecting a five-star restaurant, but even guys back in Rusty Mud Creek wouldn't take a first date to the Chinese version of a firehouse spaghetti dinner. My benefit of the doubt did a one-eighty and flew the coop.

Elvis the Accountant wasn't colorblind; he was cheap. With a capital *cha-ching*.

Elvis opened the restaurant door and led me directly to the empty buffet line. I glanced around the room. The only other diners were an octogenarian couple. I had the sinking feeling this evening would turn out as bad as my non-date with Jason. The only difference being this time I'd get fed.

That is, if I really wanted to eat gluttonous gray vegetables, pork, and chicken with a side of library paste rice—all of which had been simmering in stainless steel chafing dishes for at least eight hours if not eight days. I was filled with a sudden longing for my mother's cooked-to-death string beans. At least they were still green when she plopped them on my plate.

I helped myself to a small amount of the least offensive looking buffet items while Elvis heaped mounds of food onto his plate. "Is that all you're going to eat?" he asked.

Before I could answer, he added a large spoonful of glop to my plate. "Don't be shy. I like a woman with a healthy appetite."

This was healthy? I now had enough sodium on my plate to carry me through the next decade. Good thing I'd inherited my mother's low blood pressure.

So here's the problem: Take away his questionable dietary choices, his fashion flaws, his Scrooge McDuck attitude when it came to a dollar, and his constant references to his mother, and Elvis the Accountant was actually an interesting guy. Not to mention good-looking.

Think cheap mama's boy accountant, and my first image would be someone who looked like Woody Allen—short and nerdy with black frame glasses and a comb-over. Elvis was close to six feet tall with a tennis pro body and a full head of wavy ebony hair that showed no signs of graying.

Before I knew it, we'd spent two hours chatting over chow mein. And although Elvis began far too many sentences with *Mother and I*, I found myself enjoying his company. And that put me in a pickle of a predicament when he asked me out for the following Saturday night. To meet *Mother*.

"Don't you think we need to get to know each other better before we introduce relatives into the mix?"

"Mother enjoys meeting the women I date."

And enjoys scaring them off, I'll bet. I changed the subject. "Have you ever been married, Elvis?"

He shook his head.

"Engaged?"

"Once."

"What happened?"

He fidgeted with his chopsticks and spoke to his plate. "She didn't get along with Mother." He raised his head and speared me with his nearly midnight eyes. "How could I commit myself to a woman who refused to accept that a son has a responsibility to the woman who gave him life?"

Danger, Will Robinson! "So you believe that a man should put his mother's needs ahead of his wife?"

"Of course." Bewilderment swept across his face. "Don't you?"

Strike two in the date column. "I'm afraid I'll have to pass on next Saturday night." And every other night from here to eternity.

So now I had three guys to avoid at the next singles thingy, and worse still, unless the group got an influx of fresh—and desirable—testosterone between now and then, I was down to my last eligible bachelor.

~*~

Saturday arrived on a beam of intense sunlight that shot its way through the crack in my Kmart Blue Light Special bedroom blinds and slammed into my closed eyelids. I buried my head under the comforter and fell back to sleep for another hour until my bladder forced me to shuffle barefoot into the bathroom.

I knew I should take advantage of my day off. I even had a car at my disposal. Saturday beckoned, but my body protested. Besides, I'd awakened in an anxiety-riddled, Jason and Elvis-induced blue funk. I tumbled back onto my mattress and fell asleep for another two hours. Only my rumbling tummy finally forced me to drag myself out of bed and into the shower.

Afterwards, still deep in funk mode, I nibbled on a piece of buttered toast and wondered whether Chet, the biology teacher, would be strike-three-and-I'm-out in my plunge back into the dating pool.

By the time I got around to dressing, it was nearly noon. I ate a fat-free raspberry yogurt that was only a week past its expiration date, then settled into pacing barefoot back and forth, coffee cup in hand, from one end of my apartment to the other. Over and over. Although spacious in dimension with a minimal amount of furnishings, the third-floor walk-up suddenly felt more confining than Ben's cluttered Victorian. I flipped on the radio to the oldies station, hoping some Lady Gaga would drown out the deafening silence that had leaped from oxymoron to reality.

However, instead of Lady Gaga, reality and Joni Mitchell smacked me upside my head with her song about not realizing what you've got till it's gone. She may have been singing about paving paradise for a parking lot, but her lyrics took on a different meaning for me.

I missed Ben and the boys. But it was more than that. Much more. I realized I'd built an unattainable fantasy around Ben and his kids, a fantasy that hogtied me. For the past few weeks, I'd experienced family for the first time in a very long time—even if vicarious and temporary. Now, halfway through playing Mary Poppins, I realized I dreaded the day the final curtain lowered, and I returned to being alone on the stage of my life.

I'd never gotten along with my own family. It's hard to see eye-to-eye with parents who are light years in the past. However, even though our differences at times had created an insurmountable chasm between us, I never doubted their love for me. And I never stopped loving them. Which was probably why I was so desperate for this date with Chet not only to work out but to develop into much more. I'd been alone too long.

Of course, masochist that I am, it didn't help that I'd complicated my situation further by falling not just for Ben, but for his three sons. After Fritzi returned, I could probably maintain some sort of relationship with the boys, but it wouldn't be the same. And would I only wind up hurting myself if I tried? What would happen when Ben found someone new to share his life? I doubted the next Mrs. Ben Schaffer would tolerate me hanging around like a love-struck puppy dog begging for a few scraps of affection.

Anyway, it was a moot point. Unless someone came along to scratch my itch enough to make me and my hormones forget Ben, I'd leave the firm the moment he found a new love, no matter that this was my dream job. I'd find another. An unrequited relationship was enough of a bummer. I wasn't about to compound my misery by hanging around to see the object of my lust go gaga over someone else. Not unless I'd found someone to go gaga over first.

Which brought me, once again, back to Chet. I didn't necessarily want to marry the man. Hell, I barely knew him. I just wanted him to make me forget Ben in any way, shape, or form other than as my boss.

Anyway, allowing myself to think about family was dumber than dumb. I'd spent three years suppressing feelings that were at this moment having a heyday dancing the Rumba up and down my nerves. *Damn!* When would I learn to leave the past in the past? Ruminating on what could never be was counterproductive to getting on with my life.

But the damage was done. Why had I gone there? I knew better than to open a door to the past. Nothing but pain existed on the other side. I swiped at the tear trickling down my cheek. I needed to get away from myself and my misery. I needed to lose myself in a noisy crowd.

I needed to shop till I dropped. Whether I could afford it or not. After all, what was another few hundred dollars of credit card debt when my sanity was at stake?

But first I needed to find my sandals.

After a quick perusal of the living room, I headed down the hall toward the bedroom. I scanned the room. One sandal lay on the hardwood floor, half-hidden by the dust ruffle. The other was nowhere in sight. Kneeling beside the bed, I blindly poked underneath, retrieving a handful of dust bunnies but no sandal. I stretched out flat on my belly and extended my arm farther. And slammed my fingers against the cardboard box I'd shoved under the bed weeks ago.

The universe was really jerking me around today. Try to escape and zap—another reminder of all I wanted to forget. But maybe the gods of the cosmos were trying to tell me something. I dragged the carton out from under the bed and stared at it. Nearly four years had passed since I packed up the broken and charred memories. If I threw them out, would I finally rid myself of the pain?

Or did I need to confront the to free myself from its stranglehold?

The thought struck like an ice ball between the eyes. Did I have the strength to view the contents of the box? Time had done little to dim my memories, but I kept them and the pain at bay by packing up the few surviving remnants. But the loss—and my guilt—even after all this time, was still far from bearable.

I'd allowed the pain and the past to rule my life for too long. Even though I'd learned to rein in my anger, I still found it hard to tackle my guilt. So I buried it in a cardboard carton along with the broken and singed detritus of life before that fateful day.

And all the therapy in the world couldn't erase the fact that if

I hadn't argued with my father, maybe he wouldn't have suffered a massive heart attack. And maybe he wouldn't have lost control of the car and plowed into the propane tank at the back of the house. And maybe he, and my mother, and my brother, and my sister and her unborn child would still be alive.

Chewing on my lower lip, I lifted a corner of the discolored packing tape and peeled it back. After taking a deep breath, I flipped open the brittle cardboard flaps and tossed aside a layer of crumpled newspaper. One by one, I removed the bubble wrapped survivors to the fireball that had decimated my family home, leaving little beyond a pile of ash.

At the time of the explosion, I sat sulking on the front porch steps, nursing my anger and frustration over parents who couldn't understand why I preferred a college degree to a new husband.

"You're thirty years old, for cripe's sake," said my father moments earlier after he'd once again charged into the same battle we'd fought for nine years. "What about children?"

"I'm a widow, Dad. Remember?"

"Of course I remember. I'm not senile, damn it! How do you expect to find another husband if you don't even date? You're wasting your life on pipe dreams, Hope. Not to mention that you've throw all of Wally's insurance money away on this nonsense and gotten yourself deep in debt with all those college loans. How do you ever expect to pay back all that money?"

"I don't consider a college degree a pipe dream or nonsense. And I'll pay back the money the way every college student does after I get my degree and begin working."

"Doing what? Drawing pictures of buildings?" He uttered a loud harrumph.

I threw my arms up in frustration. This was an old argument.

Nothing I said would ever convince him I knew what I was doing.

"Mark my words, young lady," he continued, waving a finger under my nose. "Ten years from now you'll be sorry you didn't listen to me. You'll be all alone with nothing but a worthless piece of sheepskin and a stack of bills to keep you company at night."

Instead of answering him, I stormed out of the house. Through the screen I heard the refrigerator door slam shut and my father mutter that we were out of beer. A moment later his Chevy pickup sputtered to life.

That was all I remember. I learned later that the initial concussive blast flung me through the air, away from the house. The others weren't as lucky. I awoke three days later to find my grief-stricken brother-in-law at my bedside. Dwayne reached for my bandaged hand as a doctor gave me the horrifying news that neither my family nor several of my internal organs had survived.

Children, whether I remarried or not, were no longer a possibility.

The explosion that hurled me across the yard also hurled to safety the few items I'd packed away in the carton. The firemen were able to rescue the singed remains of my parents' wedding album, a chipped Waterford crystal vase brought over from Ireland and handed down through several generations, and my mother's slightly melted and misshapen gold wedding band which she kept in a dish on the kitchen windowsill while she washed dishes. Nothing more.

And because I had moved back in with my parents after Wally was killed, all my personal memories had also gone up in smoke. No family photos, no yearbooks, not a single memento of three decades of my life.

I picked up the wedding album and carefully removed the

bubble wrap. Why this when little else had survived? I ran my fingers across the cracked white leather and gold embossed letters that commemorated Charlie and Dorothy Morgan's wedding day. As a very little girl I used to cuddle next to my mother, the wedding album perched between us.

"Oh, Mommy! You look like a fairy princess in that pretty dress."

"Someday, you'll wear this dress, Hope, and Daddy will walk you down the aisle just like Grandpa walked me."

And I did. And he did. And then Wally went off to Kuwait and came home in a body bag. And other than a grave on the other side of town, there was no tangible evidence that any of it had ever happened. And I felt guilty about that, too, because poor Wally had deserved better than a wife who mourned him only as a friend and not as a lover, let alone a husband.

One by one I flipped through the sooty pages, neither recognizing nor remembering most of the smiling faces. Other than my parents, the remainder of the people filling the pages meant little to me. My grandparents' generation was long dead, as were most of my parents' siblings. The mines and mills of Western Pennsylvania chewed up men and spit them into early graves.

I turned to the last page, a waving Mom and Dad standing beside an early sixties Chevy. I wondered if they had driven all the way to Niagara Falls with the *Just Married* sign whitewashed on the rear window and the shoes tied to the back bumper.

I was about to close the album when a loose picture slipped out from between the last page and the back cover. The snapshot was not of my parents' wedding but taken several years later at the county fair, according to the notation written on the back in my mother's perfect Palmer style penmanship.

Faith - 7, Hope - 5, Charlie - 3
Butler County Fair

Faith, Charlie, and I sat astride a Shetland pony. Faith held the reins, her arms wrapped around me, my arms wrapped around Charlie. My father's Kodak had captured three giggling youngsters and one extremely bored looking pony.

I have a dim memory of the day but not the pony. When I think of those yearly trips to the county fair, I remember little more than a chronic sour taste in my mouth. And to think I once wanted to be an astronaut. *Ha!* Dad needn't have bothered with the roller coaster years later. All he had to do was remind me of the Ferris wheel. Or the whip. Or the merry-go-round. When it came to amusement rides, I was an equal opportunity hurler.

I studied the three pinkie-sized laughing faces, trying to see if my face gave any indication of whether the photo was taken pre- or post-cookie toss that year. But something else caught my attention. Something I hadn't noticed at first. I blinked, refocusing my eyes, convinced they were playing tricks on me, but the uncanny resemblance remained.

A moment later the phone rang.

TWENTY-THREE

"Hope! Thank goodness you're home. I'm near my wit's end."

I recognized the caller at once. Le could read a shopping list out loud and make it sound like a nineteenth century melodrama. "What's wrong?" I asked, expecting a disaster along the lines of a world shortage of mechanical pencil lead.

"Look, I know it's your day off," she said, barely coming up for air, "and I'm sorry, but I can't reach Ben. He's not at home, and he isn't answering his cell. I don't know what else to do. We're up to our eyeballs in barf here. You've got to come get the boys before we have an epidemic on our hands."

Barf? Seemed like the theme of the day. Just the thought had me lowering my head to my knees and sucking up air. Were the triplets sick? I hadn't counted on dealing with toddler hurling when I signed on to Mary Poppins them for a few weeks. And why were they with Le? I thought Ben was looking forward to a weekend alone with his sons. "I don't understand," I said. "You have Ben's boys, and they're sick?"

"Not yet, but mine are, and the triplets were supposed to spend the night with us. You've got to come get them before I have five kids heaving all over the place. God, am I glad I caught you." She paused for a moment, then gasped. "Oh, gosh. You aren't going out or...anything, are you?"

"Or anything?"

"I mean, I'm not interrupting something, am I? You know, like dinner plans? A date?"

Date! I glanced at the clock. Chet was picking me up in less than three hours. Where had the day gone? Had I really spent the last several hours on the floor with my parents' wedding album? "Yes," I said. "I have a date picking me up at six."

Le cursed under her breath. "What am I going to do with them? They can't stay here."

True. No one wanted those boys away from Le's sick kids more than I. If they caught a stomach bug, I'd be the one dealing with the fallout. Just the thought had me turning a non-complementary shade of pea green, and I didn't need to glance in my bedroom mirror for confirmation. "I'll come get them. Ben's probably in a dead-cell zone. You know how he is about those kids. He'll probably be calling to check on them soon anyway."

"Thanks, Hope. I owe you big time."

"Wait! Don't hang up."

"What?"

I had to ask—even if it was none of my business. Even if I suspected the answer was one I didn't want to hear. "Why were the triplets spending the night with you?"

"Oh. I thought you knew."

"Knew what?"

Le's voice grew brusque, her words terse. I could hear the anger she fought to contain. "Zeke and Paco fixed him up with a blind date." Her voice dipped to a conspiratorial whisper. "The guys think Winnie and I don't know. They've been plotting all week, acting like high school jocks trying to get the campus dweeb laid."

"Oh." I hung up the phone without waiting for Le to say more.

~*~

"Jessie pukeded," said Scotty as I ushered the boys into the back seat of the mid-sized sedan Ben had rented and prayed I wasn't about to hear a graphic retelling of Barfarama at the Wang residence.

"Let me see if you can fasten your own seatbelts," I said, hoping to distract the triplets and change the subject. Ben and I had switched cars for the weekend, and he had the toddler seats in the LX.

"It was yucky," said Teddy, screwing up his face as he yanked on the shoulder harness clasp. He stretched it across his lap and inserted it into the buckle. "I did it! See?" A megawatt smile reached from ear to ear.

I ruffled his hair. "Good going."

"The thwow-up was gween and smelly and got all ova the table," continued Teddy. "We was eating ice cream."

"Then Davey pukeded and his was bwown," continued Scotty, reveling in his recounting of the event, "only he turned his head, and it got all ova his daddy's shirt and legs and on the dog and evweything."

"Wonderful," I muttered. "Now how about that seatbelt?" I pointed to the strap. Scotty quickly complied.

"It was weal gwoss!" said Woody, speaking up for the first time while still engrossed in fitting the two parts of his belt together.

After the third belt clicked in place, I reached across the back seat, checking each boy's handiwork. When I got to Woody, I paused and stared at him. There was definitely an uncanny resemblance between Woody Schaffer and three-year-old Charlie Morgan, Jr. Was that spooky or what?

"Hope?"

Woody was also the spitting image of his father. Besides, Ben had said hazel eyes ran in Marion's family. But who knew? If you traced our family trees back far enough, maybe we were forty-second cousins fifteen times removed. Stranger things had happened. During the 2004 presidential election, hadn't someone discovered Bush and Kerry were related?

"Hope!"

I shook myself back to the present. "So, did you eat the ice cream?"

All three shook their heads. "And I'm weal hungwy," said Woody.

"Me, too," said Teddy.

"And me," chimed in Scotty.

"So let's go home and make sundaes," I said. Maybe by then I'd be able to track down Ben and still get back to my apartment in enough time to change for my date.

But when I swung into Ben's driveway, I was surprised to see his car parked near the walk. *Shit!* What if Ben was home all along and hadn't answered either phone because he was in the middle of some X-rated escapade? An image of a naked Ben and some faceless bimbo popped into my head. Their bodies entwined. Stretched out on the Oriental carpet in front of a roaring fire. *Don't go there, Hope.*

Now what do I do? A Bachelor of Fine Arts degree didn't exactly prepare me for situations like this. Damn him! Weren't his kids traumatized enough? I couldn't let them walk in on their father screwing some bitch.

"Why we sitting in the dwiveway?" asked Scotty.

"I gots to pee," said Woody.

"Me, too," chimed in Teddy.

I glanced at the boys through the rearview mirror. They had already unbuckled their seatbelts. Woody and Teddy were wiggling in their seats, their legs tightly crossed. Scotty, always the perceptive one, wrinkled his brow, his Sherlock Holmesian mind, no doubt, trying to decipher my behavior.

"Hold it in, guys." I cut the engine, reached for my cell phone, and punched in the house number. Giving Ben a few seconds warning might spare all of us some major embarrassment—and hopefully, keep the boys from seeing something they shouldn't.

"Hello?" Ben picked up on the second ring. His voice sounded perfectly normal. Not that Ben's voice wasn't normally sexy as hell, but I detected no signs of having torn him from the throes of passion.

"I hope you're decent," I said without preamble as I opened the car door for the triplets, "because the boys and I are about to walk in the front door."

"Hope? What's wrong?"

"Potty run." Woody, Teddy, and Scotty raced for the house. I followed close behind. "You've got about ten seconds if the front door is unlocked. A few seconds more if it's locked."

"What?"

Teddy pushed open the door. He and Woody made a beeline down the hall toward the powder room. "Too late now," I said, disconnecting the call.

I held my breath as I stepped over the threshold and darted a quick glance left and right to the rooms on either side of the foyer. No Ben. No bimbo. No discarded clothing draped across the furniture or scattered on the floor. "So far, so good," I muttered. Maybe Ben had come to his senses and passed on the bimbo offer. "Or maybe she's already upstairs in his bed."

"Huh?"

I spun around, surprised to see Scotty standing behind me. "I thought you had to go potty."

He shook his head. "That was Woody and Teddy, not me. Is Daddy in bed?"

Before I could answer, Ben called from the second-floor landing. "Hope?" He started down the steps. Fully clothed. Even his blue paisley tie was still securely knotted. "Why aren't the boys at Le's? What's going on?"

"Le's kids got sick, and she couldn't reach you. So she called me."

"And that strange phone call a moment ago?"

"Le said you had a date. When I saw your car in the driveway, I was worried the boys might burst in on something."

Ben grimaced. "I see."

No, I doubted he did. But that was as it should be. I'd purposely infused my voice with a light, flippant tone to mask my own fears of what might be waiting inside the house.

"Who that?" Scotty pointed toward the stairs.

I stared in the direction he indicated. So much for laying fears to rest. There, at the top of the staircase, stood a candidate for Playmate of the Decade. No, scratch that. This woman qualified as Playmate of the Century.

She wore a skimpy red strapless number that looked more negligee than cocktail dress. And covered about as much. Her legs seemed to go on forever. Cascading waves of honey blonde hair fell over her bare shoulders, calling attention to a pair of breasts threatening to spill out of the top of her dress. One of her hands caressed the oak banister as if it were a lover, the other held a wine glass near lips too pouty to be natural.

Good thing I'd vowed to find someone to take my mind off Ben because if this was the type of woman who turned him on, I didn't stand a chance. Once more I mentally crossed my fingers, hoping Chet and I wound up pushing all the right buttons for each other later that night. Seemed to me I deserved a bit of good Karma for once. First Jason. Then Elvis. Now the Bimbo Barbie from Hell. How lucky could a girl get?

Bimbo Barbie spoke. "Ben?" Slowly, she descended the staircase, her four-inch zebra print Alberta Ferretti vamps clicking against the polished wood. Her gaze fixed on me; her pout deepened. "I thought we had the evening to ourselves."

Woody and Teddy scampered back into the foyer, stopping short when they spied the woman. Neither spoke, but Woody sidled up to me and slipped his hand into mine. Teddy stepped closer to the foot of the stairs. His angel fine brows knit together as he studied the woman. Hands on hips, Scotty tilted his chin up at his father and waited for an answer to his question.

Ben stared at the woman, then his sons. I bit my lower lip to choke back a chuckle, even if I was beginning to feel like the heroine of a Greek tragedy.

With what seemed like a forced smile, Ben began the introductions. "This is Mrs. Glassman, guys. Say hello."

Teddy mumbled something indiscernible.

Woody buried his face in my thigh.

Wrinkling his nose in distaste, Scotty defiantly disobeyed his father's directive and squeezed his lips together.

"They're a bit shy around strangers," said Ben. He scowled at his sons, then offered Mrs. Glassman a shrug of his shoulders.

But Mrs. Glassman wasn't paying attention to either Ben or his sons. Her attention was still firmly riveted on me, as if sizing up a prospective rival. "And you are?" she asked.

Call me clueless, but I couldn't fathom how someone like her could consider me a threat, but it was certainly a boost to my ego. I squared my shoulders and returned her scrutiny. "Hope Morgan. I work for Ben."

"You're the nanny?" The question was asked with more than a hint of condescension.

I smiled a cocky smile. "Among other things." My reply had the desired effect. Mrs. Glassman narrowed her gaze and pursed her lips. I could see her wheels spinning.

"Why's she here?" Scotty asked.

"Mrs. Glassman and I are having dinner together this evening," said Ben. "She wanted to see our house first."

Especially the master bedroom, I thought.

Ben's date, obviously put out by the change of events, exhaled an overly dramatic sigh. "This one's a very direct little boy, isn't he?"

This one? She wouldn't score any brownie points with Ben by showing annoyance toward his children. The woman had hardly acknowledged the triplets' presence, much less spoken to them. And now she had the audacity to refer to Scotty as if he were an inanimate object! I glanced at Ben, waiting for him to react. If he didn't, I might—even if it wasn't my place. I'd love to toss Bimbo Barbie out on her lipo-sucked rear-end.

Ben cleared his throat. "Uhm, Vanessa. Under the

circumstances, perhaps we should postpone our dinner."

I bit down on my tongue to keep from yelling. Ben's response was hardly the strong rebuke I'd expected.

"I don't see why." Vanessa batted her false eyelashes, employing a well-worn trick from the Bimbo Bag of Wiles. "You have a nanny."

"Today is Hope's day off," explained Ben.

"So? She's here now. And we do have reservations in the city." She glanced at the delicate gold watch adorning her left wrist. "Which we're never going to make if we don't leave within the next few minutes."

I stared at Vanessa Glassman. The woman was nothing more than a blonde version of Marion, selfish and self-absorbed to the core. She executed a practiced head toss, complete with the prerequisite hand flip of her shimmering locks and a pouting of her deep crimson lips.

I rolled my eyes, hoping Ben saw through her machinations but doubting he would. Men's brains were generally too low on their anatomy, and Ben already had a negative track record in that area. That's why women like Vanessa and Marion wielded such power in both the bedroom and the boardroom while those of us with normal looks or worse fought for every scrap of attention and success. Tits and ass won out over brains and talent every time.

Luckily, I wasn't a man and as such, was immune to Vanessa's bag of tricks. And I sure as hell wasn't about to be manipulated by her. Ignoring Vanessa, I spoke directly to Ben. "I have a date this evening and don't even have time to watch the boys while you bring Mrs. Glassman home. You'll have to bring them with you." And with that I spun on my heels and walked out of the house— but not before I noticed the perfectly put together Mrs. Glassman turning the exact same shade of red as her dress.

TWENTY-FOUR

"We's hungwy," said Woody after Hope closed the door behind her.

"Hope pwomised us sundaes," said Scotty, his hands on his hips, his head tilted back to look up at Ben.

"Wiff whip cweam," said Woody.

"And cherries," added Teddy.

"Then she should have stayed to make them for you," said Vanessa. She crossed the foyer, placed her half empty wine glass on Marion's ornate Victorian bench and retrieved her shawl and purse. "Your father has to drive me home." After adjusting the shawl around her shoulders, she glared at Ben. "Now."

Now had taken on an entirely different meaning for Ben after the birth of his children. He glanced at the boys, all three of them casting evil eyes at his date, and weighed his options. Three cranky three-year-olds or one annoyed blind date? Hardly a difficult decision in his mind. "Why don't we all have sundaes first?"

"Her, too?" asked Scotty, pointing to Vanessa.

"Of course. I'm sure Mrs. Glassman would love to have sundaes with us." He turned to Vanessa. "Wouldn't you?"

She offered him a tight smile. "What do you think?"

Ben wasn't sure whether her wrinkled nose was an indictment of his suggestion to eat dessert with his kids or the dessert itself. "I can offer you cheese and crackers if you prefer. And another glass of wine."

"We gots 'merican," said Teddy. "The white kind."

She ignored Teddy. Picking up her wine glass, she drained the remains in one gulp and handed the empty glass to Ben. "Wine will do," she said.

Ben took the glass and headed toward the kitchen, the boys scampering ahead of him. Vanessa might be annoyed over the aborted evening, but he certainly wasn't. Not now that he'd seen her true nature. Zeke and Paco might think mind-numbing sex was the answer to his and every man's problems, but sex for the sake of sex had never held much allure for him. As beautiful a woman as Vanessa Glassman was, she left him cold. He wouldn't be rescheduling their dinner date.

Besides, no way was he getting involved with a woman who wasn't crazy about his kids. Been there. Done that. And the boys bore the psychological scars to prove it. Vanessa had scored a big fat, red "F" on the Scotty-Woody-Teddy Test.

To Ben's amusement, she had also flunked the Hope Morgan test. At one point the tension in the room had soared so high that Ben thought the two women were about to square off in a cat fight.

Until Hope showed up, he hadn't been able to figure out why he was dreading an entire evening with Vanessa. The woman was both beautiful and intelligent. Yet, after half an hour in her company, he was bored to death with her. When he saw Hope walk through the front door, he finally realized why. Vanessa wasn't Hope.

So, I'm back to Square One, he thought, scooping fudge ripple into four bowls. Tempted by forbidden fruit.

~*~

Half an hour later Ben sat stuck in traffic, his three restless sons in the back seat and one highly critical Vanessa Glassman seated next to him. "What a waste of a Saturday night," she muttered. "Next time, please make certain you have backup care for your children."

There wouldn't be a next time, but Ben decided against mentioning it. Instead, he took a deep breath and stabbed at the radio controls. After several minutes of sports and inane commercials, the traffic report confirmed what he already knew. Northbound traffic on the Garden State Parkway was at a virtual standstill. He was halfway between exits going nowhere fast.

"I'll bet that nanny of yours didn't have plans for this evening," continued Vanessa. She removed a gold compact from her handbag and began blotting her nose and chin. Ben hated when women touched up their makeup in public. He wondered how she'd feel if he trimmed his nose hairs during a date? "I could see it in her eyes," she continued. "She just wanted to spoil our evening, and you let her."

"I don't care if her date was with her television and a slice of pizza. It's her day off. End of discussion."

"I don't see why."

"Are we there yet?" asked Teddy.

"Soon, pal. We're stuck in traffic."

"Why?" asked Scotty.

"I don't know," said Ben. "Maybe there's an accident up

ahead."

"What kind of accident?" asked Woody.

"How should we know?" snapped Vanessa. "Sit back and behave."

"I am!" shouted Woody.

Ben glared at Vanessa. "I'll handle my sons, if you don't mind." He glanced into the rearview mirror. Woody's bottom lip trembled. "Of course, you are, Woodster. How about a video, guys?"

"Nemo!" shouted Scotty.

"Nemo!" chimed in Teddy.

"That okay with you, Woods?"

"Okay," he mumbled.

Ben started the video for the boys, then gripped the steering wheel. He never should have let Zeke and Paco fix him up with Vanessa Glassman. What were they thinking? The woman was a Marion clone. And now his kids were paying for his need for a bit of recreational mattress gymnastics. Thank goodness he'd declined the sexual appetizer Vanessa offered prior to dinner. Walking in on such a scene might have placed his kids in therapy for the rest of their lives. Hope had thought more of his sons than he had. She'd anticipated the worst and tried to protect them with a warning phone call.

For several minutes Ben stared ahead at the endless line of unmoving vehicles before finally cutting his engine. He saw no point in wasting fuel or adding to the already excessive levels of pollution in the Garden State. As if on cue, several cars around him did likewise. Five minutes later two police cars and an ambulance zipped past him on the shoulder, but the only other movement came from the southbound lanes on the opposite side of the concrete median.

With the boys content in the backseat and Vanessa pouting beside him, Ben's thoughts wandered back to the conversation that had taken place when Hope arrived with the boys. Something about her tone of voice and choice of words gnawed at him. As they continued to sit in traffic, he mulled over her words and the feisty way she'd handled Vanessa's condescending attitude toward her.

Among other things.

Ben grinned. With one well-calculated phrase Hope leveled the playing field.

I'll be damned! Sweet, unpretentious Hope. He thought her hostile reaction toward Vanessa was over his date's less-than-effusive response to the triplets. In a few short weeks Hope had become extremely protective of his sons, even challenging *him* on several issues concerning their wellbeing.

But maybe there was more to Hope's spunky response than he first realized. Was it possible she'd reacted to Vanessa in the same manner and for the same reason Vanessa reacted to her? Did the tension in the room have less to do with the children and more to do with him?

For the first time Ben wondered if Hope might be as attracted to him as he was to her. He hoped not. For her sake. She deserved far more than he could ever give her. She deserved to build a life with a man free of complications and responsibilities to others. Not someone like him, a man who came with the fallout of broken dreams.

The traffic in front of him began to inch along. Ben started the engine and as they crept forward, he replayed every scene, every conversation between the two of them he could remember, trying to see himself through Hope's eyes, attempting to get inside her head and analyze each nuance, every verbal and silent exchange. He hoped he was jumping to the wrong conclusion, but in the end he couldn't be certain.

And he could think of only one way to find out.

TWENTY-FIVE

Chester "Chet" Buchanan loved children and didn't live with his mother. And yes, I asked.

He shook his neatly trimmed head of maple syrup colored hair and chuckled at my first question, which I asked as we drove to dinner in his late model red Mazda Miata convertible. Chet scored bonus points right off the bat by asking if I preferred the top up or down. When I chose down, the twinkle in his deep blue eyes suggested I'd tallied a few points on his score sheet.

"Would I be teaching school if I didn't like kids?" he asked as we zipped down the street.

"I've known a few teachers who acted like they hate kids, even if they never came out and said so."

He thought for a moment. "A few of my colleagues would qualify, but they're more equal opportunity misanthropes. They hate everyone. Me? I like to think you get what you give. Treat a kid with kindness and respect, and you'll get treated likewise."

Chalk up another few points for Chet.

LOIS WINSTON

I waited until we arrived and were seated to ask my second question, mentally adding a few more points to Chet's plus column for his restaurant choice. He'd picked an upscale northern Italian bistro with real linen on the tables and not only a maître d' but waiters and a wine steward. There wasn't an all-you-can-eat buffet line in sight.

"Do I live with my mother?" Chet asked, repeating my question. He laughed. "Let me guess. You had a date with Elvis."

"Bingo."

"And he brought his mother along?"

"He was saving that for our second date. The one we're *not* going to have."

"Too bad. She's a real trip."

"You've met her?"

"He brought her along the first time he came to a singles event."

"You're kidding."

He made the sign of the cross over his heart. "Honest to God. Someone not so tactfully suggested he leave her home the next time. The guy is clueless."

"It's too bad. He really is an interesting guy when he's not talking about his mother. Part of me feels sorry for him."

"And the other part?"

"Let's just say there's a creepy Norman Bates type subtext I'd rather not explore."

"I know what you mean. So now that we've gotten the important stuff about me out of the way, tell me all about Hope Morgan."

I gave him the condensed version as we nibbled on antipasto and sipped Merlot.

Instead of finding it strange that I would agree to help Ben out while Fritzi recuperated, he commended me. "Shows a lot about your character."

"In what way?"

"You're a person others can count on in a time of need. And from what you've told me, your boss sounds like one needy guy right now. Poor bastard. Three little kids, no wife, no help. I wouldn't want to be in his shoes."

And with that I added another dozen bonus points to Chet's scorecard. The man appreciated how I'd jumped in and helped Ben out during a family crisis. Unlike Jason, he hadn't assumed any sexual ulterior motives. Chet Buchanan had definite boyfriend potential. I began to relax and enjoy myself.

When he kissed me goodnight at the door to my apartment, I *really* began to enjoy myself. The kiss hinted of things to come, things I wouldn't have minded coming right then and there. I hated to see the evening end. Even so, I didn't want to appear desperate. I might be horny, but I'm no slut who spreads her legs to cap off a first date. So I broke the spell and stepped out of his arms.

"That was nice," he said.

I responded with a smile and a nod, a bit too discombobulated to trust my voice just yet.

"Any chance you're free tomorrow?"

"Possibly. What did you have in mind?"

"A drive in the country? Lunch at a little out-of-the-way inn I know?"

I took a deep breath. Time for a reality check. There was something else I had to know first. I stepped back and with hands on hips, assessed him. "Explain to me why you're available."

He raised both eyebrows. "Excuse me?"

"You, Chet Buchanan, are too good to be true. How come some woman hasn't snapped you out of circulation yet?"

He laughed. "Actually, one did a few years ago."

"And?"

"And it didn't work out."

"No one since?"

His eyes twinkled; the corners of his mouth twitched into a grin. "Not until tonight."

It took every ounce of willpower I could muster to keep from inviting him into my apartment, but in the end, my Rusty Mud Creek-Bible Belt morals won out over my libido. Sometimes being a good girl really sucks.

~*~

I spent much of that night analyzing my scant sexual history. Wally and I were both virgins when we married. Our sex life, the little there was before he went off to play marine and got himself killed, hadn't lived up to all the fireworks and exploding rockets I'd read about in romance novels. And since I had no other basis for comparison, I chalked the books up to what they were—fiction. Female orgasm was a myth as far as I was concerned and remained so until one night when Wally was soldiering in Kuwait, and I worked up the nerve to do a bit of self-exploration. That's when I finally discovered my G-spot and the guilty pleasures of vibrating plastic.

Still, I had decided I must have a lower-than-normal libido because even self-gratification came in last on my to-do list while pursuing my degree. When my nighttime companion sputtered and died, I didn't even bother to replace it. Most nights I was too damned tired to even notice that something was missing in my life.

And that was fine with me.

Until my libido slammed smack into Ben Schaffer and decided it was time to make up for lost time. So now the question was—would said libido be satisfied with Chet Buchanan, or would sex with Chet be as unfulfilling as it had been with Wally? And would I have the courage of my convictions to find out? No matter how great the itch, making the leap from thinking about recreational sex to actually doing it was still a colossal mega-hurdle for me—thanks to all that Rusty Mud Creek-Bible Belt morality.

And then there was also the question of whether I really wanted to sleep with Chet. I suppose if I were really being honest with myself, I'd have to admit I was using him to chase away my desire for Ben. I'd convinced my body to respond to Chet the way I wanted it to respond to Ben.

But maybe I just needed to stop analyzing my urges and worrying about antiquated morality. I was an adult, wasn't I? Maybe it was time to close my eyes and take a plunge into the deep end of the pool.

~*~

The following evening after a day in the country and an elegant lunch at what turned out to be a five-star, Michelin-rated inn, I invited Chet to stay for a candlelight picnic of wine, cheese, baguette and me. We had finished the wine, finished the cheese, finished the baguette, and were working on me. Our bodies were entwined on the couch, his mouth nibbling on my left breast when his watch alarm sounded. Without lifting his head, Chet felt for the remote on the coffee table and switched on the television.

"What are you doing?"

"The Yankees are playing the BoSox," he mumbled around my nipple. "I've got a hundred bucks riding on the game."

I pushed him off and refastened my bra.

"Hey, we don't have to stop." He gave me a sheepish grin. "I can multitask."

"Multitask?" I threw his shirt at him. "What am I, something on your to-do list? Change the oil. Watch baseball. Fuck Hope?"

He shook his head. "I don't know what you're getting so upset about. Think of it as background noise. Tune it out if you don't want to listen."

I picked up the remote, clicked the television off, and gave him an ultimatum. "Baseball or me."

He grabbed the remote and turned the game back on. "I'll make you a deal. Baseball now. You later."

Unbelievable! And he called Elvis clueless? Chet Buchanan had just forfeited all those points he'd racked up. I reached for the remote and once more depressed the off switch. "Baseball now. Me never. Goodbye, Chet."

TWENTY-SIX

A business dinner Monday evening kept Ben from arriving home until after the boys' bedtime. The house was quiet when he entered except for the murmuring of voices that spilled down the staircase. Making his way upstairs, he stood outside the second-floor den. Behind the slightly ajar door he listened to the woman he shouldn't have feelings for calming his young son's fears. From his vantage point Ben could see Hope stretched out on the overstuffed sofa. Woody, dressed in his Elmo pajamas, snuggled against her chest. One of Hope's arms curled around the child's slightly trembling body. Her other hand stroked his sleep-disheveled hair.

"She was scawy, Hope. Big and wed with sharp teef, and she twied to eat me, but I wan away."

Hope brushed a kiss across the top of his head. "Nightmares can be very scary, Woody, but you know that they're not real, right? The monster-lady wasn't here when you woke up, was she?"

Woody shook his head. "Daddy made her go away."

Ben didn't need to stretch his imagination very far to surmise the identity of the big, red monster-lady in Woody's dream. He could now see how negative an impression Vanessa had left on at least one of his sons on Saturday.

Hope continued soothing Woody. "Daddies are good at getting rid of monsters. They learn how in Daddy School."

"They do?" Woody twisted his head to face her.

"Sure."

"Why?"

"Because they love their little boys and don't want mean dream monsters scaring them."

"Did Daddy make Mommy go away 'cause she was mean and didn't wuv us?"

Woody's words slashed through Ben's heart. He had wanted to give his sons a life of love and happiness. He failed. Miserably. Thanks to their mother. He started to enter the room but froze at Hope's next words.

"Your Mommy loves you very much, Woody, but sometimes grownups get sick."

"Mommy's sick?"

"Not like tummy-ache sick." She stroked Woody's cheek. "Sometimes people get sick in their heads."

"Like when I felled down and got a bump, and it huwt?"

"No. This is a sick that keeps grownups from showing how much they love you."

"Jessie's Gwanpa got sick in his head. Jessie said he kept fowgetting things. He didn't even know his name. Then he died and went to Heaven. Did my Mommy fowget she loved me, Hope? Did she die?"

Ben saw Hope wince.

"Oh, no, sweetheart. Your mommy just had to go away. Maybe someday she'll get better and be able to love you. Then she'll want to come back."

Woody twisted out of Hope's arms. Sitting upright, he turned to face her. "I don't want her to come back. She's mean. I want you to stay and be my mommy." He threw his arms around her. "I wuv you, Hope."

Hope hugged Woody to her chest, rocking him in her arms. "And I love you, Woody. Very, very much."

Throwing his head back, Woody stared up at her, his eyes filling with tears, his lower lip trembling. "But you going away when Fwitzie comes back."

"I have my own apartment."

"I 'member. You lives on top of Minnie's Mouses. Daddy takes us there to see the animals sometimes."

"So you know I'm not far away, and we can visit."

"I don't want you to leave." Woody buried his face in Hope's neck and began to sob.

"Hey, don't cry. I have a secret to tell you."

Struggling to sniff back a fresh set of tears, Woody cocked his head and once more stared up at Hope. "You do?"

"Uh-huh. Just for you."

"Not Teddy or Scotty?"

"No. This is just a Hope and Woody secret."

"Tell me, please!"

"Promise you won't cry?"

He brushed the back of his hand under his nose, sniffing loudly. "I pwomise."

Reaching across his body, Hope retrieved a tissue and dabbed at Woody's damp face. Ben felt unshed tears pooling behind his own eyes. "When I was at my apartment over the weekend," she said, "I was looking through some old pictures of my family, and you know what I discovered?"

"What?"

"I found a picture of my younger brother Charlie when he was your age, and guess what?"

"What?"

"He looked just like you, Woody."

"Just me and not Scotty or Teddy?"

"Hmm." With exaggerated facial expressions and cocking her head from side to side, Hope studied Woody for several long moments. "Well, maybe a little like Scotty and Teddy but exactly like you."

"Can I see it?"

"I'll bring it over the next time I go back to my apartment. But only if you promise to climb into your bed and go back to sleep."

"Okay, but don't fowget the picture." Woody wriggled off the sofa and raced across the room, plowing right into Ben's legs. "Daddy!"

Ben scooped him up into his arms. "Hey, there, Woodsman! What are you doing up so late?"

"I had a bad dweam, but I'm okay now."

"I'm glad to hear that." Ben glanced over at Hope. "Thank you."

Hope looked flustered. "How long have you been standing there?"

"Long enough."

~*~

"I didn't know what to say to him," said Ben after Woody was tucked back in bed. "Part of me wanted to take him in my arms and never let him go, but part of me was afraid I could never make things right for him. I froze." He paused halfway down the steps and turned to face Hope. "I'm grateful you were with him. I wouldn't have handled the situation as well as you did."

"Of course you would have."

"No." Ben shook his head and continued down the stairs and into the library. Hope followed him. Striding over to the bar, he removed the stopper from an ornate crystal decanter and filled a matching glass with whiskey. "Join me?" he asked, holding the tumbler out to her.

"Thanks."

Ben poured a second glass for himself, downing it in one long swig. Then he poured himself another.

Hope settled herself into one of the leather chairs, tucked her legs underneath her body and sipped at her drink. "You don't give yourself enough credit, Ben. Considering the circumstances, I think you're doing a pretty good job of handling things."

"Because of you. You seem to possess an intuitive understanding when it comes to the boys. I constantly struggle with my decisions, always second-guessing whether I've made the right ones when it comes to their wellbeing. Not you. Somehow you always know exactly what to do or say to ease their pain."

"Do I? I'm worried about them. What happens when your housekeeper returns? You heard Woody. He wants me to stay and be his mother. Won't I just wind up hurting the boys even more when I leave?"

Ben turned his back on her. Instead of addressing her fear, he changed the subject. "I started boxing up some of Marion's collections over the weekend. I've made arrangements to store them for a while. She might change her mind and want them eventually."

From behind him Ben heard her sigh. Frustration echoed in her voice. "Ben, you have to deal with this. You can't just ignore it and hope it goes away."

He slammed the nearly empty glass down on the desk, sending the few remaining droplets of whiskey flying up into the air before scattering across the polished wood and dripping onto the carpet. He spun around and confronted her. "Damn it, Hope! I don't have any answers! Not for you. Not for the boys. Not for myself."

"Ben, I'm sorry...I didn't mean to..." She rose from her chair and took several steps closer until she stood inches from him. Reaching out, she placed her fingertips against his cheek.

"Don't!" He grabbed her wrist, yanking her hand from his face.

"I only meant—" She never finished her sentence.

TWENTY-SEVEN

In the next instant Ben's lips captured mine, his breath sucking the words from both my lungs and my mind. His tongue plundered. And against my better judgment, I surrendered, my entire body tingling from head to toe. Ben kissed me as no one had ever kissed me before. These were not the tentative kisses of high school dates. Or the sweet but passionless kisses of my dead husband. Nor the suggestive hinting-of-more-to-come kisses from Chet. Ben kissed me with a raw and primal need.

His cock sprang to life, pressing hard into my belly. Waves of heat and desire coursed like a river of fire through my veins, pooling between my legs and turning me into the epitome of every romance heroine I'd ever read about. Never again would I doubt the truth of those love scenes I once scoffed at. I now knew every word had to be true. I wrapped my arms around him and molded myself into his body. I wanted more. Wanted him to rip my clothes off and take me right there. On the desk. On the carpet. On the tile hearth. I didn't care where. I needed him now. Needed him to pound inside me until I experienced all those fireworks and exploding rockets I'd read about but never experienced with another person.

For weeks I'd wanted this moment, no matter how hard I'd worked to replace Ben in my dreams. Screw the singles scene. I wanted Ben. I'd wanted him from the moment I first saw him. And now I knew he wanted me.

Or did he?

With a sudden jerk, he tore his lips from mine, pushed me away, and stumbled backwards into the desk. "I'm sorry," he said. Panting, he swiped the back of his hand across his mouth. His face, at first ashen, grew red with embarrassment. "That never should have happened. I don't know what came over me. It was a mistake."

A mistake? I clamped a hand over my mouth and bit down on my lower lip to stifle the cry forming in my throat. No! He wanted me. I felt that hard, searing need pressing against my belly. Why was he now denying what had burned so intensely between us only moments before? "Why?" I asked, forcing the word through the lump of tears. "Talk to me, Ben."

He refused to look at me. With his jaw firmly set in a sullen scowl, he leaned against the mantle and fixed his gaze on the cold hearth.

"I know I don't compare in looks to Marion or Vanessa," I whispered, "but am I less appealing than a dead fire?"

His body stiffened, his only acknowledgment of my question. I stood staring at him, waiting for him to speak. When he continued to stare into the hearth, I left the room, grabbed the car keys, and fled to my apartment.

TWENTY-EIGHT

With his fists pressed against his throbbing temples, Ben stood at the window and watched Hope drive off. He had accomplished the one thing he wanted to avoid—hurting her. *Fool!* And he couldn't even go after her to explain. Not with the boys asleep upstairs. Disgusted with himself, he stalked back into the den and picked up the phone.

"Let me get this straight," said Zeke after Ben related the evening's events. "You thought if you kissed her, she'd reject you, and you'd get over this thing you have for her?"

"That about sums it up. Only I overdid it, and she didn't reject me."

"No duh, man."

"What's that supposed to mean?"

"It means you're one blind son-of-a-bitch if you haven't noticed the way Hope Morgan's been mooning over you since Day One."

"You're wrong. She's never—"

"You're right, Ben. You are a damn fool."

"Thanks a lot, pal."

"Hey, look. Just because the chemistry wasn't right between you and Vanessa—"

Ben snorted. "Vanessa Glassman was good for one thing. She made me realize how much I want Hope."

"I'm warning you, Ben. You're courting disaster if you continue down that road."

"No, you're wrong. Hope is everything that's been missing in my life. I finally realized that tonight when I watched her comforting Woody."

"Wise up, man. Sure, Hope might enjoy playing mommy to the triplets. For now. But remember, she knows it's a temporary gig. Mark my words. If you pursue this relationship, one day she'll wake up and realize she's sacrificing her life for someone else's kids. She'll make a beeline for the nearest exit before you know what's hit you."

Zeke's warning stabbed at his heart. Without saying another word, Ben hung up the phone. After Marion's desertion, he found it difficult to disagree with his friend's dire prediction.

TWENTY-NINE

Now what? I hurled myself onto my couch, too numb to cry, too angry to think. In little more than ten hours I needed to be back at Ben's house to watch his kids when he left for work. Was I supposed to pretend nothing had happened? Right. That would work—not. But that's exactly what I expected from Ben. Mr. Denial. After all, given his marriage to Marion, the man was a champion of the art of refusing to see what was smacking him right in the face.

My life sucked. Here I was, nearly thirty-four years old, practically on the cusp of middle-age, and my love life had consisted of one practically platonic marriage, a series of jerk dates, and rejection by the one guy that every cell in my body told me was *the* guy. How pathetic was that?

I couldn't not go back in the morning, though. I had to put my hurt and my heart aside and think of those little boys. No matter how much Ben had humiliated me, I couldn't pull a Marion. I promised him six weeks, and six weeks is what he'd get. I could tough it out for the remaining two weeks. Once Fritzi returned, I'd apply for work at another architectural firm.

If I were lucky—not that I had any sort of track record in that arena—eventually the pain would recede to that place where all my other pain resides. Life would go on. But I'd learned my lesson. Never again would I allow my heart to control my head. Love was nothing more than a masochist's implement of torture. I'd lived without it this long; I could live without it forever.

~*~

Hours later I woke to a repetitive thumping. Forcing open one eye, I glanced around, surprised to find myself in the living room. Still fully clothed, my upper body rested against a sofa cushion; my lower body sprawled across the faded oval braid rug that covered part of the hardwood floor.

I opened my other eye and brought my watch to within an inch of my nose. Six o'clock. God, in an hour I had to face Ben. Grabbing hold of the coffee table, I pushed myself to my feet. Ever muscle in my body screamed out in protest. The thumping continued. Disoriented, it took me a moment to realize someone was pounding on the door. "All right," I yelled. "I'm coming." I forced my legs to carry me across the room. "Who's there?"

"Ben."

His voice hit me like an ice water typhoon. "Go away."

"Hope, please. I need to talk to you."

"Leave me alone. I don't start working for you for another hour." I covered my ears with my hands and headed for the bathroom.

With a slam of the door, I stripped off yesterday's clothes and stepped into the shower. Adjusting the water to only a few degrees shy of scalding, I stood under the nozzle and allowed the biting spray to pummel my sore muscles. And my even sorer ego.

After thirty minutes I'd depleted my supply of hot water. The ache in my body had diminished. Too bad the same couldn't be said for my other aches.

What nerve! How dare Ben show up at my door after the humiliation he'd subjected me to last night!

Twisting off the spigots, I grabbed a towel and stepped over the edge of the tub. After drying myself, I wrapped a fresh towel around my damp hair and shrugged into my thick terry robe. Then I padded barefoot toward the kitchen to start a pot of coffee. Although I'd probably need an intravenous caffeine drip to get me through the day.

It was then that the smell hit me. Fresh coffee. Coming from my kitchen. I turned the corner and froze. My mouth moved, but no sound came out. Ben stood at my kitchen counter, calmly pouring coffee into two of my mugs. When I finally found my voice, I shouted, "You have your nerve! How the hell did you get in here?"

He offered me one of the steaming mugs. "Minnie gave me a key."

I grabbed the mug with both hands. "*My* landlady gave *you* a key to *my* apartment?"

"I was worried. You were pretty upset when you left last night."

"That was nine hours ago!"

"I couldn't leave the boys alone."

Of course not. Even if Ben had come to his senses, he couldn't have followed me last night. But he could have called. "Ever hear of a telephone?"

"Would you have answered?"

Probably not. And even if I had, I would have hung up on him.

Still...worried or not, it didn't excuse what he'd done to me. "Well, as you can see, I'm perfectly fine, so you can leave."

He didn't. Instead, he pulled out a chair and took a seat at my kitchen table. "I'm not leaving until I've said what I came to say."

"Then you'll say it to the four walls, because I won't be here." I started for the doorway, but Ben reached out and grabbed my wrist. Coffee sloshed over the rim of my mug and splattered onto my robe. I stared at the brown stains, then glowered at Ben as I yanked my arm to wrench myself free of his grasp.

"For the record," he said, pulling me closer, "I think you're far more beautiful than either Marion or Vanessa."

I froze but kept my back to him.

"I should have told you that last night." He stroked my wrist with his free hand. "I should have told you many things, but I was just beginning to admit them to myself. I kept trying to deny my own feelings."

I glanced over my shoulder. His eyes were filled with remorse, and despite any effort on my part to the contrary, my traitorous body was melting at the sound of his voice. "Your own feelings?"

"About you." He paused. "I came on too strong. I didn't want you to think I was forcing you into something."

I finally turned around and challenged him. "Did I respond like you were forcing yourself on me?"

He shook his head. "That was part of the problem. You weren't supposed to respond at all. Not the way you did, anyway."

He wasn't making any sense. "You didn't want me to think you were coercing me, but you didn't want me to respond to your advances?" He loosened his grip. I withdrew my hand and leaned against the kitchen counter. I tried to steady myself with several deep breaths, but Ben had me too rattled. His presence, his voice, his words—all worked against me. So much for all those vows I'd made myself last night.

Ben rubbed his forehead. Pushing back the chair, he rose and began pacing around the tiny kitchen. "Damn it, Hope, I come with too much baggage. Can't you see that?" He halted his pacing and spun around to confront me.

I shook my head.

"Those should have been your words, not mine," he continued, pointing an accusatory finger at me. "You should have the sense to know that. You were supposed to push me away and say, 'I'm sorry, Ben, but I don't feel this way about you. I just want to be friends.'"

"You wanted me to lie to you?"

"Yes!"

I opened my mouth to protest.

"No." He turned his back on me. "Hell, I don't know." He slammed his fist into the wall. "I thought I had it all figured out. You'd rebuff my advances, and I'd get you out of my system." He spun around. With three long strides he crossed the room, stopping within inches of me. "You screwed up my not-so-well-thought-out plan, and now I don't know what to do about you, Hope Morgan."

Okay, just throw me into a tailspin, why don't you? I stared at him, his coppery eyes filled with doubt and confusion, deep creases obscuring his boyish features. "You could kiss me," I said.

He scowled. "Haven't you heard anything I just said? I have three children."

"I love your three children."

His frown grew into a scowl. The lines on his forehead deepened. "I'm your boss."

"So fire me."

The scowl transformed into a smirk. A slight glint of amusement appeared in his eyes. "Ah, Hope, and have you go to one of my competitors?"

"Ben?"

"Hmm?"

"Shut up and kiss me."

"Oh, God." He dipped his head, meeting my lips. "This is all wrong," he murmured. "You deserve so much more."

"I don't want more. I want you." The towel slipped from my head. Ben brushed back the damp hair that fell across my face and moaned. "You have no idea how hard I've fought this."

"So stop fighting it."

And he did. He kissed my brow, my eyelids, my nose. His lips traveled across one cheek and down my jawbone to my chin, then back up to my lips. I trembled in his arms.

He journeyed to my neck, alternately nipping and sucking until my trembling grew to writhing. I clung to him, my robe falling open, my bare breasts pressing against his chest. His index finger drew a line from the base of my neck down to my cleavage, and I shuddered. He dipped his head and drew a nipple into his mouth. The bud was already hard as a marble, pebbled and ripe and waiting for him. His hand reached for its twin, rolling it in his fingers while he sucked at the other, sucked until I gasped and moaned and gasped again. I ground my hips against him and reached for his belt buckle.

"No." He stilled my hand and straightened. Taking half a step backwards, he reached for the sides of my robe and drew them back across my body, cinching the tie. "We're not doing this."

I stared in disbelief. "You just did it again!"

"I don't want to hurt you." He stroked my cheek with the tips of his fingers.

I swatted his hand away. "So you'd rather leave us both in a state of constant sexual frustration? Don't touch me unless you plan to finish what you start."

Ben's face tightened. "Is that all you want from me? A quick screw?" He yanked at my robe. "If that's it, then let's get it over with here and now. We can both get it out of our systems and go on with our lives. Where do you want it? On the floor? The kitchen table?"

I jerked away, drawing my robe back across my breasts. "Don't talk like that! You know that's not what I want."

His body relaxed. "No, I didn't think so." Slowly his gaze traveled the length of my torso. "You'd better put some clothes on before I lose my resolve. Then we'll try to make some sense of all this."

"Ben?"

"Hope, please. Get dressed. I can't take much more of looking at you like that."

When I returned several minutes later, I found Ben sitting in the living room. He held up the snapshot of Faith, Charlie, and me on the pony. I had purchased a frame for it on Sunday and placed it on one of the end tables. "This is the photo you told Woody about, isn't it?"

I sat down beside him. "Yes."

"Not a very large photo but I can see the resemblance, especially around the eyes and mouth." He placed the frame on the coffee table. "I looked through your bookcase for a photo album. I thought maybe you'd have a larger picture, and I wanted to see what your brother looked like over the years. I couldn't find one."

I picked up the photo and placed it back on the end table. "You won't. There was a fire. That's the only picture of any of us that survived."

"What about recent photos? I'd love to see what the Woodster might grow up to look like."

I turned away from Ben and inhaled sharply. Too sharply. He noticed.

"Hope?"

I shook my head. "I'm the only one who survived the fire."

Ben reached for my hand and urged me into the seat next to him. "I'm sorry. When did this happen?"

Don't go there. We needed to talk about the future, not the past, but he'd popped the top on my private can of worms, and there was no way those insidious little buggers were going to let me squish them back into my own private hell. "Three years ago," I finally said.

"Your parents must have been devastated."

Damn, he wasn't going to leave this alone. "They died, too."

"God." He wrapped his arms around me.

And then I did something that shocked me as much as Ben. I admitted what I'd admitted to no one but myself. "It was my fault," I whispered into his chest.

He pulled away and stared at me. "The fire?"

I rose from the couch and walked to the window. Staring out into the early morning traffic, I told him everything. Well, almost everything. I told him about Wally, our nearly platonic marriage, and his subsequent death. About my parents not understanding my need to be more than a secretary and their disapproval of me using Wally's life insurance to help finance an education they believed useless. About putting that education before everything else until it was my one reason for living. About the argument my father and I had moments before he suffered the heart attack and plowed the car into the propane tank. About the baby Faith was carrying. I stopped short of telling him the baby was mine and that I could never have another.

"I packed up the few surviving remnants of the fire and didn't open the box again until the other day," I said.

Ben strode across the room and grabbed my face between his palms. "Look at me. You can't blame yourself for what happened. Not arguing with your father wouldn't necessarily have changed things."

I pulled away. "Wouldn't it? Sure, he may still have died from a heart attack, but maybe he would have been sitting in his recliner, watching football at the time, not starting up the car. Everyone else would still be alive."

And I'd still be able to have children.

Ben shook his head. "If you continue to live with this guilt, it will eat away at you. Trust me. I know."

"Because of Marion?"

He nodded. "You don't know the half of it."

I wanted to say, so tell me, but I didn't. Apparently, we both hid secrets too painful to voice. "We're a great pair, aren't we?"

"We shouldn't be a pair. Every part of me is screaming out against...this."

"This?"

"Us."

"Which is why you're fighting both me and yourself. Denying your own feelings. Your own needs."

"If you knew what was good for you, you'd keep your distance," he said.

"Why?"

"I told you why."

We were going around in circles. "And I've told you none of that matters to me."

"Well, it should. What if things don't work out? What if you get hurt?"

I threw my arms up, then smacked them on my thighs. "What if I do? That's a risk everyone takes."

"You deserve a relationship without complications. Without being burdened by someone else's mistakes."

"Is that what you're really worried about, Ben?"

"What do you mean?"

"Or are you more worried that I'll change my mind and leave. Like Marion did." He looked away. "That's it, isn't it?"

"It's been suggested."

"By whom?"

"Does it matter?"

"Yes, I think it does."

At first, I didn't think he'd tell me. I sat back down on the sofa and folded my arms across my chest, waiting. Finally, he said, "Zeke."

"Zeke? Why doesn't that surprise me?" Of all the staff minus Marion, Zeke was the one person from whom I often felt negative vibes. Now I knew why.

"He meant well."

"Yeah, right."

"You don't understand. He warned me about Marion, but I didn't listen. Now he's warning me about you. He's convinced you'll tire of the responsibility and walk out on me and the boys."

I slammed my palms onto the coffee table and leaped to my feet. "On what basis? What have I ever done to make him think I'm anything like Marion? Didn't I offer to step in when she walked out on you and the boys? Haven't I put those kids first from the moment I met them? And who the hell anointed him Dr. Phil?"

"Look, it's just a feeling he has. The same feeling he had once before. I ignored him then, and look what happened. This is more about me than it is about you. Zeke's been my friend for a long time. He cares about me. He doesn't want to see me hurt again. Or see the boys hurt."

"Well, at least there's something Zeke and I can agree on. I don't want to see you hurt, either. Or the boys. But damn it, Ben! Love is always risky. And always complicated. Sometimes it works, and sometimes it doesn't. I don't know about you, but I'd rather take that risk and fail than live my life wondering if I let you talk me out of the most wonderful thing that has ever happened to me." I reached for his hand. "To us."

His face filled with anguish. "You seem so sure of yourself. Maybe Zeke is wrong. But don't you see, I'm not only risking my heart this time around. I'm risking the boys' hearts as well. I don't have the right to do that."

"You can't protect them from life, Ben. I love you. I love them. Isn't that worth the risk?"

He shook his head. "I'm gun-shy. I've already made one huge mistake by rushing into a relationship for the wrong reasons. Five people have suffered because of it. I won't let that happen again. I don't want to hurt you like I hurt Marion. And I don't want my children to suffer any more than they already have."

"What are you telling me? That you won't even try? Is that

what you really want?"

He turned away from me and spoke to the wall. "I have to think of the boys. What I want doesn't matter anymore."

I stepped in front of him and poked him in the chest. "Maybe it should. Maybe that's the greatest gift you can give your sons. Don't become a martyr to protect them, Ben. It will only backfire on you. Look at me. I lived the life my parents expected me to live because I was a dutiful daughter. And I was miserable. It drove a wedge between us. The same thing will happen to you and the boys if you continue down this path. Zeke doesn't know what the hell he's talking about."

Ben walked back to the sofa, sat down, and lowered his head into his hands. "I don't know. Maybe if we take it slowly. Very slowly."

I sat down beside him, a glimmer of hope growing in my belly. "Define slowly."

He thought for a moment. "Little by little. No sex until we're sure it's going to work." He raised his head and grimaced. "Even if it kills me."

"And me." I laughed. "You know, you're certifiable, Ben Schaffer."

"Probably."

I threw my arms up in surrender. "Fine. No sex. It's not like I've had any in over a decade anyway."

That caught his attention. "You're kidding, right?"

"Wally was it. First. Last. Only. And believe it or not, I was fine with that until I met you." I saw no point in mentioning my deceased handy-dandy plastic partner. We were talking relationships here, and a relationship with a vibrator isn't exactly a relationship a girl brags about.

"I'm sorry."

"Stop saying that. I'm not a charity case. If you've got it in your head that the only way we're going to succeed is by following some antiquated courtship rules from another century, then so be it. I'm going to prove Zeke wrong one way or another."

"This isn't about Zeke. You need to understand—"

I waved yet another excuse away before he could finish and rose to my feet. "Whatever. I suppose we'd better have a chaperone. Or three. Where'd you leave the boys?"

THIRTY

"The boys are downstairs in the store with Minnie," said Ben.

"Downstairs? Today is Tuesday. The store is closed."

Ben chuckled. "The animals don't know it's Minnie's day off. They still need to be fed."

"Of course."

He reached for her hands. "Are you all right?"

"No." She shook her head. "I'm sleepy and confused and frustrated and..." She offered him a wry smile. "and strangely enough...somewhat happy. I think. All at once but not necessarily in that order. Does any of that make sense?"

He kissed her cheek. "It does."

Holding up both hands palms out, Hope drew back and scowled. "Wait a minute. I agreed to no sex. Nowhere did we discuss cheek pecking."

He pulled her back into his arms.

She tilted her head back. "So holding's allowed? I'm going to need these rules in writing, you know."

"Holding's allowed, smart ass."

"Good." She pressed deeper against him. "Because I wouldn't want to risk overstepping my bounds."

Ben began to respond to the way she rubbed against him. He stepped back, grasping her shoulders and allowing several inches of distance between his groin and her belly. "Damn, you're not going to make this easy, are you?"

"I have no idea what you're complaining about now."

"Sure, you don't."

She shrugged from his grasp and closed the distance between them, wrapping her hands around his chest as she lowered her head to his shoulder. "The man doth protest too much. I just want you to hold me."

Ben removed her hands and once more backed up. "I think we need those chaperones before the best of my intentions fly south. Besides, Minnie's expecting us downstairs for breakfast. She'll be sending out a search party if we don't show up soon."

~*~

Hope expressed surprise at finding Edwina waiting for them in Minnie's apartment. "Winnie? What are you doing here? Why aren't you at the office?"

Winnie gaped at her. "Girl, are you that far gone? It's Fourth of July. National holiday." She hitched her thumb in Ben's direction. "Even Simon Legree here gave us the day off."

Ben watched the color creep into Hope's face. "Fourth of July. I forgot." That explained her yelling at him earlier about still having an hour before she needed to be at work. She'd forgotten she had the day off.

Hope gave Winnie an odd look. "So let me get this straight. It's your day off, and you got up at the crack of dawn to visit your

216

aunt?"

"Hell, no. I came last night." Surrounded by the triplets, she sat on the floor in Minnie's living room. She held her ever-present cup of coffee in one hand, a wiggling ball of brown and white fur in the other. "Isn't he the most precious thing you've ever seen?" She held up the puppy for Hope's inspection. "We're going to name him Cappuccino."

"He's a twiplet," announced Scotty, "just like Woody and Teddy and me."

Edwina nodded to two puppies snuggled between her crossed legs. "This one's Espresso," she said, pointing to the darker of the two, "and his brother here is Latte." She stroked the fur of the tan puppy nestled up against her thigh.

"I take it you picked out the names?" asked Hope.

"Who else would choose names like that?"

Teddy jumped up and ran to his father. Bouncing up and down, he tugged on Ben's jeans leg and asked. "Can we keeps them, Daddy? Aunt Minnie says we can if you do. Please, daddy. Please!"

Ben tried to mask his horror. Three kids. Three dogs. One already frazzled single parent. He tried to reason with his sons. "I don't know, guys. Taking care of one puppy is a big responsibility, let alone three. Maybe we can get a dog in a few years when you're older."

"No!" Scotty sprang to his feet, placed his hands on his hips, and stamped his foot. "I wants a puppy now!"

"Me, too!" added Teddy.

"Please," whined Woody. "They wuv us."

"What's all the commotion?" asked Minnie, entering the living room and heading for the massive pine plank dining table that filled one corner of the room.

Ben scowled at her. As roly-poly as her niece was statuesque, the lively septuagenarian was dressed in a multi-colored dashiki and matching turban. An assortment of silver wrist bangles covered both wrists. Carrying a platter of freshly baked cinnamon buns in one hand, a pitcher of milk in the other, she stopped and eyed the crowd suspiciously.

"Did you promise my sons this litter of puppies?"

After adding the pastries and milk to the abundance of food already filling the table, Minnie approached the triplets. "What did I tell you?"

"That we could have doggies," said Teddy, staring up at her, his eyes filled with hope.

"When?"

All three boys hung their heads.

Minnie cleared her throat.

"When Daddy says we can," mumbled Scotty.

"End of subject." She gathered up the puppies and placed them back with their mother. "Time for breakfast. Go wash your hands."

Ben breathed a sigh of relief. He'd nearly given in, especially when he looked into Teddy's pleading eyes. Even if he knew he'd immediately regret it. He had a hard time saying no to the boys, an overreaction to Marion's strictness, no doubt. But the care and feeding of three untrained, non-housebroken puppies would fall to Hope—at least for the next two weeks, and then to Fritzi. He wasn't willing to dump any more responsibility on either woman.

As Ben herded the boys off to the bathroom, he noticed Winnie placing a hand on Hope's forearm and whispering something to her. When Hope glanced at him and blanched, he knew he was in deep shit.

By the time Ben returned from hand-washing duty, he could see that Hope had worked herself up into full dagger-glaring mode. Before he could speak, she grabbed his arm and dragged him into the kitchen. "What's wrong?"

"Does everyone know what happened last night?" She whispered the question in a clipped, angry tone.

He decided to feign innocence. "I don't know what you mean."

"You know exactly what I mean, Ben Schaffer. You told Edwina what happened last night. Who else did you tell? Minnie? Zeke? What did you do, hold a conference call to solicit their opinions?"

"Hey, girl, don't get so upset."

Hope spun around to find Winnie standing in the doorway. "And why not?"

Winnie stepped farther into the kitchen. "Because Ben didn't say much of anything. He didn't have to."

She stole a glance at Ben, and he nodded. "What do you mean?"

"Honey, I've known Ben a long time. I can read him like a book. And you, well, those big hazel eyes of yours say it all. A person would have to be blind not to see the two of you have the hots for each other."

Hope frowned. "It's that obvious?"

"Well, maybe not to your average rocket scientist. After all, they're pretty dense and single-minded. But to the rest of us?" Winnie paused. Cocking her head, she eyed Hope. "Yeah, I'd say it's pretty obvious. So, I repeat the question, because you didn't answer me before. Are you okay?"

Hope glanced once more at Ben before offered Winnie a weak

smile. "I'm surviving."

"Surviving ain't good enough. Not for you *or* Ben. You two need to be thriving."

"And you need to stick that nose of yours out of other people's business and back on your own face where it belongs," said Ben. "Hope and I can manage our own affairs, thank you very much."

"Not very well from where I stand," Winnie retorted.

"Then maybe you need to stand somewhere else," said Ben.

"Everyone to the table," called Minnie, from just beyond the kitchen where she was apparently eavesdropping.

Grateful for Minnie's intervention, Ben headed toward the table. Behind him he heard Edwina's stage whisper to Hope. "Don't worry. We'll work on him for you."

Just what he needed. Now he'd have to deal with Edwina and Zeke squaring off in a battle to control his sex life.

THIRTY-ONE

The next two weeks were both the longest of my life and the shortest. Each day Ben left earlier for the office and returned later than normal. When he was home, he spent most of his time with the children. After tucking them in bed at night, he concentrated on cataloging and boxing up Marion's extensive collections.

He did everything in his power to keep his distance from me, like I was some evil sexual temptress. How else could I interpret his behavior? The evening after I offered to help him pack up Marion's junk, he came home with a rush rendering assignment for me. So I spent the next several nights at the drawing board in his office while he wrapped and packed in the front parlor.

Ben wasn't cold. Just distant. Physically. On the outside we interacted with the children and each other as before, but other than an occasional cheek peck, he maintained a clear line of demarcation between his body parts and mine. I wanted to scream.

One night I did. "Good Lord, Ben! Even the Puritans spooned!"

"They wore more clothing," he said. "When I take you into my bed, I don't expect you to be wearing anything."

I fisted my temples and groaned. "If we're not going to do it, can we please not talk about it?"

"As you wish." He turned his attention back to packing china.

I picked up a lace pillow from the sofa and hurled it at his head. Then I stormed out of the room and headed upstairs to my half-finished watercolor of the soon-to-be-built Lake Hopatcong Shopping Plaza.

~*~

And then it was over. Every wonderful minute of each of the six weeks I'd spent with Ben and his sons. Fritzi Fitzgerald returned. Healed and healthy, she jumped back into her triple role of housekeeper-nanny-caretaker. Teary-eyed, the boys said their goodbyes to me and I to them. Ben returned the rental car, and before I could say *supercalifragilisticexpialidocious*, I found myself back in my own apartment. Within five minutes the silence was driving me crazy.

Fifteen minutes later my phone rang.

"Will you have dinner with me this evening?"

"Ben?"

"Now that we're no longer living together, I thought we might start that courtship."

"So this is an official date?"

"Only if you accept. You haven't said yes yet."

"Yes! Yes! Yes!"

"Well, if you're not sure, Hope..."

"Ben?"

"Hmm?"

"Can I at least expect a real goodnight kiss?"

I heard his deep sigh through the phone lines. "We'll see."

We certainly will. I was going to make damn sure of it. I hung up the phone, grabbed my keys, and headed out the door. I'd start by a quick trip down the street to the drug store for the necessary supplies.

Only the trip didn't turn out to be as quick as I anticipated. Bewildered, I stood in front of a long aisle filled with row after row of hair coloring products. I hadn't dyed my hair since high school when I defied my parents because, according to Madonna, "Being blonde is definitely a different state of mind."

Unfortunately, I hadn't followed the directions quite as carefully as I should have, and the end result was more brassy green than blonde. To teach me a lesson, my father refused to let my mother take me to the beauty salon for a much-needed repair job. I spent the next year wearing hats and scarves until my natural color grew in enough to cut off the evidence of my disobedience.

This time I'd take my time. Studying the back of each box, I ultimately selecting one that promised silky, natural golden highlights with a minimum of mess and fuss.

"Hair coloring for dummies," I mumbled, as I headed for the manicure supplies. The selection of nail enamels proved equally extensive, but after a few minutes of debating the merits of various shades, I settled on a delicate tint of opalescent peach. Although I found the reds and purples daring and tempting, I wasn't after a Bimbo Barbie look. I'd leave that to women like Vanessa.

In the next aisle I added a bottle of tangerine and melon aromatherapy bath oil and a facial mask gel.

One item to go. I wheeled the shopping cart into the next aisle. Not that I had to worry about pregnancy, and I certainly wasn't harboring any STDs, but given what I knew about Marion...well, it wasn't beyond the realm of possibilities that she may have picked something up from her geriatric Italian Stallion and passed it along to Ben.

I stopped in front of the rack and stared at the selection confronting me. *Good Grief!* If I thought I had trouble picking out hair coloring, the variety of condoms boggled my less-than-experienced mind. Ribbed. Smooth. Lubricated. Unlubricated. Natural. Latex. *Glow-in-the dark? Flavored? Edible!*

I don't think so.

I reached for the most innocuous box of regular latex condoms I could find, then hesitated. What the hell. Placing them back on the rack, I grabbed a box of chocolate-flavored ones instead. Might as well live dangerously. I tossed the package into my cart and headed for the checkout counter.

I walked the few blocks back to my apartment, and before heading upstairs, I stopped in the pet store to retrieve my week's worth of mail from Minnie.

Once inside my apartment, I sorted through the stack of letters and advertisements, dividing the mail into two piles, keepers and recycling. Bill. Bill. Junk mail. Bill. *You may have already won.* Definitely junk mail. Credit card offer. More junk mail. Another bill.

Office of the District Attorney? The nondescript white envelope had been forwarded from my former address in Pennsylvania. A jury summons, no doubt. I was about to open the envelope when I noticed the New York City return address. Political junk mail. I tossed the unopened letter into the recycling pile.

Several months ago, the Pittsburgh District Attorney had lost her prolonged battle with ovarian cancer. The city was about to hold a special election to replace her. Obviously, one of the candidates had solicited the aid of another big city D.A. to sway voters with a letter of support. *Sorry, buddy. I'm now a New Jersey resident.*

Leaving the two piles on the coffee table, I grabbed my bag of purchases and headed for the bathroom.

THIRTY-TWO

Standing in the hallway outside Hope's apartment, Ben hesitated before ringing the doorbell. His decision to call her within minutes after dropping her off earlier in the day had been pure impulse. The more he thought of it, the more he realized every action he had ever taken toward Hope was either based on impulse or fighting those impulses. Yet, he couldn't deny the fact that the moment she stepped from his car and disappeared inside her apartment, he'd felt loss seep into his bones.

Part of him wanted to wave the white flag, say the hell with it, and take her to bed. She wanted it. He wanted it. Why fight it? *Because your best friend warned you against it, and he was right the last time.*

"You're too desperate, Ben. Step back and think about what you're doing. Besides," Zeke had said, "you're not in love. It's a rebound romance, and they wear thin very quickly. We've both seen it dozens of times in people we know who have gone through divorces. Just hang in there and ride out the storm. You'll be doing both you and Hope a big favor."

"I've fallen for her, Zeke. I can't help it."

"Yeah. You once said the same thing about Marion."

"This is different. Hope's different."

"You don't have much of a basis for comparison, buddy. Don't go turning her into a saint. No one's that sweet. Not even Hope. I saw that for myself her first week in the office. What are you going to do when she walks out and tramples you and the boys in her wake?"

"What makes you so certain she'd do that?"

"What makes you so certain she won't?"

"You don't know her the way I do. She's not Marion." Ben found it difficult to accept Zeke's cynicism, but he knew Zeke had his best interests at heart. Which was probably the only reason he hadn't told his friend to go fuck himself each time he railed against Hope.

But Zeke's reservations weren't the only reason Ben had refused to act on his feelings toward Hope. He didn't deserve the love he saw shining in her eyes. He was a flawed man, and because he'd grown to care so deeply for her, he wanted her to have better. No matter how she protested to the contrary. Yet, if he really believed that, why was he standing outside her door in a stuffy hallway, dressed in a summer suit and carrying a bouquet of roses?

Ben scowled at the flowers nestled in the crook of his arm. When he walked into the florist shop, he'd had no idea he was entering a minefield. Pick the wrong color rose, and your life could explode in your face. Foolish fellow that he was, he'd thought you picked flowers to complement a room's décor. Or because it was someone's favorite color. When he'd mentioned Hope's living room color scheme to the florist, she smiled condescendingly and pointed to a decorative chart hanging behind the counter.

In flowing calligraphy and dotted with illustrations, *The Language of Flowers* told him more than he ever wanted to know about the hidden meanings behind various blossoms.

He wondered who the hell came up with such absurd nonsense. Certainly not the guy on TV who constantly hawked his dial-a-bouquet business. Men's minds just don't work that way. Had to be the guy's wife. But there it was, spelled out in front of him, and much to his annoyance, the snippy saleswoman had informed him that all women were well versed in such details.

After studying the chart for several excruciating minutes, Ben quickly eliminated coral. The color indicated desire. Even if he *had* foolishly called Hope, he was adamantly convinced it was not in her best interest for them to pursue any type of relationship—no matter how much he desired her. Scratch coral.

Red and lavender were also out. Maybe he was only kidding himself. Still, he wasn't about to announce to the world in general and Hope in particular that he'd fallen in love with her, let alone at first sight as lavender roses indicated. But hadn't he already admitted as much to her? Still, no point driving the point home thorn by thorn.

Ben eyed the bundle in his arm and grunted. Love at first sight only happened in the movies and romance novels. His life was far from either. Besides, he hadn't fallen in love with her. He had just fallen *for* her. There was a big difference. His reaction was purely hormonal, wasn't it? Which was why he refused to act on his urges. And why he would continue to rebuff her advances—even if it killed him.

So what the hell are you doing buying her roses then, hotshot?

Ben had considered yellow roses but talk about hidden

meanings! According to the chart, today yellow could signify joy, freedom, gladness, or even slight love, but historically it meant a decrease of love or even infidelity. That made about as much sense as the stupid chart in general. Did a two-timing Victorian husband bring home a dozen yellow roses to his wife after spending an evening with his mistress? Did the wife then place the flowers in a vase or throw them in the philanderer's face?

Complicating matters even more, further down the chart Ben learned that mixing yellow and orange roses implied passionate thoughts. No, he'd stay away from the yellows, thank you very much.

Then there were the pinks. Lighter shades implied grace, gentility, and admiration. Darker shades said, "thank you." Now he was getting somewhere. Hope was graceful and gentle beyond words. He greatly admired her and fully appreciated the sacrifice she had made for him over the past six weeks. Yes, pink was perfect.

So here he was, quaking outside her door like a pimple-faced adolescent about to go on his first date. Time marches on, but some things never change. Taking a deep breath, he depressed the buzzer.

A moment later the door swung open, and Ben's myriad of reasons for not getting involved with Hope Morgan flew from his brain. He needn't have worried about the hidden meaning behind rose colors. The bulge in his trousers spoke for him. "You look beautiful," he managed to say, although how he forced the thought into words was anybody's guess. She literally took his breath away.

He had seen Hope in a business setting. He had seen her in a home setting. Sometimes she wore a suit or a dress, sometimes jeans or shorts or a casual jumper. He had even seen her in a robe and towel. Yet, nothing could have prepared Ben for the sight of her this evening.

"Thank you. Are those for me?" She pointed to the roses.

Ben didn't think he'd ever felt so awkward or tongue-tied—not even as a teenager. But then again, he'd never been sucker punched by Eros. He definitely would have remembered. "Yes." He placed the cellophane-wrapped package in her outstretched arms. "From me and the boys. A...a thank-you for all your help over the last few weeks." There, he'd kick-started his brain, making clear the meaning of the flowers, thus preventing any later misunderstandings.

"From you *and* the boys?" Hope's eyes twinkled. Her lips turned up in a slight smile as she bowed her head to inhale the heady fragrance. "I see. They're lovely."

"Your hair," he said, captivated by the way the soft curls framed her face and fell across her breasts. "You've done something to your hair."

And everything else for that matter. Wearing a calf-length, flowing white sleeveless dress made of some soft gauzy material, she reminded him of an angel. A very sexy, desirable angel. Damn if she didn't positively glow! Ben took a deep breath. He had to get hold of himself. If he didn't remove them both from the apartment soon, every ounce of his resolve would evaporate in a rush of testosterone.

"I decided to lighten it a bit." She turned and headed toward the kitchen. "Come in. I'd better put these in water."

Against his better judgment but as obedient as a puppy dog, he followed her down the hall and into the small kitchen. Leaning against the counter, he watched as she removed a heavy crystal vase from the cabinet above the refrigerator.

"This belonged to my great-grandmother." She ran her finger along the chipped edge of the rim. "She brought it over from Ireland. Somehow it survived the fire."

"First time you're using it?"

She nodded as she filled the vase with water. "It's time." One by one, she separated a stem from the bouquet, snipped its bottom, and placed it in the container. Once finished, she added the baby's breath and ferns the florist had included with the spray, carefully arranging them among the blossoms.

Ben's tension increased as he watched her work. He was at a loss to explain how the hell she managed to turn a simple chore into an act of seduction. Yet, she had. He couldn't watch her slender fingers move along the thin, firm stems of the roses without imagining their sensuous exploration of his body. When she paused for a moment and bit her lower lip in concentration, he held his breath, imagining her nipping him in a place that normally didn't see the light of day.

He couldn't take much more. If he didn't get them both out of her apartment and into a public setting soon, he might as well forget every good intention he had. The heat suffusing his body was turning into a raging inferno. "Hope, we have to go. Now."

She lifted the vase and smiled sweetly at him. "I'll just put these in the living room and grab my purse."

As Ben trailed after her, his gaze never left her tight little butt. With each step he followed the seductive sway of her hips as her buns undulated back and forth. Back and forth. Back and forth. Beads of sweat sprang up across his brow, and he wondered if she had the slightest notion of her ability to reduce a grown man—a grown man with three toddlers—into a goddamn quivering bowl of Jell-O.

Hope draped a flimsy lace shawl across her shoulders, retrieved a small white purse from the coffee table, and paused, smiling up at him. "I'm ready."

But when Ben saw the hint of mischief twinkling in those big hazel eyes of hers, he had the answer to his question. Underneath Hope's sweet angel exterior beat the heart of a seductive witch. "Not tonight, Mrs. Robinson," he muttered to himself. "Not if I can help it." For her sake he'd make certain he could. Even if it meant an hour-long cold shower before he hit the sack. Alone.

~*~

The moment Ben escorted Hope into The Springside Inn, he knew he'd been sabotaged. Recommended by Le, the restaurant, located in the rolling hills of Morris County, was far from what he expected. Steeped in Revolutionary War history, she had said. Delightful ambiance. Quaint charm. With a description like that, Ben expected rustic Colonial à la Martha Stewart, not a romantic, candlelit enclave more suitable to The Left Bank of Paris.

His architect's eye took in his surroundings. A stone fireplace, perhaps the only original remnant of the Eighteenth-Century building, stood against the back wall. Deep teal wainscoting covered the lower half of the remaining three walls. A brass chair rail separated the paneling from a lavender, teal, and plum floral print paper. Reproduction Louis XVI chairs, upholstered in the same floral print, sat at each table. Plum louvered shutters covered the windows. Verdigris glazed terra cotta tiles covered the floor. Tiny white twinkle lights hung from the perimeter of the paneled ceiling.

"Oh, Ben, this is lovely!" Hope gazed up at him. Her eyes, normally larger than should be legal, grew even wider with delight. Her lips, glossed and inviting—too inviting—parted in awe.

Ben pasted a smile over his scowl. "I'm glad you like it. Le recommended it."

The maître d' led them to a small corner table draped in lavender linen and partially shielded by a wrought iron trellis and large Oriental vases of dried hydrangeas. A water lily-shaped candle, floating in a blown-glass bowl, provided the only additional light.

"Somehow I don't think Le and her husband come here with their kids," said Hope, scanning the room.

Ben glanced at his menu, written in French with prices to match. If Le weren't such a damned good engineer, he'd strangle her. *Some friend!* This was the kind of place where guys popped the question. Ben wanted to discourage Hope, not propose to her. "No, I doubt they have a children's menu." He raised his head to discover Hope staring at him.

"Not what you expected, is it?" The hint of a smile playing at the edges of her mouth.

"What?"

"The restaurant."

"Why do you say that?"

"For one thing, those deep furrows that creased your forehead the moment we entered the building." Her smile grew. "Besides, this is a rather romantic setting, and you keep telling me we shouldn't get involved."

"We shouldn't."

"So you've said."

Before Ben could reply, the sommelier appeared. "A bottle of champagne, sir?"

Hope giggled.

Ben began to feel as if he were the victim of a huge conspiracy.

"Damned if I do, damned if I don't," he muttered.

"Pardon, sir?"

"Why not?" Ben handed him the wine list. "A bottle of your best."

Hope raised an eyebrow.

"Thank you, sir." The wine steward departed.

The strolling violinist appeared.

THIRTY-THREE

Poor Ben, I thought, sipping my champagne as the solo musician serenaded us with Debussy. The man was so entrenched in his crazy notion of protecting me from being hurt by him that he couldn't see how right we were for each other. Apparently, even Le saw it. Why else would she recommend a restaurant like this? If only Ben would drop his defenses long enough, I was certain nature and a heaping dollop of chemistry would do the rest. But Ben fought his feelings for me at every turn.

I figured I might as well order dessert. It certainly didn't look like I'd be sampling any other chocolate-flavored confection this evening.

I reached across the table and placed my hand over his. "Tell me something. Would you be more relaxed at McDonald's?"

He turned his hand, laced our fingers together, and spoke to our interlocked hands. "I feel as though I have an angel perched on one shoulder and a devil on the other. They're taking turns bashing me over the head with a baseball bat."

"I don't need protecting, Ben. I'm not some young kid. I know my own heart."

"Do you? Do you really have any idea what you'd be letting yourself in for?"

Here we go again. I yanked my hand away, nearly tipping over my water glass. "Damn it, Ben! You're beginning to sound like a broken record. Stop treating me like a child."

"I'm a man with lots of baggage, Hope. Three children and an ex-wife who could come back at some point and create even more problems. For me. For my kids. For you. I don't know that I can believe she'll stay away for good. She's too unpredictable."

"You're a foolish, pig-headed man who's afraid to live! That's what you are." I tossed my napkin onto the table and jumped to my feet. "Take me home, please. It's perfectly obvious you don't want to be here with me."

Ben stood. He placed his hands on my bare shoulders. "Nothing could be further from the truth. Please. Sit down."

I hesitated.

"Please, Hope."

I studied his sad brown eyes and worry-lined features. Reaching up, I traced an index finger along one deep crease. "Then why do you act that way? Everything you say and do confuses me."

I took a deep breath. "I love you, Ben. There, I've said it. I love you, and now I want to know how you feel about me. Don't tell me what's best for me or why we shouldn't or can't love each other or throw up Marion or your kids or the fact that you're my boss. Just tell me the honest to God truth about how you feel."

His gaze never left mine as he took hold of both my hands and brought them to his lips. "God help us both. I love you."

Then he dipped his head, replacing my fingers with my lips,

and I fell into his arms, clinging to him as though he were my salvation. In a sense, he was. Corny as it sounds, with those three words Ben released my soul and liberated my heart. He delivered me from the longing and loneliness that had plagued me for too many years, offering in their place, the promise of a shared future.

My head spun, my heart pounded as his kiss, possessive yet gentle, traveled from my lips to every neuron in my body. Goose bumps erupted up and down my arms. My legs trembled. My scalp tingled. All from a kiss. A kiss that ended far too quickly. I moaned. "Don't stop. Please don't ever stop."

"We have an audience," he whispered as he stepped back, slowly skimming his fingers down my arms until he clasped my hands.

A moment later the room echoed with applause. I spun around to find the other diners clapping their hands and offering their congratulations. Heat raced up my neck and into my cheeks. "Oh God." I bit down on my lower lip and eyed Ben. "Now what do we do?"

He held my chair out for me. "We sit down and eat our dinner."

I stared at the platters that must have arrived during the heat of our embrace. "And then?"

Ben's face clouded over in a thoughtful expression. Instead of answering, he speared a morsel of lobster and placed it in his mouth.

At least I was making progress. Maybe I wouldn't order dessert after all.

THIRTY-FOUR

The road to hell is paved with good intentions, thought Ben, trying to concentrate more on his meal than the invisible line he'd just crossed. He'd spoken from his heart when he told Hope he loved her, but once upon a time, he'd spoken those words to Marion, and look where that got both of them.

Maybe Zeke was right.

Shortly after his birth, Ben's parents fell victim to the pervasive drug culture of the time. Although various relatives and foster parents raised him and cared for him, Ben grew up believing they did so, not out of love but Christian duty.

As he looked back on his life with Marion, Ben wondered if love had ever been a part of their relationship. On either side. Never having felt truly and completely loved before, perhaps his childhood insecurities had led him to confuse lust for love.

He hoped he'd matured enough not to make the same mistake with Hope, but how could he know for sure? Besides, Hope didn't deserve a man who couldn't tell the difference. He knew from experience, that at least with him, the road they were about to travel led to only one destination: heartache.

Yet, there they were, poised on the brink of a journey toward disaster. How'd he let it get this far? He was a grown man with responsibilities—three children and a business to run. No longer a horny adolescent, he should be able to cap his raging hormones. But even as the thought rattled around inside his head, he knew when it came to Hope, hormones where only a part of the problem. She'd penetrated his soul.

They spoke little the remainder of the meal, communicating instead mostly with their eyes. On the drive back to her apartment he held her hand, occasionally raising it to his lips. By silent agreement they both knew how the evening would end. Words had become superfluous.

Ben draped his arm around her shoulders as they climbed the two flights of steps leading to her apartment. On the small landing outside her door, in the soft yellow glow of the overhead bulb, he took her in his arms once more. "I think you're a witch," he murmured, burying his face in her hair. "You've trapped me in some goddamn magic spell."

"If so, I'm not a very good one. I can't even get you to finish a kiss." Lifting her head, she tossed him a wry smile. "Much less anything else."

"Have patience. There's an old saying, 'Good things come to those who wait.'"

Hope wrinkled her nose. "I can put up with the cliché if you're that good."

"Open the damn door, and you might get lucky enough to find out just how good I am."

She reached into her handbag, retrieved her key, and unlocked the door. For a moment they stood on the threshold, staring at each other, but he was losing control fast. "Damn, I need you," he said.

"Show me."

Ben leaned into her. "Now how can I pass up a challenge like that?" He bypassed the preliminaries. No sweet, tentative kisses. Nothing subtle. He plunged right into a heated lip Lambada and tongue Tango, leaving no doubt as to his intentions. But just to make certain, he sent his hands off on a mission of exploration, one heading north, the other south.

Hope responded with an eagerness that nearly knocked him off balance as she rubbed her body against his. Ben pressed her against the landing wall, and she began a bit of exploration of her own. When her fingers made contact with his groin, he thought he'd explode.

They practically tumbled into the apartment. Ben kicked the door closed with his foot. Too impatient to find her bed, he led her to the sofa. Damn, he was hard! He wanted to take his time, to enjoy every excruciating minute, but Hope wasn't making it easy. She had already unfastened several buttons on his shirt and was reaching for his belt buckle.

"Slowly," he mumbled, as much to himself as to her. Reaching behind her, he fumbled with her zipper.

She shivered in his arms. "You first."

Easier said than done. *Slow* had disappeared from his lexicon. And apparently from hers. Tugging the dress down her arms, he lowered her backwards onto the cushions and unclasped her bra. With her body trapped beneath his, he began nibbling on her shoulder. He'd force himself to go slowly if it killed him.

And with what Hope was doing at that moment, he just might

die because even trapped beneath him, she had managed to spring the crown jewels and wrap her fingers around him. He hadn't thought he could grow any harder than he already was.

"Wait." He pulled away from her and sat back on his heels. He needed to cool things down a bit, or this would be over before they got to the good part.

"Why?" she asked.

"Because there's something I want to do first." He leaned forward and his fingers skimmed across her silk panties. He dipped his fingers beneath the elastic and deep inside her. Her muscles contracted around him. Her breathing grew more rapid and shallow. Ben found her clit and rubbed it between his fingers. Her body clenched.

Panting, she writhed beneath him. "Ben, please. Come inside me."

"I am inside you."

She arched her back. "Not like this."

"Not yet." Withdrawing his fingers, he slipped her panties down her legs, placed his hands beneath her buttocks, and lowered his head.

"Oh God!" Hope gasped, then began panting again. Faster. Harder. Until she shattered beneath him.

He drew her into his arms, brushing strands of hair from her damp cheeks. And froze. Jeez, had he hurt her? He held her at arm's length and studied her face. "What's wrong?"

Hope shook her head. "It's never...I've never..." She took a deep breath and grinned. "Wow."

"Wow, huh?" He laughed off his worries. It had been a long time since he'd experienced *wow*. He'd like to experience a little *wow* of his own. But then it hit him. He wasn't prepared for *wow*.

"Your turn," she said.

Ben stilled her hand. "I didn't plan for this. I don't have any condoms with me."

Hope flashed him a devilish smile. "I do."

He raised an eyebrow. "Just happened to have some on hand, huh?"

She slipped her hand from under his and ran a finger up and down the length of his penis as she spoke. "I needed to pick up a few things at the pharmacy today, and...well...it is a good idea to be prepared for an emergency."

He eyed his throbbing cock. "So you consider this an emergency?"

Her entire hand replaced her finger as she continued stroking him. "Wouldn't you?"

Ben sucked in his breath. "Definitely a witch," he muttered.

He slipped from her grasp, stood, and pulled up his pants. Lifting her to her feet, he slipped one arm around her waist, the other behind her knees, raised her into his arms, and carried her down the hall. When they reached the bedroom, he deposited her on the bed. Hands on hips, he leaned over her, eyeing her in the moonlight. "I can't take my eyes off you."

"Forget the eyes. I'd rather have your hands on me. Along with the rest of your body. Preferably naked."

"Hard to resist an offer like that." He stripped off his clothes and joined her on the bed.

Hope sat up and bent over his groin, teasing his penis with puffs of her hot, moist breath and flicking the tip of her tongue against him.

Ben groaned. Grabbing her head between his hands, he urged her lips to take him.

"I've never done this before," she said, coming up for air.

"Could've fooled me."

"Does it feel good?"

He shuddered. "Oh, baby, you have no idea."

She lowered her head once again, but Ben stopped her. "No, you're going to make me lose control."

She laughed. "I'm counting on it."

"Not like this. I want us to come together." He flipped her onto her back. "Where are they?"

Hope pointed to the nightstand.

Ben yanked open the drawer, found the box, and tore open one of the foil packets. Deftly, he sheathed himself, then hovered above her before slowly lowering himself into her.

He withdrew nearly entirely before sliding back inside her. With long, slow strokes he repeated the process, gritting his teeth to maintain a control he was a flicker away from losing. Hope's rapid-fire pelvic thrusts weren't helping—no matter how good they felt. She kept trying to speed things up; he needed a timeout. Ben eased away from her. "In a hurry?"

Wide-eyed she shook her head and fought for breath. "Yes! I mean no. Oh, God, Ben, I can't think straight with what you're doing to me! Please!" She reached up and grabbed his shoulders, lowering him back onto her.

Enough torture. He sank back inside her and increased his momentum to a four-legged mattress rock and roll that sent them both hurling into The Land of the Big O.

~*~

Later, propped up against the headboard, Ben watched Hope sleep. So much for slow old-fashioned courtships, he thought, stroking her hair. The silky strands, kissed by the waning moonlight, slipped through his fingers. He liked the shimmering highlights she'd added. He liked everything about her—including her dogged determination to go after her heart's desire—even if he thought she was nuts to want him.

He reached for the box of condoms. Studying them in the dim light, he chuckled softly. *Chocolate-flavored condoms!* Had she chosen them for him or herself, he wondered. "What am I going to do with you, Hope Morgan?"

Beneath his arm, he felt her stir. Her eyes fluttered open. "Ben? Is something wrong?"

The understatement of the year. No matter how good she made him feel, whether he loved her or not, in his heart he was still convinced Hope was better off without him. Only how could he give her up after tonight? She'd never leave willingly, and he'd cut out his own heart sooner than deliberately hurt her. "I have to leave."

She rolled to her side, removing the leg draped across his thigh. "What time is it?"

"Late. Nearly three."

"I wish you could stay."

"You know that's not possible." He tossed the quilt aside. Swinging his legs over the side of the bed, he reached for his boxers.

She stroked his back, leaning her cheek against his shoulder blade. "I know."

He stepped into the shorts, standing to pull them up over his hips. He was hard again—with just the touch of her hand on his back. He glanced at the box of condoms, knowing several remained, but hesitated. No. If he didn't leave now, he'd never leave. Grabbing the rest of his clothes, he headed for the bathroom.

When he reappeared a moment later, fully dressed, he found Hope standing in the middle of the bedroom. She had donned her robe and turned on the bedside lamp. Ben cradled her cheeks with his palms and placed a chaste kiss on her forehead. "Go back to bed, sweetheart."

"I'll walk you to the door." She draped her arm around his waist. With her head leaning against his shoulder, they headed for the living room.

THIRTY-FIVE

I leaned my forehead against the cool pane of the front window. As I watched the receding taillights of Ben's car disappear around the corner, my body thrummed from the vibrations of the air conditioner humming away in the adjacent window.

Or did I tingle from hours of lovemaking? I had never felt so loved, so wanted. How could Ben think what we'd shared was wrong for me? Yet, he did. I saw it in his eyes before he left, saw the doubt written across his features. He didn't think he was good enough for me. He thought he'd wind up hurting me. And deeper down, he thought I'd wind up hurting him and the boys. No matter how many times I protested to the contrary, Ben, pig-headed, stubborn man that he was, thought he knew what was best for all of us.

And according to this self-appointed arbiter of my love life and future happiness, he wasn't it.

I may have won the first skirmish, but the war to knock sense into Ben Schaffer was going to be long and hard fought. But worth every bloody battle. If nothing else, I knew my heart, and that heart told me we belonged together.

I turned to head back to the bedroom, pausing to pick up the mail scattered on the braided rug in front of the couch. At some point one of us must have kicked the piles of bills and junk mail off the coffee table. I resorted the envelopes and carried the two stacks into the kitchen. Dropping the important envelopes on the table, I tossed the junk mail in the paper recycling bag I kept next to the refrigerator.

"I'll deal with it tomorrow," I mumbled to myself, the words fighting over a yawn as I traipsed off to bed. "Ben and bills. I'll figure everything out tomorrow. Like Scarlett O'Hara."

~*~

Five hours later I sat at the kitchen table staring at the bottom entry in my checkbook. With a grimace I glanced at the stack of envelopes piled neatly in front of me, knowing without looking inside any of them that the total sum of what I owed far exceeded the meager balance in my checking account.

"Looks like another month of minimum payments and loan shark bank fees," I grumbled to the credit card statements lurking in the pile. "At this rate I'll get out of debt just in time to retire. And with my luck Social Security will have gone belly-up decades before."

I tore open the envelopes one by one, sorting the bills into three stacks—utilities, credit cards, and the one non-government college loan that didn't come with the traditional six-month grace period. I'd take care of the gas, electric, and phone first. Thanks to my Mary Poppins stint, I hadn't spent much time in my own apartment. So at least those bills were minimal.

After adding up the damage on my pocket calculator, I stared at the LED display. I had enough to get me through until next payday. Barely. Thanks to succumbing to mall temptation, but I blamed that on Ben. His car automatically headed for one of the three local malls whenever I had any time to myself.

I rose to refill my coffee cup and spied one remaining unopened envelope lying face down on the table. Crap! I tore open the envelope, removed the lone sheet of paper, and stared in puzzlement. This wasn't a bill. And it wasn't the political solicitation I'd originally assumed when I consigned the letter to the recycling pile yesterday.

I sank back into the chair and read the short letter several times.

Dear Ms. Morgan,

As you are most likely aware from recent media coverage, our office, in conjunction with the attorneys general of several other states, is conducting an investigation into the illegal trafficking of human eggs. According to insurance information obtained through a search warrant of the fertility clinic where you were treated, we believe you may be one of the victims of this crime.

In order to expedite our investigation, we would like to send one of our attorneys to Butler County to ask you some questions regarding your experiences while under the care of Dr. Anthony Wolfowitz. Please contact this office at your earliest convenience so that we may set up a time that is mutually agreeable.

Sincerely,
Lawrence J. Piedmont
Assistant District Attorney for the Borough of Manhattan

I tossed the letter on the table. Fertility problems? Not me. Faith was the Morgan sister with fertility problems. I was her solution. Not that it made any difference in the end. Faith was dead, and so was the baby I'd given her. Lawrence J. Piedmont had his facts mixed up. I'd call his office tomorrow morning to explain.

Unless there was no mix-up. I read the letter again. Donor egg harvesting wasn't covered under my insurance. Or Faith's. She paid the fertility clinic directly for my procedure. No claim should have been filed. But the procedure would have been covered if Faith had her own eggs harvested for in vitro. The D.A. must be investigating Dr. Wolfowitz and the clinic for insurance fraud.

The scumbag! No wonder insurance coverage was sky high. Faith and Dwayne had depleted their life's savings and hocked their future to pay that man, but it obviously wasn't enough for the greedy bastard. I shoved the letter into my purse. I'd call Lawrence J. Piedmont, Esquire from work tomorrow and offer him whatever assistance I could. It was the least I could do in Faith's memory.

I spent the remainder of Sunday waiting for a call from Ben— a call that never came.

~*~

Butterflies the size of pterodactyls dive-bombed in my stomach as I stood in front of the office entrance Monday morning. My life had changed dramatically in the six weeks since I'd last stepped through the double glass doors on the fifth floor of the former warehouse. Marion was gone. Ben and I were now lovers. How would he react to me on the job? How should I react to him?

And why hadn't I heard from him since he left my apartment in the wee hours of Sunday morning?

I'd never had a lover, much less one that was also my boss, but I'd heard more than enough about the downside of office romances. The Dorfman-Hewitt mess was never far from Ben's mind. He managed to bring it up every time he launched into one of his we-shouldn't-get-involved lectures. I was tired of hearing about Chuck Dorfman, his vengeful secretary, and the lawsuit destroying Ben's biggest competitor.

Nerves or no nerves, I couldn't stand in the hallway forever. *Here goes nothing. Or everything.* I pushed opened the door.

"Hey! Welcome back, Hope." Tony was the first to greet me. The gangly computer guru waved both arms from across the room.

Paco, Nigel, and Freddie followed suit with an equally effusive greeting. Zeke, his nose buried in papers spread across his desk, mumbled a hello without glancing up. No one else had made it into the office yet. I headed for my drawing board.

As the day progressed, the first thing I noticed was the lack of the tension that permeated the loft before Marion's departure. The second was Zeke's coolness toward me. The third was Ben's absence. Knowing how Zeke had tried to thwart any relationship between Ben and me, I guess I shouldn't have been puzzled by his attitude. But where was Ben?

"He's pitching up in Westchester County," said Winnie when I worked up the courage to ask her. "Big one."

That small bit of information offered me a heaping dose of reassurance. From having lived under the same roof as Ben for six weeks, I knew the man became totally obsessed before a presentation. Making a good impression at those initial meetings meant the difference between an offer to submit a proposal and a thanks-but-no-thanks handshake. Pitching had everything to do with marketing and very little to do with talent.

And marketing had been Marion's forte, not Ben's. As aloof as the former Mrs. Ben Schaffer had appeared in the office, she apparently had a knack for winning over clients. Ben was a behind-the-scenes guy, far more comfortable at his drawing board or computer than in a boardroom. Under the circumstances, I now understood why he hadn't called. He'd probably spent every available moment on Sunday preparing for the meeting.

During my nanny stint, the rest of the team had finished up the preliminaries on the Woodmere Resort project. I arrived back in time to begin my part of the campaign, a dozen detailed renderings of the interiors and exterior, based on the computer-generated prototypes designed by Ben, Paco, Nigel, and Freddie. By five o'clock I was nearly done with the first of the watercolors.

"Quitting time," said Winnie, bending over the drawing board to inspect my work. "Hmm. Nice. Maybe after it's built the client will treat us all to a weekend. Doesn't look like a place I could afford otherwise."

"You and me both." The pricey Woodmere Resort, to be located in The Berkshire Mountains of Massachusetts, would cater to celebrities and the elite of New York and Boston. All others need not bother calling ahead for reservations.

I scanned the room. Zeke, Winnie, and I were the only ones remaining in the loft. "Go ahead. I'll lock up if Zeke wants to leave. I only have about an hour's worth of work left on this. Might as well finish it up tonight and start fresh on another one tomorrow."

"Suit yourself. Just don't forget to go home. I don't want to walk in tomorrow morning and find you asleep at your drawing board."

I waved her off. "Don't worry." But the truth was, I had no desire to rush back to my empty apartment.

I also wanted to speak privately to Zeke. I couldn't continue to ignore his hostile vibes. When he was forced to speak to me, his words were curt, his body language stiff. Zeke had been friendly and encouraging when I first began work at Schaffer-Merrick, but after the first few days, I'd noticed a change. At first, I chalked it up to my overactive and sleep-deprived imagination as I struggled to finish the Scarpetta watercolors. Now I knew his behavior had nothing to do with my own paranoia.

He had no right to transfer his hostility toward Marion onto me. I wasn't Marion, and history wasn't going to repeat itself. Besides, my relationship with Ben was none of his business. Better to confront him on his change of attitude and get it out in the open before it festered and boiled over.

I pushed away from my drawing board, squared my shoulders, and walked across the room to his desk. "I'd like to speak with you."

He lifted his head and glowered at me. "I'm busy."

I glanced at the newspaper spread open across his desk. He was working a crossword puzzle! "Poinsettias."

"What?"

"Forty-one across." I tapped the paper with my index finger. "Christmas flowers. The answer is poinsettias."

"I tried that. It doesn't fit."

"It does if you spell it correctly." I picked up a pencil and inserted the word. "Now everything else will fall into place. Thirty-four down is—"

Zeke yanked the pencil from my hand. "I know what thirty-four down is." He scribbled in the five-letter word, then quickly filled in the remaining blanks. "You think you have all the answers, don't you?"

His animosity rocked me. "No, I don't, but now that you're no longer busy, I'd like to find a few." I placed my hands on my hips and returned his glare. No way was I going to let this man intimidate me. "What the hell's eating you?"

Zeke slammed his fist on the desk. "You want to know what's eating me? You are!"

"Me?" I stepped back, shaken by the venom in his tone. "What have I done to you?"

"You're messing with my best friend's head, and I don't like it. He's been through enough, damn it! Stay away from him."

I couldn't believe my ears. "What gives you the right—?"

"Friendship gives me the right." His voice shook with anger. A thick blue vein throbbed at the side of his head. "That fucked up basket case he was married to nearly destroyed him. I'll be damned if I'll give you the opportunity to finish the job."

"Who the hell appointed you emperor?" Every muscle in my body trembled with rage. "My relationship with Ben is none of your goddamn business."

He leaned across the desk, sticking his face inches from mine. "I'm making it my business. We both know you're not going to stick around, Hope." I opened my mouth to protest, but he cut me off with a sneer. "You'll be bored with him and his kids in less than six months. He knows it, too. He's just too far gone and pathetic to do anything about it."

His words burned like acid. Tears stung my eyes, but I refused to give him the satisfaction of seeing me reduced to a sniveling ninny. "You don't know anything about me. I love Ben. And his sons. I'd never hurt them."

"You already have!"

"That's enough, Zeke!" I spun around to find Ben standing in the doorway. Fists clenched, he glared at his friend. "Clear out."

"Ben—"

"Now, Zeke, before I forget that we're friends."

Zeke shot me one parting glare before heading for the exit. "I'm doing this for you, man." He grabbed Ben's arm.

Ben jerked from his touch. "I know. It's what's keeping me from firing you. Now get out of here."

Zeke pushed open one of the glass doors and strode from the office. Ben stared after him. I slumped against Zeke's desk, still trembling from the altercation.

"What are you doing here?" he asked, striding across the room toward me. Anger clouded his face. Annoyance peppered his words.

I froze, uncertain how to react or what to say. "I had work I wanted to finish up." Forcing one foot in front of the other, I made my way back to my drawing board. Standing beside my workstation, I lifted a brush from the water jar, swished it back and forth, then wiped it on a paper towel. I heard Ben follow me, felt him hovering behind me.

He reached over, removed the paintbrush from my hand, and added it to the can of brushes on the workstation. With his other hand he scooped aside the hair that draped over my shoulder. "I've missed you," he said, bending to nuzzle my neck.

I laughed as I spun around and fell into his arms. My body shook so hard that I lost my balance and nearly sent us both tumbling to the floor.

He steadied us by grabbing onto the edge of my drawing board. "What the hell's so funny?"

I shook my head and gulped in some air. "I was so...oh, Ben, I was so worried. When you didn't call, I thought you were having second thoughts, and then after what Zeke said—"

He clasped his hands on either side of my face and stared into my eyes. "Zeke had no right to say what he did to you. He acted out of guilt."

"Guilt? I don't understand."

"Twelve years ago, Zeke saw through Marion the moment he met her. He tried to warn me. When I refused to listen, he held his peace rather than risk our friendship. He blames his silence for my mistake."

"And he's afraid history is repeating itself with you and me. He accused me of being just like Marion. He said I'd leave and hurt you and the boys just as badly."

"I know. I heard."

I wrapped my arms around his waist. "I love you, Ben. I could never leave you. Not in six months or six years or sixty."

"I know that, too, but I fought it, thinking I knew what was best for you. The truth is, I still don't have any answers, Hope. I don't know what to do about you. About us. I can't see into the future."

"None of us can, but you can't stop living because you once made the wrong decision."

"And I can't keep listening to Zeke. I made a mistake a long time ago. It was a whopper, and it had far-reaching consequences, but hearing Zeke tear into you just now made me realize that he still thinks I'm that same person."

"And destined to repeat the same mistakes for the rest of your life?"

"Hell no. Zeke needs to realize you're nothing like Marion. That I'd never be drawn to another Marion. Not after what I've lived through."

THIRTY-SIX

"How did your meeting go?" Hope asked, as they sat at the approach to the Lincoln Tunnel. As usual, traffic was backed up for blocks. Impatient drivers on either side of Ben's Lexus voiced their frustration with blasts of their car horns, despite the sign warning of steep fines for honking.

"I can never read those stuffed shirts. Who knows what they're thinking behind their phony smiles and cursory nods?" He inched the Lexus up a few feet. "Marion was the people person of the firm, not me. She was always so much better at the politics involved in charming and winning over clients. I've been thinking maybe I should have Winnie start searching for a marketing person to replace her."

Hope chuckled.

"What's so funny?"

"It's just that I can't picture Marion as a people person, much less a charmer. If what you say is true, your ex-wife's a regular chameleon."

"Yeah. A goddamn chameleon. Too bad she never saw fit to use any of that charm on her own kids."

Hope reached across the console and placed her hand on his thigh. "How are they doing?"

"They miss you."

"It's only been two days."

He covered her hand with his. "Come home with me. Have dinner with us."

"That's hardly fair to your housekeeper."

"Nonsense. Fritzi always prepares more than enough dinner to accommodate an extra mouth."

"You're sure she wouldn't mind?"

Ben squeezed her hand. "Trust me. She won't mind." He turned to look at her, this woman he shouldn't want as much as he did.

"Hmm...decisions, decisions."

"Oh? Got a date?"

"With a tuna fish sandwich. The question is, do I give that up for you and the boys and a home-cooked meal? Maybe I should toss a coin."

"Maybe you should stop being a little tease and just say yes."

She stared at the traffic, her face pensive. "Under one condition."

"What's that?"

She shifted in her seat, turning her body to confront him. "When we get back to the house, you call Zeke and try to straighten things out with him. I don't want him blaming me for coming between the two of you."

"That's so like you. Always thinking of others, always putting everyone else's needs before your own."

"That's not exactly true."

"Isn't it?"

Her mouth twitched into a smile. "Of course not. I got you, didn't I?"

~*~

The triplets attacked them—or rather Hope—as she and Ben walked through the front door.

"Hope!"

"Hope!"

"Hope's here!"

Ben stood to the side of the foyer and watched as his sons ran to his lover. His heart swelled three sizes as he watched the way Hope greeted the boys. Kneeling to their level, she held out her arms and swept them into a group hug. The hallway echoed with the sound of her laughter. Tears gathered behind Ben's eyes. Try as he might, he couldn't recall a single memory of Marion hugging her children, let alone acting overjoyed to see them.

"Don't like her much, do they?" A Serving spoon in hand, a smile playing at the corners of her mouth, Fritzi leaned against the kitchen door, observing the commotion. "Maybe I should be jealous?"

Ben navigated his way around the tangle of bodies sprawled on the Oriental runner and wrapped his arm around his housekeeper. "Not to worry. You're irreplaceable, and you damn well know it." He planted an affectionate kiss on her cheek.

She blushed twelve shades of red as she playfully hit his arm with the spoon. "Flatterer! Where've you been? Dinner was ready ages ago. Go get everyone washed up."

"Yes, ma'am." Ben turned back to the melee and clapped his hands. "Okay, men. You're going to hug the stuffing out of Hope.

Go wash your hands for dinner."

"Can Hope stay for suppa?" asked Woody. With a worried expression on his face, he glanced up first at Fritzi, then his father.

"Of course," answered the housekeeper. "You think we're going to make her stand and watch while we eat?"

Woody broke out in a belly laugh. Scrambling to his feet, he headed for the powder room, his brothers close on his heels. Chuckling, Ben followed them down the hall.

THIRTY-SEVEN

"'Bout time we had some laughter in this place," mumbled Fritzi, her short, compact body hustling back into the kitchen.

I followed her. "Can I help with anything?"

Fritzi shook a head of tightly permed, light brown curls as she slipped on a pair of oven mitts. "Everything's been done for over an hour. Sure hope dinner isn't ruined." She opened the oven door and peered inside. "I was just about to give up and feed the boys and myself."

I'd taken an immediate liking to Fritzi Fitzgerald when we briefly met upon her return Saturday morning. "We were stuck in traffic at the entrance to the tunnel."

She eyed me over her shoulder. "And he forgot how to use his cell phone?"

I felt my cheeks flame, but the rush of heat had nothing to do with the open oven door. "I don't think he realized the time."

"Mind on other things, huh?" She winked before turning her

attention back to the oven. With a loud grunt, she removed a large roasting pan and set it on the stove burners. "He drove into the city today?"

"Ben was up in Westchester at a prospective client's most of the day." I reached for a serving spoon and dish. As Fritzi lifted the leg of lamb from the pan and placed it on a carving board, I spooned the parsleyed new potatoes and baby carrots into the dish.

"Ah, that explains his rotten mood all day yesterday. Wanted to kick him out of the house, I did. Told him he should go see you." She turned and shook the carving knife at me. "Might've put a smile on that sour puss of his."

My mouth dropped open.

Fritzi chuckled. "Don't act so surprised, missy. You think I couldn't tell the moment I walked in this house day before yesterday?"

"But I...I mean we...never...hadn't..."

Fritzi offered me a smug smile before she turned her attention back to the lamb. After carving a few slices in silence her eyes misted over. Her voice took on a dreamy quality. "Had over thirty years of happiness with my saintly husband before I lost him. When that man looked at me, his eyes would sparkle with a special light. Always set my heart to dancing."

"Ben isn't sure we're not making a big mistake."

Fritzi shifted her attention back to me. "A man can utter insincere words of love till the cows come home. He can plaster a phony smile across his lips and pledge his undying devotion till he's blue in the face, but believe me, missy, there's no way on God's green earth he can fake that special look."

"What are you telling me, Fritzi?"

"I'm saying, I see that same fire in Ben's eyes whenever he looks at you." She paused, her clear blue gaze studied me for a moment before she continued. "And I never saw it when he looked at his missus."

Before I had time to mull over Fritzi's words, Ben herded the boys back into the kitchen.

Throughout dinner, in-between the flying conversations, the spilt milk, and the laughter, I stole quick glances in Ben's direction. Each time I caught a tender look on his face, a unique sparkle in his eye. After each quick peek I heard Fritzi clear her throat. Finally, I turned to her.

"Convinced?" she asked.

"Eat your carrots," said Ben, pointing to Teddy's plate. "About what?" He glanced at Fritzi.

"I don't like cawwots," said Teddy.

"Yes, you do," I said. "You ate carrot soufflé last week when I made it."

"That was cawwots?" Scotty's voice rose several octaves in indignation.

"But that was good," said Woody, joining Teddy's protest. "This is just yucky cawwots."

"Eat," said Ben. He swung his head around to face Fritzi. "Convinced about what?"

Fritzi offered him a pleasant smile. "Girl talk. Doesn't concern you."

"I'm beginning to sense a conspiracy," he said.

"What's a 'spiwacy?" asked Scotty.

"You and your brothers refusing to eat your veggies. Now finish up or no dessert."

As if choreographed, the three boys sighed in unison, each

spearing a carrot and offering it a frown and a *yuck* before slipping the fork into their mouths. They repeated the exaggerated act until all three plates were empty.

"I want Hope to wead us our stowy tonight," said Woody, crossing his arms over his chest.

Ben glanced at me. "My punishment for making them eat their vegetables. What do you say?"

"I suppose it could be arranged."

"Huh?" Puzzlement clouded Teddy's face.

I laughed. "Yes, I'll read to you. Who gets to pick the book tonight?"

"It's my turn," said Woody.

~*~

After dinner the triplets staged a rebellion, refusing to take their bath unless I bathed them. "Can I put in for overtime?" I asked Ben as I ran the water in the massive claw foot tub.

"You could say no."

I glanced over at the boys. Seated on the tile floor between us, they busily worked at untying and removing their sneakers. "Never." I tweaked Woody's scrunched up nose. The child, his head bent in concentration, was working out a knot in his lace. "Need help?"

"I gots it!" He offered up a huge grin of accomplishment, kicked the shoe off, and stood to pull down his shorts.

One by one Ben lifted the naked little boys into the tub and stood back to watch as I handed them each a washcloth and bar of soap. "Don't forget behind the ears."

"We won't," said Scotty, lathering his belly.

"And necks," added Teddy.

"Yes, necks, too," I said.

When the children were scrubbed to my satisfaction, I rinsed them off. Wrapping each little body in a large towel, Ben lifted them out of the tub and rubbed them dry. "Now go get into your PJ's" he said.

"And then a stowy?" asked Woody.

"And then a story," I said.

Bundled in navy blue terrycloth, the boys scampered down the hall to their room. Ben and I followed.

"Wait." He reached for my hand, drew me into his arms and lowered his head until our lips nearly met. "You're wonderful. Then he kissed me. Hard and deep but not nearly long enough.

"This one," said Woody, tugging at my skirt.

"Oops!" I quickly stepped out of Ben's arms, but Woody appeared oblivious to the heated embrace. Dressed in a one-piece blue sleeper decorated with Donald Duck and his nephews, he held up a book. I took the slim volume from his hands and stared at the title—*Are You My Mother?*

THIRTY-EIGHT

Ben leaned against the doorway and listened as Hope read to his sons. She had settled on the floor, her back propped against Scotty's footboard. Woody sat in her lap. Scotty and Teddy, sprawled on the carpet on either side of her, nestled their heads against her thighs.

He wondered how much of a coincidence Woody's choice of book had been. Were three-year-olds capable of devious ulterior motives? His sons were bright. He never doubted that for an instant, but was Woody perceptive enough to formulate a message of double meaning in his choice of reading matter? Ben had always thought Scotty, with his probing questions and leadership qualities, the smartest of the triplets. Woody certainly surprised him this evening.

Ben studied the shy, sensitive tyke. With his thumb firmly ensconced in his mouth, he hung on every word Hope read.

When Hope came to the last page, the boys, their lids heavy with sleep, climbed into their beds without complaint. Ben tucked them in, hugging and kissing each boy, then watched as Hope did the same. He turned off the light and together they walked from the room. "Go on," he said at the top of the steps. "I'll be down in a minute."

He watched Hope descend the stairs, then quietly walked back to the boys' bedroom. Standing in the shadows, he listened to the whispered conversation taking place.

"Daddy kissed Hope," said Woody.

"Good," said Scotty.

"When's Hope gonna be our new mommy?" asked Teddy.

"Weal soon," said Scotty.

Ben slumped against the wall and closed his eyes. "Shit." He loved Hope, but he refused to saddle her with instant motherhood, no matter how much she cared for his sons. Zeke was right about one thing. He came with too much baggage for her. Maybe for anyone. If the burden began to overwhelm her and she left, she'd hurt the boys far worse than their mother had. They knew Marion didn't love them. And they were smart enough to realize Hope did. For now.

Ben crept back downstairs. His life would be a hell of a lot easier if Hope Morgan had turned out to be a nasty bitch with a huge wart on the end of her nose.

Ben felt himself slipping back into the indecision that had plagued him from the moment he first admitted his feelings about Hope to himself. And Zeke. Who should he believe, his best friend who'd known him for years and tried to warn him against Marion? Or Hope, who claimed she'd love him and his sons forever? His heart, which had failed him once? Or his head, which told him this relationship was neither in her best interest or that of his children?

And why, after everything he'd said to her earlier, did he

continue to fight the best thing that had ever walked into his life? The questions stopped him cold in his tracks.

"Is something wrong, Ben? Did you speak to Zeke?"

Hope's concern-filled questions drifted up the staircase and smacked him upside his head. What had he been thinking? How could he consider giving her up? The mere sound of her voice turned him on. He'd been hard since he kissed her. Hell, if he were going to be honest with himself, he'd been hard from almost the moment he first laid eyes on her.

Descending the last few steps, he reached for her hand and dragged her toward the door. What he had in mind was best left for the privacy of her apartment. "The hell with Zeke. Let's get out of here."

Minutes later, after telling Fritzi he was leaving to take Hope home, Ben drove them silently down the quiet streets. One hand gripped the steering wheel; the other locked on Hope's thigh. Sexual tension filled the car. His. Hers. His need had taken on a life of its own. Hope's slightly trembling thigh muscle and her occasional glance in his direction communicated her own need. She laced her fingers with his and squeezed his hand.

Five minutes later, he pulled the Lexus into the small parking lot behind her building. They climbed the stairs to the third floor, and before she could unlock her apartment door, Ben pinned her up against the wall of the dimly lit landing.

When their lips parted for air, she smiled, a devilish twinkle playing in her eyes. "Déjà vu?"

Ben grinned. "Worked before. Why mess with success." He kissed her hard as he pulled her skirt up over her thigh. Hope thrust her pelvis toward him and sucked his lower lip between her teeth as she reached for his zipper.

Ben tore his mouth away from hers and stilled his movements. Her eyes sprung open. "Don't stop."

"Don't close your eyes. I want to see them when you come."

She nodded. As they stared at each other, his fingers engaged in Mission G-Spot.

Hope squirmed.

"More?"

She bit her lower lip and nodded.

He sped up his pace. "Faster?"

She gulped. "Stop teasing me."

"Say it."

"Faster." Her voice whimpered.

Ben paused. "I can't hear you."

Her pupils widened. "Faster," she cried between gulps of air.

Ben raised an eyebrow as he went back to work on her. "Like this?"

"Oh, God!" Her eyes glazed. Her gulps grew to short pants, the pants to groans as she rode his hand until finally, with a loud moan, her body grew rigid, then limp in his arms.

"Wow. Again," she said, trying to catch her breath. "You should patent those magic fingers of yours."

He withdrew his hand and grinned at her. "Enjoy yourself?"

She grinned back at him. "Give me a minute to land back on earth. Then it's your turn."

He nodded toward the staircase. "Maybe we should go inside. I may be a bit more vocal than you were."

She arched her brows and scowled at him. "What? I wasn't loud enough for you?"

"Apparently not loud enough for Minnie to hear over her TV."

"Or maybe she's got her ear to the door, waiting to hear more."

"Not Minnie. She would have opened the door to watch, phone in hand so she could give Winnie a blow-by-blow description."

"Speaking of which..." Hope unlocked her door and dragged him inside.

They never made it to the bedroom. Again. But this time they didn't even make it to the couch. Kicking off her shoes, Hope dropped to her knees and reached for his belt buckle. "I don't get to sit down?" he asked.

She lifted her chin and smirked at him. "You made me stand."

"You weren't exactly standing on your own if I remember correctly."

Her eyes sparked a challenge as she pulled his pants down around his ankles. "Don't be a wuss, Schaffer."

"I'm not a—" Ben swallowed the rest of his sentence as Hope sucked him into her mouth. What her lips and tongue and mouth did next blew more than his mind. Yet, as incredible the experience, when she released him and rocked back on her heels, and he sank to his knees, she'd only whet his appetite. Within moments he was rock hard again. Even at eighteen he'd never recovered that quickly. Either Hope definitely was a witch, or his body was trying its damnedest to make up for three years of solo sex.

Ben lowered them onto the braided rug. One moment they were tearing off each other's clothes; the next moment he was inside her, fucking her as though his life depended on it. And maybe it did.

She came quickly. Her clenched muscles continuing to pulse around him for several moments after he exploded inside her. He figured Hope had some catching up to do, too. He wasn't complaining. There was something very arousing about a woman who came within moments of him entering her. Which probably explained why he wasn't as limp as he should be, even after coming twice in less than ten minutes.

Still, she probably would have preferred something a bit longer than a blitzkrieg quickie. As they lay unmoving, catching their breaths, he offered her an apology. "I'm sorry. I don't know what came over me."

She twisted to face him and swatted his bare chest. "Don't you dare apologize for the most incredible experience of my life, Ben Schaffer!"

He grinned. "It was pretty spectacular, wasn't it?"

"Magnificent."

"Extraordinary."

"Stupendous."

Except suddenly Ben thought of something, something he probably would have remembered had he been thinking with his brain and not his dick, something he would have remembered had they made it to the bedroom. "Sonofabitch," he muttered. "I don't believe it. What the hell was I thinking?"

Hope's eyes grew wide. She sat up. "Damn you! Don't you dare start. Not now. Don't ruin it with another one of your you-deserve-better, I-come-with-too-much-baggage lectures. Not tonight."

He ran his hand along her spine, stroking her back. "No." Sighing, he sat up and planted a kiss on the top of her head. "I'm through fighting my feelings for you. I think I pretty much proved that a few minutes ago, didn't I?" But now he had a new worry. And a two-ton lump of concrete weighing down his chest. *Sometimes, Schaffer, you can be such a fucking idiot.*

Hope's eyes filled with worry. "Then why do I see fear written all over your face?"

He shook his head. "Because you and I just had unprotected sex. Things between us are complicated enough. We don't need an unwanted pregnancy added to the mix."

She turned away from him but not before he saw the tears pooling in her lower lids. "We don't have to worry about that."

Her words pried the concrete off his chest. "You've started taking the pill?"

She shook her head and turned back to him but kept her eyes closed. "No."

"That patch thing?"

"I'm not using any birth control, Ben."

The concrete slammed back onto his chest. "Then how can you say we don't have to worry? Damn it, Hope, we acted like reckless teenagers."

She inhaled sharply. "When I told you about the fire, I didn't tell you everything."

Pulling her knees up to her chest, she wrapped her arms around her legs and lowered her head. Her eyes remained closed as she continued speaking. "The explosion hurled me into the front yard. I spent three days in a coma. When I woke up, the doctors told me I'd suffered massive internal injuries. They removed my spleen and...and several other organs." She opened her eyes and stared into his. "I have no female plumbing, Ben. I can't have children. Ever."

Ben bit back his anger. Life was so fucking unfair. Hope was a woman who should have a passel of rugrats scampering around her legs, yet she'd never have even one. He didn't know what to say to her. So he chose not to say anything. No words could ease the pain he saw in her face. Instead, he drew her into his arms and kissed away a stray tear that dribbled down her cheek. Then he rose, pulled her to her feet, and led her down the hall to the bathroom.

He pulled a clean bath towel from the rack and placed it on the commode lid. "Sit," he said.

"What are we doing in here?"

He leaned over the tub and twisted the spigots. As water gushed from the faucet, the room fill with steam. "Ever since I saw you bathing the boys this evening, I've had this incredible fantasy. You. Me. A tub. And this." He reached for the bottle of bubble bath sitting on the edge of the tub and squirted a generous amount under the stream of water.

~*~

Once again, at three in the morning he left her bed. Reluctantly.

THIRTY-NINE

When the early morning commuter train to New York pulled into Garwood station the next day, Ben was standing on the metal platform of one of the cars, waiting for me to board.

"You never spoke with Zeke, did you?" I asked after we found two empty seats.

He shook his head. "I'll take care of it this morning. Don't worry. Zeke will come around. He's just worried about me."

"He hates me, Ben."

"No." He patted my hand. "Actually, he likes you very much."

Right. "He has a funny way of showing it."

"Trust me."

We didn't speak much the remainder of the train ride. I had a feeling Ben was trying to convince himself of the assurance he'd offered me. Once in the city, we walked hand-in-hand through the crowded streets toward the office. Ben remained deep in thought, his brow creased with worry lines. A block from the loft he steered me into Bagel Bob's, directing me to an empty table at the back of the shop. "Wait for me here."

"But—"

He bent down and placed his index finger against my lips. "Trust me."

Several minutes later he reappeared with Zeke in tow. From my seat in the corner, I watched them approach. Ben's face was set in stern determination. Zeke wore an expression of annoyance.

"Sit," Ben ordered his friend as they arrived at the table. Zeke glared at him, but he pulled the chair out from under the table and complied. "Now start talking. Both of you. I'm going to get us some coffee." He glanced at his watch. "We're not leaving here until this is resolved. Understood?"

"Come on, Ben!"

"I mean it, Zeke. We'll stay all day if that's what it takes. You're my best friend. I love Hope. She's not Marion. I don't want you to accept that grudgingly. I want you to understand why I feel the way I do about her. Now start talking." He stalked over to the counter.

Zeke grunted and grumbled something under his breath, but he did start talking. This time instead of blowing up at me, he began to explain in painful detail how he had reluctantly sat by and watched Marion manipulate Ben from the moment they met. "Because of his childhood, Ben was starved for love. Because of hers, Marion was starved for love, acceptance, and attention. She gave him just enough of what he craved to keep him constantly fawning over her.

"He began to worship her, and she drank it up. Right from the beginning the entire relationship was constructed on an unstable foundation, but he didn't see it. I recognized it, but I was powerless to stop him. All I could do was hang back and watch, knowing someday he'd wake up and need me. Only by the time that happened, it was too late."

Throughout his monologue I sat with both my hands and my mouth firmly clasped. When he paused, I jumped in. "I understand your apprehension, and I appreciate your concern and love for Ben, but you have no right to project your feelings for Marion onto me."

"Don't I? Ben has a history of being attracted to the wrong type of women."

This was going well. *Not.* I reigned in my contempt and kept my voice passive. Well, as passive as possible under the circumstances. "One mistake doesn't make for a history. He was young and naïve."

"And still is."

This time I couldn't keep the snicker from escaping. I placed my hands on the table and leaned forward. "Is that your professional opinion, *Doctor*?"

He mimicked my move, his face coming within inches of mine. "Yeah, it is. I listen to my gut, and my gut's telling me history is repeating itself."

"You're not much of a friend if you don't give Ben credit for learning from his mistakes."

"I give Ben plenty of credit. I've known him a hell of a lot longer than you have."

"Then maybe you're too close to the situation to be objective about it. Or me. Marion was a victim. Her personality was shaped by circumstances beyond her control. She never had a chance. You tell me alarm bells went off in you the moment you met her. Can you honestly look me in the eye and see any of the warning signs you saw in her? Can you honestly tell me that there's *anything* in my personality, *anything* you've observed, that Marion and I have in common?"

Zeke stared at me for the longest time, as if trying to find some similarity that would prove his theory. Finally, he shook his head. "No, I guess not."

Score Round One for me. "Look, I'm no psychologist, but if you ask me, your guilt over what happened to Ben has made you paranoid and overprotective."

Zeke grimaced, nodding to Ben as he returned with three cups of coffee. "What you call *paranoid and overprotective*," he said, "I call looking out for a friend."

Ben passed around the coffees, then took a seat. "Pretend I'm not here."

Easy for him to say but I tried. "Ben's a grown man, Zeke. He doesn't need you as his protector. He needs you as his friend."

Zeke pounded his fists on the table. "I am his friend, damn it! Everything I've ever done has been out of friendship for him."

I frowned at his outburst and cast a quick glance at Ben. He, too, was frowning.

"I'm sorry," Zeke mumbled, lowering his voice. He clamped his hands together on the table and stared at them.

I reached over and placed my palm on top of his tightly clenched fists. "Then prove your friendship. Allow him a second chance."

He raised his head. His eyes held a challenge. "How do I know you won't hurt him?"

I thought for a long moment. "I'm afraid I don't have the answer to that—"

He interrupted me mid-sentence and turned to Ben, "See? What did I tell you?"

I glared at him as I finished my sentence, my voice more forceful. "—any more than you can be certain your wife won't someday hurt you."

Zeke yanked his hands out from under mine. "My wife would never—"

"Don't." I raised my hand to stop his fresh tirade. "Come on, Zeke. No matter how happy we are, no matter how much in love, no one can predict the future. Not you. Not Ben. Not me."

Ben spoke up. "She's got a point there, buddy."

Zeke stared at Ben.

"Admit it," said Ben. "You're no Nostradamus."

"I suppose."

I continued. "If you drive a wedge between us, Zeke, we'll all lose. I want to be your friend, and I don't want Ben to lose you as his."

His icy glare began to melt. His features softened. He nodded at Ben. "Okay. I'll trust your judgment this time. You're right. She's nothing like Marion."

Ben wrapped his arm around my shoulders and grinned. "No, she's not."

"Yeah, Marion would have told me to go fuck myself." Zeke shot me a warning, then spoke directly to Ben. "Just don't prove me wrong. These last few years have been hell, man."

"For all of us."

With a tenuous truce established, the three of us headed back to the office. Ben seemed happy with the outcome, but I couldn't help feeling that Zeke was just waiting for me to slip up. He didn't seem like a man who liked being proven wrong.

~*~

That evening, I again joined Ben for dinner with the boys and

Fritzi. Afterward, Ben and I returned to my apartment, and once again Ben left my bed hours before the sun rose. The pattern continued for the remainder of the week. I began to wonder if it would continue that way for the rest of our lives. Or at least until the triplets went off to college.

~*~

On Saturday we piled the boys into the Lexus and headed for the Jersey shore for a day of romping in the ocean and building sandcastles that brought admiring comments from the scores of other beachgoers. "You're missing a marketing opportunity here," I said after Ben finished sculpting an intricate turret.

He peered over his sunglasses. "How so?"

"Watch." I grabbed a stick and began digging in the sand, forming a large raised rectangular sign.

Ben read out loud. "*Schaffer and Sons, Architects of Distinctive Sandcastles, Shopping Complexes, Resorts, and Office Buildings.*" He chuckled. "Not a bad idea."

"All you need is a strategically placed bucket filled with business cards."

Scotty stared down at the writing in the sand. Pointing to the first word, his face lit up in recognition. "That's my name. Schaffer."

"Very good," said Ben.

"Where's Hope's name?" asked Woody. "She helped, too."

"And deserves equal billing," said Ben. He grabbed the stick from my hand. Kneeling in the sand, he altered the wording.

Morgan, Schaffer, & Sons. I fought back a smile, silently, rolling the words around in my head. Definitely more appealing than Schaffer-Merrick. How long would Ben keep Marion's name attached to the company she'd abandoned? I shielded my eyes from the sun and glanced up at him. His face showed no emotion. Damn those dark sunglasses that kept me from seeing his eyes. And his heart.

FORTY

Sunday morning Ben woke to a trio of bouncing bodies scampering across his bed. Thunder boomed. Lightning crackled. Frightened, the children buried their heads under his blanket and huddled close.

Twisting his body from under the melee, Ben focused bleary eyes on the nightstand clock. Five-forty-five. He'd fallen into bed less than three hours ago. Stifling a groan, he tried to comfort his sons. "Hey, guys. It's just a loud boom. Nothing to be scared of."

"I don't like loud booms," whined Woody. "They hurt my head."

"Me, too," said Teddy and Scotty at the same time.

Yawning, Ben tried to convince his sons to settle down and go back to sleep for a few hours. The boys, wide awake, had other ideas.

"I'm hungwy," said Teddy.

"Me, too."

"And me."

Bowing to the pressures of his sons' imminent starvation, Ben forced his body into a sitting position and reached for his robe. "Okay, let's see what we can find in the kitchen, but keep it down. You'll wake Fritzi."

Ben poured bowls of cereal for each boy, then settled them in front of some obnoxious cartoon before heading back to the kitchen to start a pot of coffee. He had a feeling it was going to be a long day.

By ten o'clock he'd poured two full pots of coffee into his body and was no more awake than four hours earlier. He was also in a bear of a mood from lack of sleep. His nights with Hope were beginning to take their toll. He picked up the phone and called her. "Wake up. I'm having a single parent crisis and need moral support. I also need your body to prop me up. I'm about to fall asleep on my feet."

She laughed. "Are you awake enough to drive?"

"Barely."

Fritzi had left for church at eight-thirty. She had plans to spend the rest of the day with a friend. Ben had no choice but to bundle the boys into their slickers and take them with him to pick up Hope.

When they arrived at her apartment, she shook her head and held out her hand. "Give me the keys. You're in no condition to drive."

Ben didn't argue. Once back at the house, she ordered him to bed.

He slept for nearly five hours.

They spent the remainder of the day playing board games, watching Disney videos, and building LEGO dinosaurs. Shortly before dinner, they lost power. The boys began to whimper about monsters coming to get them. Hope suggested they build a fire and pretend they were camping in the woods—not the brightest of ideas, considering the ninety-degree heat, hundred percent humidity and no air conditioning, but the boys were all for it, so who was he to argue? Once he stoked up a roaring blaze in the library fireplace, they feasted on popcorn, hot dogs, and roasted marshmallows.

When Teddy dropped a sticky marshmallow on the arm of one of the leather chairs, he began to tremble. "I...I'm sowwy. I didn't mean it."

"No big deal," said Hope. Scooping the gooey glob onto her index finger, she popped it into the child's mouth. Teddy's eyes grew wide with astonishment.

Ben didn't have to be a mind reader to know what his son was thinking. Marion would never have allowed the children to eat in the library. Had one of the boys been caught with food in any room other than the kitchen, he would have suffered a blistering lecture and severe punishment. There was no telling how she would have reacted to the gummy mess smeared over the dark green leather chair.

To Hope, Ben realized, the dropped marshmallow was an accident. Nothing more. Grabbing one of the flashlights, she left the room, returning a short time later minus one sticky finger and carrying two damp paper towels. "Want to help?" she asked Teddy, offering one of the towels to him.

Ben watched, not only as she helped Teddy wipe off the chair, but at how Scotty and Woody took in the action from the sidelines. Their mother had always reacted to them with disdain and annoyance. Hope responded with love and guidance. The boys stared in mesmerized fascination.

Thoughts of Marion reminded Ben of the unpleasant situation facing him the next day. He hadn't seen his ex-wife since the night of Scarpetta's dinner party. He had no desire to see her tomorrow, but circumstances deemed otherwise. Thanks to Dr. Leo Bussey.

~*~

Marion arrived nearly forty minutes late for their meeting with assistant district attorney Lawrence J. Piedmont. After waiting twenty minutes past their scheduled time, the lawyer's secretary ushered in his next appointment, thereby keeping Ben and Marion waiting even after Marion's appearance.

"This is ridiculous," she complained, pacing the length of the small anteroom. She glanced down at her watch, something she'd done every two or three minutes since arriving thirty minutes earlier, and impatiently tapped her foot against the worn linoleum. "I'm leaving for Buenos Aires at five. I can't hang around here all day."

"If you'd arrived on time, we'd be done by now," said Ben. "You're not the only person in the world with commitments."

"This entire meeting is a waste of time. I'm only here because of Giovanni's attorney."

"What do you mean?"

"He suggested I might get subpoenaed at a later date if I didn't cooperate now."

A door on the opposite side of the waiting area opened. "You can come in now Mr. and Mrs. Schaffer."

"It's Scarpetta," said Marion, breezing past the secretary as if she owned the place. "Countess Giovanni Scarpetta."

"Sure. Whatever," mumbled the woman, eyeing Ben with puzzlement. She closed the door behind them and commenced with the introductions. "Assistant District Attorney Lawrence J.

Piedmont. Mr. and Mrs..." Marion shot her a supercilious look. "...excuse me. *Countess* Scarpetta and Mr. Schaffer."

"Thank you for coming," said the prosecutor, rising to shake their hands. "Please." He motioned to two chairs in front of his desk.

Ben took one, Marion the other, crossing her legs to expose several inches of smoky gray silk-covered thigh. Ben gritted his teeth.

"Ms. Reeves will be taking notes," said Mr. Piedmont as his secretary settled into a chair off to the side. "Now, I take it you're familiar with the case we're investigating?"

Ben nodded. "You think there might be a possibility that Dr. Bussey stole some of my wife's—"

"Ex-wife," Marion corrected him.

"—some of my *ex-wife's* eggs during her harvesting procedure? And sold them to other patients?"

"That's one of the possible scenarios." He turned to Marion. "Did Dr. Bussey ever mention how many viable eggs he retrieved from you and the number he transplanted after fertilization, Mrs. Schaffer?"

"I am no longer Mrs. Schaffer." Marion leveled an icy glare at the prosecutor. "Please do your best to remember that, Mr. Piedmont."

The lawyer clasped his hands together on his desk and returned her glare. "Forgive me for saying so, ma'am, but most of the couples I've questioned are far more concerned over the possibility that they have children they were unaware of, rather than whether I've addressed them properly." He paused for a moment. "Now, if you don't mind, I'd appreciate an answer to my question."

"Your question is irrelevant," said Marion.

"Excuse me?"

Annoyed by Marion's hostile attitude, Ben cleared his throat and answered for her. "What my ex-wife means, Mr. Piedmont, is, due to a past medical problem, she didn't carry our children. We used the services of a surrogate."

"I see." Piedmont glanced over at his secretary, then back at Marion. He spoke in a level, measured tone as if he were trying to control his temper. Under the circumstances, Ben thought the man was exercising admirable restraint. "Let me rephrase the question then. Did the doctor ever mention the number of eggs he extracted from you as well as the number he implanted in your surrogate?"

"None."

"I don't understand."

Marion exhaled a sigh of impatience. "What's not to understand, Mr. Piedmont?"

"According to the insurance records, you underwent a procedure to extract eggs. Are you saying this information is incorrect? Did Dr. Bussey use eggs from the surrogate instead of your own?"

"I have no idea whose eggs the doctor used."

"What!" Ben gripped the arms of his chair. He couldn't believe his ears. A chill dread crept up his spine and settled in his bones. "Marion? What the hell's going on here? What are you saying?"

She turned on him, her eyes filled with disdain. "You didn't really think I was going to subject myself to that sadistic procedure, did you? Do you have any idea what's involved? The massive hormones I'd have to inject into my body? The possible side effects? Just so you could have children?" She snorted. "I think not."

Her words hit him like a box of free weights dropping on his head. Suddenly everything began to make horrible sense. Seething with rage, Ben jumped to his feet and leaned over her, his face a mere inch from hers. "You're saying you're not the boys' mother?"

"Of course not."

"Then who is?" he shouted, grabbing her shoulders.

Marion cringed. "Take your hands off me." She pushed him away. "Sit down, and stop yelling, Ben. You're making a spectacle of yourself."

Ben felt the veins throbbing in his neck. He let go of her. Clenching and unclenching his fists, he fought back an overwhelming urge to strangle her. "Answer me, Marion, or I'll wring it out of you!" He took a deep breath before repeating his question. "Who is the mother of my children?"

"How the hell should I know? I paid Bussey for donor eggs. He used them in the surrogate."

"Good Lord!" Ben slumped against Piedmont's desk. All these years and he'd never suspected a thing. Zeke had been right. He'd always seen only what he wanted to see when it came to Marion. The life partner he wanted her to be. "You were never going to tell me, were you?"

"I saw no reason. Look how you've overreacted as it is." She rose to her feet, smoothing down her skirt and picking an invisible speck of lint from her jacket.

"Overreacted?" Ben nearly choked on the word. She had no idea of the enormity of her deception, of the traumatic implications of her selfishness.

"You got your precious children, didn't you?" She nearly spit the words at him. "That's all you ever cared about. Not me! You never loved *me*, did you, Ben? Just *them*. Everything was for *them*!" She turned to the lawyer. "I see no further reason to waste my time here. Good day, Mr. Piedmont." She spun on her heels and left the office, slamming the door behind her.

An eerie silence fell over the room. Ben felt a hand on his shoulder and turned to find Piedmont's assistant standing beside him. "I'm sorry, Mr. Schaffer. Can I get you a drink or something?"

He nodded. "Please." Shaking, he sat back down in one of the chairs across from the lawyer's desk. Piedmont took the chair Marion had vacated. The secretary retrieved a bottle of whiskey and a shot glass from a cabinet in the corner of the room and handed them to her boss. He filled the glass halfway and offered it to Ben.

Ben stared at the golden liquid for a moment before tossing it back in one gulp. Resting his elbows on his knees, he braced his forehead with his hands. "Is there any way of finding out who my children's mother is?"

"I wish I could help you, Mr. Schaffer, but I don't see how. Bussey was tipped off. By the time we arrived with a search warrant, he'd destroyed all his records. The mother could be any one of hundreds, maybe thousands, of in vitro patients. At this point we don't even know how many clinics are involved."

"What about DNA testing?"

"It would only help if all the patients agreed to the testing, and as of now, we don't have a clue as to how many patients are involved. The investigation is being conducted over several states. So far, three other attorneys general are involved. And that could be the tip of the iceberg. We may never know how extensive Bussey's operation was unless he decides to cooperate. So far, he's not talking."

Ben stared at the lawyer. "How could something like this happen?"

Piedmont stood and returned to his desk chair. "Bussey was considered one of the leading experts in his field. He had a remarkable success rate. Much higher than other specialists. We now suspect that was because he borrowed from Peter to pay Paul."

"I'm not following you."

"I'm no fertility expert, but from what I understand, often when a woman undergoes a harvesting procedure, the doctor may only retrieve a few good eggs. Of those, sometimes only one or two might develop into a viable embryo after meeting up with the sperm. And none might take hold once implanted in the womb."

Ben began to understand. "So Bussey increased the odds by also using eggs from other women? And I'm assuming his patients didn't know he was implanting them with strangers' eggs as well as their own?"

"Exactly. Except he was also selling eggs to patients, as in the case of your wife. His crime was spurred by both ego and greed."

Ben nodded. "I see how he could have done this with his own patients, but you said the investigation covers several states."

"Dr. Bussey often lectured to fertility doctors and their staff at medical conferences across the country. He was also something of a ladies' man. A nurse or technician in every port, so to speak."

"And these women went along with his scheme?"

Peidmont shrugged. "Some women will do anything to keep their man coming back for more. Once a week, they'd pilfer the egg bank, taking an egg or two from each patient, then alter the records. The doctors at the clinics had no idea."

"So what happened?"

Piedmont placed the pen on his desk, leaned back in his chair, and grinned. "One of Bussey's babes found out about the others. In this business I've learned never to underestimate the vengeance of a woman scorned. She bargained immunity for herself, then blew the whistle on him and the operation."

"Will you contact me when you have a complete list of patients?" asked Ben. "I have to know who the mother of my sons is. Surely, you can understand that."

"I sympathize with you, Mr. Schaffer, but we're in the very early stages of this investigation, and it gets more complex with each passing day. We'd hoped to rely a good deal on insurance records, but we're running into problems."

"How so?"

Piedmont stood, lifted a sheaf of papers from the corner of his desk, and waved them at Ben. "Besides allegedly operating a black market in eggs, the greedy bastard dabbled in insurance fraud. Your insurance company paid out a claim to harvest eggs from your wife. That harvest never took place." He tossed the papers back onto his blotter. "Other discrepancies have shown up as well. We have no way of knowing how many more we'll find as we continue the investigation. I still have dozens of interviews to conduct."

"I see." Ben stood. Placing the glass on the corner of the lawyer's desk, he extended his hand. "If I can be of any further help, Mr. Piedmont—"

The prosecutor shook his hand. "I'll be in touch if and when I have any answers for you, Mr. Schaffer."

~*~

Ben had no desire to go back to the office. He'd kept his meeting with the district attorney to himself. Zeke knew of the investigation, and Ben supposed the others did as well by now, but no one mentioned it to him. Maybe they were waiting for him to broach the subject. He was glad that, at least until now, no one had.

He hadn't told Hope. She knew nothing of the circumstances surrounding the triplets' conception and birth, let alone his and Marion's involvement in the Bussey mess. Ben couldn't remember making a conscious decision to withhold the facts from Hope, but for some reason—why he didn't know—he'd never spoken of it. Maybe because he wanted to rid himself of all memories of Marion's involvement with the boys, somehow hoping that it would help heal the wounds she'd inflicted on all of them.

Ben wandered aimlessly around the streets of Lower Manhattan, anger, guilt, and confusion roiling inside him. At some point in the future his sons would have to be told the truth. All other considerations aside, there were medical factors involved. Ben believed all children, whether biological or adopted, had a right to know their genetic history. Such information could be crucial to their future health. Marion's selfishness had denied his children that right. But the likelihood of ever obtaining any knowledge of their biological mother seemed remote at best. Thousands, Piedmont had said. There could be thousands of possibilities, ruling out the hope of any DNA testing.

He also owed Hope the truth. Everything he'd learned today complicated their relationship even further.

He knew how she'd react. She'd smile, and take his hand, and tell him they'd face the unknowns together. That was Hope. Sweet, loving Hope. But she had no idea what she was getting herself into, and it was unfair of him to expect her to shoulder the fallout of someone else's selfish behavior. Still, he knew she would. That realization both filled him with joy as well as sadness. Hope's love for him might lead her down a very rocky road.

FORTY-ONE

"Hey, Hope."

I glanced up from my drawing board and across the room to where Le was calling to me. "Hmm?"

"Want to grab some lunch with Winnie and me? We're heading over to The Salad Shack."

"Sorry. Can't today. I've got to head downtown for an appointment." I turned to Winnie, coming up from behind me. "I may be a bit late getting back. I don't know how long this is going to take."

"Anything wrong?" she asked, taking a sip from her ever-present coffee cup. "You're not looking for another job behind our backs, are you?"

"Of course not. Don't be so paranoid. I just have to straighten out a health insurance records snafu."

Winnie groaned. "Good luck. Leave a trail of breadcrumbs. If you're not back by next Wednesday, we'll send out a search party."

"I don't think it will be that bad. I only have to provide them with some information."

"Ah, a babe in the bureaucratic woods." Winnie tossed Le a wink. "Poor kid doesn't know what she's in for." She turned back to me. "Listen, honey. Maybe I should tag along. As office manager, I'm used to dealing with those heartless bastards. They'll grind you into fine powder and blow you off in a gust of hot air, especially if it's over money. Which bean-counting behemoth are you dealing with?"

"Actually, I'm meeting with someone down at the district attorney's office."

Winnie raised an eyebrow.

Le wandered over to Hope's drawing board. "Did you say the district attorney's office?"

"Why?" asked Winnie.

"It's got something to do with an investigation they're conducting. Apparently, one of my doctors billed my insurance company for a procedure he never performed. I take it from the gist of the letter I received, that the guy is suspected of multiple violations."

"Lot of that going around lately," muttered Le.

"Huh?" Her remark puzzled me. "What do you mean?"

Le looked at Winnie.

Winnie looked at Le.

"You don't know?" Le asked. Her eyes grew wide with disbelief.

"Know what?" I was beginning to feel very uncomfortable with the conversation.

Le turned to Winnie. "She doesn't know."

Winnie frowned into her coffee mug. "Well, I'm sure as hell not going to be the one to break the news. Not my place." She speared Le with a threatening glare. "Or yours."

"What are the two of you talking about? What don't I know?"

"Ask Ben," said Le and Winnie in unison.

I stared at both of them. Neither offered another word of explanation, and Ben had left the office earlier in the morning. I scanned the room. Apparently, none of the rest of the staff had paid any attention to the conversation because they were all buried in their work. Either that or they were purposely avoiding eye contact with me.

Paranoia nibbled at my stomach lining. Nothing Le and Winnie had said made sense. If I had the time, I might have been able to badger some additional information out of them, but that would have to wait. If I didn't get my rear in gear, I'd be late for my appointment with Mr. Piedmont.

"Fine. Be secretive," I said, grabbing me purse, "but be forewarned. I intend to resort to torture when I return. And if that doesn't work, there's always bribery. I have at least five dollars in my wallet."

"Five dollars?" Le's face lit up. Dropping to her knees, she clasped her hands and held them to her chest. "Oh, Hope, you've got me already. Uncle! Uncle! I'll tell you the secrets of the universe for five dollars!"

Winnie shrugged. "Gee, I would have sold my soul for a mocha frappachino."

I smirked at both of them. "Very funny, you two." Swinging my purse over my shoulder, I headed for the door. "I'm out of here."

"Don't forget the breadcrumbs," called Winnie.

During my subway ride downtown, I ruminated over Le and Winnie's comments. My humorous remarks had been meant to diffuse their discomfort over divulging something Ben apparently wanted to keep from me. But what? And why? Although Ben and I shared a bed at night, in some ways I was still very much an outsider when it came to the tight-knit band of friends.

I supposed that was to be expected. After all, their relationship spanned more than a decade. I entered the picture less than three months ago. The new kid on the block. I wondered if I'd always feel like the little sister forcing her way into the big kids' clubhouse.

~*~

"I'm afraid Mr. Piedmont is running behind schedule," said the receptionist when I entered the assistant district attorney's office and introduced myself. "Please have a seat. He'll be with you shortly."

I noted the time on the wall clock behind her desk. I had a rendering to complete before the end of the day. Zeke had handed me the roughs as soon as I walked into the office that morning, saying Ben needed the finished art for a meeting first thing tomorrow. "Do you have any idea how long it will be?" I asked. "I'm on my lunch break."

"Probably at least twenty minutes. Maybe more. One of Mr. Piedmont's earlier appointments showed up late and threw our entire morning schedule to hell. He's skipping his own lunch to catch up. I'm sorry. Would you rather reschedule?"

I thought for a moment. I was here. Might as well get the whole thing over with. My meeting with the prosecutor shouldn't take more than five minutes once I got to see him. "No, that's all right. I'll wait."

Thirty minutes later I was finally escorted into the assistant district attorney's office. After the receptionist introduced me to the prosecutor and his secretary, I took the seat offered me.

Mr. Piedmont studied me for several seconds, a curious expression settling across his haggard face before he cleared his throat and finally addressed me. "May I ask your age, Ms. Morgan?"

"Nearly thirty-four."

"I see." He smiled. "That explains it."

"Explains what?"

"Forgive me. You look closer to twenty-four. So you were..." He pulled a pair of tortoise shell glasses from his shirt pocket. After perching them on his nose, he referred to a file in front of him. "...twenty-nine when you underwent in vitro?"

"No."

He lifted his chin, slid the glasses down the bridge of his nose, and peered at me. "You weren't twenty-nine?"

"I didn't undergo in vitro."

The assistant D.A. scowled as he scanned the paper a second time. "According to records we obtained from Dr. Wolfowitz's clinic—"

"I'm afraid there's been a mistake, Mr. Piedmont. I tried to straighten this out over the phone, but after explaining the mix-up, the woman I spoke with still insisted I see you in person."

He set the paper aside and removed his glasses. "What sort of mix-up?"

"My sister Faith underwent in vitro at Dr. Wolfowitz's clinic. I was her egg donor."

His bushy gray eyebrows arched toward his receding hairline. "You're not Faith Morgan?"

"No, I'm Hope Morgan."

He placed his glasses back on his nose and rifled through a

sheaf of papers. After pulling out several pages, he read through them, muttering under his breath. "My mistake, Ms. Morgan. A clerical mix-up on the part of my staff."

"Then you don't need to discuss anything with me?" I rose to leave.

"Please remain seated. This investigation does involve you."

I sat back down. "I don't understand."

"You will shortly. How many eggs did Dr. Wolfowitz retrieve from you?"

"He may have mentioned the number, but I don't remember. He implanted three in Faith, but she lost two of them."

"Your sister will probably remember. I'll need to contact her."

I glanced down at my lap. I'd twisted my fingers into a throbbing knot. "My sister died in a fire more than three years ago."

"I'm sorry. The baby?"

I swallowed the lump of granite in my throat. "Died with her, still in utero."

Piedmont glanced at his watch, then over at his secretary. He removed his glasses again and massaged the bridge of his nose. "Ms. Morgan, do you know why our office asked you to meet with us?"

"Not really. Insurance fraud?"

"In part."

"But why would the Manhattan district attorney's office be involved? Dr. Wolfowitz's clinic is in Pittsburgh."

He leaned forward, resting his forearms on the stack of papers in front of him. Both the furrows in his forehead and the frown lines at the corners of his mouth deepened. "You aren't familiar with this case, are you, Ms. Morgan? Haven't heard anything about it on the news? Read an account in the papers?"

"No." I couldn't remember when I last had time to watch the news or read a paper.

Piedmont looked like he was about to tell me I had two weeks to live. Suddenly, the theme from *The Twilight Zone* began to play between my ears. "What's this all about, Mr. Piedmont? Why am I here?"

Instead of answering, he turned to his secretary, "Jemma, why don't you get Ms. Morgan some coffee?"

She placed her notepad and pen on the desk and stood. "How do you take it?" she asked me.

My stomach began to churn a vat of acid. Coffee sounded like a very bad idea. The theme from *The Twilight Zone* grew louder. I shook my head. "I'm fine, thanks."

"Tea?"

"No, nothing." I turned to Piedmont. "Look, could we get on with this? If you have something to tell me, say it. You're really beginning to creep me out."

Piedmont made eye contact with his secretary, then nodded for her to take her seat before he turned to me. "I'm afraid I have some very upsetting news, Ms. Morgan."

As he spoke, *The Twilight Zone* theme crescendoed into eardrum-shattering range. This wasn't happening. I stared at Piedmont and his assistant. They both sat perched on the edges of their chairs waiting for me to say something. Anything.

"Ms. Morgan? Are you all right?" The lawyer rose from his seat and walked around to the front of his desk. I watched his approach as if he were part of a dream. No, not a dream. A nightmare. A cataclysmic nightmare.

I finally found my voice. "You're saying I may have children?"

Piedmont nodded. "If Dr. Wolfowitz didn't implant all your

eggs into your sister, some of them may have wound up in the hands of Dr. Bussey. We can't know for sure. What we do know is that one of Dr. Wofowitz's technicians has admitted to stealing eggs for Dr. Bussey. He fertilized those eggs and implanted them in his own patients."

"But you don't know if any of my eggs were taken?"

"No."

The realization of his words settled like a huge chunk of Gibraltar in my stomach. "And you may never know?"

He shook his head. "We definitely will never know. As you might assume, the nurse didn't keep records of whose eggs she stole. All I can assure you is that the parties involved will be prosecuted to the full extent of the law."

I jumped out of my chair and launched into a tirade, anger and frustration exploding from my mouth. "Excuse me, Mr. Piedmont, but whoop-de-fucking-do. So this Dr. Bussey and his cohorts get sent off to some white-collar prison for a few months? Big fucking deal. What about me? I have to live with this for the rest of my life. Am I a victim or not? Do I have children out there somewhere or not? You've turned my life upside-down and for what? What was the point of dumping this on me if you can't give me any answers?"

I collapsed back into the chair, covered my face with my hands, and began to cry. Three years ago, I lost the baby I'd given Faith. Now I'd learned I may have lost many more. Somewhere, other women might be raising the babies I could no longer have. I glared at Piedmont through my tears. "Damn you, I was better off not knowing."

To his credit, Piedmont hung his head. When he answered me, his words rang with remorse. "I'm sorry I had to hurt you, but I'm bound by the law."

I stood up, inhaled a deep breath, and swiped at my cheeks. Through sheer willpower, I forced one foot in front of the other. I had to get away from this office. From this man who had just shattered my life. Why had I opened that damn letter? If only I'd tossed it back with the recycling. "I have to get back to work," I said.

Mr. Piedmont reached for my arm. "Maybe you should wait until you've calmed down a bit, Ms. Morgan. Ms. Reeves will escort you to the lounge."

"No!" I jerked away from him. "Leave me alone. You've done enough damage." I yanked open his office door and raced down the hall.

I didn't bother waiting for the elevator. Finding the stairs, I sprinted the four flights, then fought my way around a crowd of people scurrying through the lobby. As I exited the air-conditioned building, oppressive summer heat slammed into my chest, sucking the remaining breath from my lungs. Overcome with dizziness, I sank to the steps, lowered my head between my knees, and closed my eyes.

How many babies? They'd be three years old now, the same age as Ben's triplets. Were they girls? Boys? Mr. Piedmont had asked about the number of eggs Dr. Wolfowitz harvested. If only I could remember. I'd tried for so long to forget.

And I'd lived the past few years believing I was alone in the world when all along somewhere someone might be raising my child or children. But who? And where? I'd never know.

Not that it mattered. If by some miracle I found out, what then? I couldn't destroy another family by demanding they relinquish their child or children to me. They were as much victims of the unethical Dr. Bussey as I was. Besides, the biological father had as much right to any children as I did.

The biological father. Some stranger's sperm may have fertilized my eggs. Some man I'd never met could be the father of my child or children. Agreeing to have my eggs impregnated with my brother-in-law's sperm had been difficult enough to accept. I'd always envisioned being in love with the man who fathered my children. That's the way it was supposed to be. But nothing in my life had turned out the way it was supposed to. Why should this startling revelation be any different?

FORTY-TWO

Ben sat at the head of the table in the conference room, his friends surrounding him. In a way he was glad Hope was out of the office. He wanted them to be alone when he told her of Marion's deception, but he also needed to tell his friends. They were his surrogate family, in some respects the only family he'd ever known until the birth of the boys. His friends had stood by him and put up with Marion for years because of their devotion to him. Telling them first might make it easier for him to tell Hope later.

After recounting his meeting with the assistant district attorney, Ben turned to his project manager and offered him a grim smirk. "This is your cue to step in with a resounding I-told-you-so, Zeke."

Instead of complying, Zeke muttered, "Fuck."

"You can say that again," added Paco.

The rest of Ben's staff mumbled in agreement. Ben buried his head in his hands. Everyone else sat in silence waiting for him to say more. Before he could, the phone rang.

"Good afternoon. Schaffer-Merrick," said Winnie. She listened to the caller for a moment. "Hold on. I'll check." She turned to Zeke. "The printer had a slot open up. He can run the Powers presentation now if we get it right over to him. Want me to go?"

Zeke shook his head. "No, I'll run it down. There are a few things I need to discuss with him." He turned to Ben. "You going to be okay?"

Ben waved him off. "Sure. Get out of here. I need to figure out what I'm going to tell Hope, and you're not exactly the best person to help me with that."

Zeke snorted, then offered Ben a wry smile. "Yeah, well for what it's worth, I'd take the direct approach—plain, simple, and to the point, but don't take my word for it." He waved his arms to encompass everyone else in the room. "Ask around."

FORTY-THREE

I needed to get back to the office. I had work to do. A deadline to meet. But when the subway pulled into the station at Broadway and Twenty-third, I stared blankly at the words on the station sign and remained seated. I rode all the way uptown, then back downtown. Finally, when the train was once again traveling north and had pulled back into the Broadway and Twenty-third Street station, I stepped from the car and headed up the stairs to the street.

A block from the office I bumped into Zeke. "Where the hell have you been? I told you that rendering had to be finished before the end of the day."

I started to cry. Damn. Zeke was the last person I'd choose to cry my heart out to, but he was there, and I couldn't help myself. The words tumbled out of me. In broken, semi-coherent sentences, as people passed us in the middle of a crowded Manhattan street, I told him everything. About my family. The fire. About Faith and her fertility problems. About the baby that had died along with my sister. My baby.

When I started talking about Dr. Bussey, Zeke grabbed my arms and shook me. "Slow down," he said, "and calm down. Take a deep breath, Hope." My body shuddered beneath his grasp. Zeke stared at me. "Now. Did you say Dr. Bussey?"

I nodded.

"Dr. Leo Bussey? The fertility doctor that was arrested several weeks ago?"

"Y...yes."

"Jeez! Does Ben know about any of this?"

"N...no. Not yet. Why?"

"Come with me." He grabbed my hand and yanked me in the direction of the office. "Look," he said, "I probably shouldn't be telling you this, but right now Ben's upstairs trying to figure out how to tell you a similar tale. Shit. This is too fucking strange."

I stopped and spun around to face him. "What do you mean?"

He grimaced. "Look, Hope, I've said enough already. Let Ben tell you the rest."

Beads of perspiration broke out across my forehead and upper lip. A cold chill coursed through my body. Suddenly, I remembered Le's and Winnie's cryptic comments of earlier and their advice to *ask Ben* when I'd questioned them. Ben had never mentioned the circumstances surrounded the triplets' birth. I assumed their conception occurred in the normal fashion—sex between their parents. "Tell me, Zeke. Was Marion one of Dr. Bussey's patients?"

He nodded.

"Then some of her eggs were probably stolen as well."

"Not exactly."

The blood in my veins turned to ice. My heart began to pound.

If Dr. Bussey hadn't stolen eggs from Marion...My mind raced with other possibilities, anything besides the first thought that popped into my head. Was it possible? I grabbed Zeke's hands and squeezed them until my knuckles turned white. My words sputtered from my mouth. "What do you mean *not exactly*?"

"Damn it, Hope, I really think you need to have this conversation with Ben, not me."

Hysteria bubbled inside me. "Tell me, Zeke!" But he didn't have to. I saw it in his eyes. "They used donor eggs, didn't they? Didn't they, Zeke?"

"Talk to Ben, Hope."

"Answer me, damn it!" I screamed, drawing the stares of passersby. A group of curious pedestrians began gathering around us. "Did they use donor eggs?"

Zeke drew his attention to the crowd forming around us and frowned. He wrestled himself from my grasp and dragged me through the crowd into a deserted doorway. Grabbing my shoulders, he pressed me up against the glass and lowered his head until it was inches from mine. "Listen to me! He didn't know. Marion did everything behind his back. He just found out today."

I stared at Zeke in disbelief. "Didn't know?" *Why would a woman who didn't want children agree to carry someone else's?*

As if reading my mind, Zeke answered my silent question. "They used a surrogate."

Oh, Ben! Everything began to tumble into place, making perfect sense. Three boys who looked nothing like their mother. Three boys with large hazel eyes—my eyes—that even a cataract-ridden old woman noticed. Three boys precisely the right age. And one of them looking exactly like my dead brother!

And Ben had never suspected a thing! I remembered his exact

words in the supermarket when I mentioned the elderly woman's comments about the triplets having my hazel eyes. *So do Marion's father and three brothers.*

"Oh, Zeke!" A fresh batch of tears spilled from my eyes, but this time they were tears of joy. "Thank you!" I flung my arms around his neck and hugged him. Breaking away, I raced for the loft.

I rushed into the building and punched the elevator button. My body trembled. My pulse raced. My head pounded. As I waited for the elevator, I leaned against the cool brick wall and took long deep breaths, but they did little to calm the excitement exploding inside me. When the elevator arrived, I pushed my way inside without letting the descending passengers exit.

A moment later, I stepped from the car onto the fifth floor and hurried through the double doors. The office area was empty. At the far end of the loft, I saw the staff huddled around the large table in the glass-enclosed conference room. Ben's back was to me. The rest of the staff concentrated on his words. No one noticed me approach.

"What the hell do I tell my kids?" Ben asked.

"The truth," said Winnie.

Ben sneered. "What? That because I married a disturbed, selfish bitch, they were the product of a laboratory one-night stand between some anonymous eggs and my sperm? That I then shoved them into some nameless incubator for nine months?"

"I wouldn't be quite that blunt," suggested Le.

"That *is* the truth," said Ben. "The God-awful truth of their conception and birth."

"I don't think it would be so bad to sugarcoat it a bit," said Nigel. "Lots of kids are conceived in test tubes nowadays."

"Or adopted," said Freddie. "My parents always told me I was special because they chose me. Tell the boys you wanted them so much, that you went to great lengths to get them. As they get older and can understand more, you can explain the situation in greater detail."

"And what do I tell them when they ask why I don't know who their mother is?" asked Ben. He dropped his head into his hands. "And how the hell do I explain all of this to Hope?"

"I don't think that will be a problem," I said, coming up behind him.

EPILOGUE

"I should have my head examined," said Ben. He chuckled as he shook the body part in question.

We were lounging in cushioned Adirondacks chairs on the brick patio of our new house, a large Colonial located a mile north of the Victorian Ben had recently sold. The moment I saw the house, with its spacious fenced-in yard and majestic oaks and maples, I declared it the perfect kid-friendly dwelling for our family.

Together Ben and I, along with the help of three lively testers, had chosen furnishings that would be both comfortable and sturdy. Country oak and pine replaced ornately carved High Victorian. Sturdy plaids and denims supplanted fragile satin and silk brocades. Cheerful warmth took the place of austere cold.

"I heard Fritzi mutter something along the lines of a frontal lobotomy last night after she discovered a mauled slipper in the dining room."

Ben groaned. "Who's?"

"Hers. They seem to have an attraction for anything fuzzy and pink."

"That's the third pair this week. Do you realize we may go bankrupt replacing slippers?"

I glanced over at the culprits in question. The three newest members of the Schaffer family were cavorting on the lawn with their human, grass-stained counterparts. A cacophony of yipping, yapping, and belly giggles rang through the soft breeze of the late summer evening. I reached over and laced my fingers through Ben's. "Things could be a lot worse. At least you waited until Minnie had housebroken the pups before caving in to the boys."

"So this is all my fault?" He gave me an I'm-not-accepting-all-the-blame-here look. "You did your share of lobbying for those three fur balls."

"And you love them. Admit it."

Ben glanced at the puppies. "They are kind of cute. When they're not chewing me out of house and home."

"Mommy! Mommy! Watch this!" Woody tossed a rubber ball over his head. As soon as the bright red ball was airborne, a chocolate brown puppy sprang into action, leaping at the rubber sphere as it bounced once, twice, three times on the grass, until he finally trapped it in his snout. "I taught Espwesso a twick!" cried Woody.

I clapped my hands. "Very good, Woody!"

Not to be outdone, Scotty and Teddy began to shout for my attention as well. "Watch me! Watch me, Mommy!" I continued to applaud as two other dogs, the tan Latte and the brown and white Cappuccino, scrambled after blue and yellow balls.

"Mommy," whispered Ben. "I like the sound of that."

"Me, too." Were the triplets mine? Statistically, the odds were against it. Even so, we had decided to go ahead with DNA testing. The results wouldn't be known for several weeks, but even if the tests came back negative, as they most likely would, it didn't matter. In my heart Scotty, Teddy, and Woody were mine. And had been from the moment I met them. As was their father.

ABOUT THE AUTHOR

USA Today and Amazon bestselling and award-winning author Lois Winston writes mystery, romance, romantic suspense, chick lit, women's fiction, children's chapter books, and nonfiction. *Kirkus Reviews* dubbed her critically acclaimed Anastasia Pollack Crafting Mystery series, "North Jersey's more mature answer to Stephanie Plum." In addition, Lois is an award-winning craft and needlework designer who often draws much of her source material for both her characters and plots from her experiences in the crafts industry.

Connect with Lois at her website, www.loiswinston.com, where you can learn more about her and her books, sign up for her newsletter, and find links to follow her on social media.